Twitterpated

OTHER BOOKS AND AUDIO BOOKS

BY MELANIE JACOBSON:

The List

Not My Type

Twitterpated

a novel

Melanie
Jacobson

Covenant Communications, Inc.

Cover image *Love Key* © Rubén Hidalgo, iStockphotography

Published by Covenant Communications, Inc.
American Fork, Utah

Printed in the United States of America
First Printing: March 2012

18 17 16 15 14 13 12   10 9 8 7 6 5 4 3 2 1

ISBN 978-1-60861-065-5

To Grant,
for your bright, happy spirit

Acknowledgments

THIS CRAZY ADVENTURE HAS TAUGHT me that writing is the furthest thing from solitary and this book would not have happened without the help of generous friends who offered advice or read countless drafts. My husband, Kenny, cheered every chapter as I wrote it and nurtured this dream. Amy Lou Bennett, my favorite (and not because you're my only) sister, read every version of this book and patiently offered opinions, revisions, and validation. My first critique partners, Aubrey Mace and Sue Marchant, promised me that I really could do this and brought their own storytelling talents to bear in polishing my manuscript. Jen Schumann offered refreshing and invaluable honesty, as well as an unerring ear for what worked and what didn't. My new critique partners, Kristine Tate and Brittany Larsen, reassured me that this story deserved to see the light of day. Christiane Woerner and Jaymee O'Rafferty read the best version I could give them and paid me the greatest compliment by forgetting to wield their mighty red pens as the story went on. Thanks to my editor, Samantha Van Walraven, who never forgets to wield her red pen and who makes my writing better for it. I owe a special thanks to Annette Lyon and Josi Kilpack, two generous and talented authors who owed me nothing and still answered every question a stranger had until I fooled them into becoming my friends. Lastly, I want to thank all the friends and family who acted completely unsurprised when I said I was going to be published: Sarah Armstrong, Colleen Strubberg, Jamie and Nadine, Aunt Linda, Nancy Ostergar, Skip and Joan, Aunt Pat and Aunt Beth, Jill and Bob, and James, who brags that I'm a writer.

Chapter 1

THE ROLLED UP YOGA MAT bounced off of my roommate's head with a satisfying thwack.

"Ow!" Sandy protested. "Are you trying to kill me?"

"Yes. Quit moving so I can hit you again."

She chose to dodge instead, her red hair streaking behind her as she ran to the other side of the dining table to use it as a safety buffer. "I don't understand why you're so angry," she said. "I did it to help you."

"Did I ask you to help?" I hoped she could hear the annoyance in my voice.

"No. But only because you're too stubborn. Why can't you see this as an amazing act of service?"

That stopped my mat-wielding for a moment. "You're trying to spin this as *service*?" I detected her smile trying to break out, and I scowled.

"You don't know what's good for you. But I do, and if you would just drop your weapons and take a look at the computer again, you'll see that I'm right."

"I'm not dropping anything," I said. "I haven't gotten to use the pillow yet." I picked up the green throw cushion off the sofa to emphasize my point.

"Trust me, Jessie. Check the computer before you hit me with anything else. They're not that bad."

"*They*?" I fought a screech. "There's more than one?"

"Yeah." She grinned. "You've got three matches. Lucky you." Her tone changed to wheedling. "I'm just trying to be a good friend."

"By signing me up for an Internet dating site without permission?" I dropped the green pillow to shove a hand through my hair. The situation had gone from irritating to embarrassing knowing that real, live boys had actually looked at the profile she had set up. "Tell me the truth," I said. "Are you crazy?"

Sandy did her best to look offended, but I could see the laughter in her eyes. "It's not a *dating* site."

"You're not even sorry," I accused her.

"Nope. You won't be either. I promise. Check the screen. If I'm wrong, I'll drop it, but there's one guy you have to see."

I threw the mat and pillow on the sofa and plopped down beside them, giving Sandy's laptop an impatient tug toward me. My own face stared back at me from the screen, cropped from a snapshot that used to show the two of us together at a barbecue the previous summer. Now it showed only me. Looking pretty good, actually. The website banner over my photo announced, "Meet one of the newest LDS Lookup members!"

"This is humiliating," I grumbled.

"Why? You look hot in that picture. I put it up two days ago, and you've already got guys lining up."

"Wrong. *You've* got guys lining up for me, which is a totally different thing."

"No, it isn't. I filled out your profile like you would."

"Like I would? I would never have filled it out. That's why I want to kill you." I grabbed for the yoga mat, but Sandy whisked it out of my reach.

"Check your profile, and tell me if I got anything wrong."

I scanned it, ignoring her while I read. She listed me as twenty-five, an accountant in the greater Seattle area, active in the LDS Church, and looking for—

"You are so dead!" I yelped. "You can't put that I'm searching for a relationship on the Internet. It's pathetic."

Sandy rolled her eyes. "It's a social networking site. Over half of the people on here are looking for relationships," she said.

The rest of the profile outlined my likes (comedies, fresh baked bread, being outdoors) and dislikes (heavy metal, mumblers, the Yankees) pretty accurately. I couldn't find much else to quibble with.

"Why would you do this?" I asked. But I already knew the answer. Her persistence in trying to jump start my social life knew no bounds.

"I'm trying to help you keep your promises," she said.

I rolled my eyes. "Promises extracted under extreme duress don't count."

She grinned. The week before, she had forced me to make a New Year's resolution to go out more by hiding my favorite ice cream behind her back until I agreed. I would have left her standing there with a quart of melted Häagen-Dazs if she hadn't waved a spoonful of butter pecan under my nose, and I folded. I promised to leave the condo every once in a while, and she gave me my ice cream back. It would be hard. I paid a stiff mortgage so I could stay in my living room whenever I wanted, and I'd spent a lot of time decorating it to make it an inviting space.

"I keep telling you this is for your own good," she reminded me.

"How come I don't get to decide what's for my own good?"

"Because you keep getting it wrong. Your work-to-play ratio is all screwed up."

"There's nothing wrong with a good work ethic. You of all people should appreciate that," I pointed out. Sandy worked at the same software company as me—Macrosystems—but in human resources, a sanitized name for the place where they do all the firing when people have bad work ethics. Sandy focused more on recruiting and hiring, but she had no problem dropping the axe when someone deserved it. She'd fired enough people over the last five years to develop bullet-proof skin, which is probably why I could practically see my complaints about her high-handedness bouncing right off her.

"You don't have a good work ethic; you have a sickness that compels you to work ridiculous amounts of overtime and waste your weekends on spreadsheets. I'm being a good friend by forcing you to mix it up a little."

"And stealing my identity for a fake dating site post is being a good friend?" I asked. I wasn't going down without a fight.

"Excuse me, but *I'm* the drama queen around here. I will not be deposed, so leave the exaggerations to me. It's not fake, and for the last time, it's not a dating site. Think *Facebook for Mormons*."

"How did you, of all people, find it?" Although Sandy and I had met through a Seattle LDS housing e-mail list, she hadn't been to church the whole time I'd known her. I couldn't picture her surfing LDS sites.

"Ah, Google. It's a wonderful thing. I entered 'find roommate a hot LDS guy,' and wham. LDS Lookup popped up right at my fingertips."

"Ha ha."

"Fine," she relented. "I checked out a ton of sites before picking this one because it has the coolest vibe. Seriously, check out the guys who sent you messages."

She yanked her laptop back and clicked the mouse a couple of times. "Look at *him.* He sent a 'Love to Know More' request."

As much as I wanted to, I couldn't resist. The profile showed a guy in maybe his late twenties, with blond hair and a nice smile. I scanned the rest of his bio and snorted. "No way," I said.

"What? He's cute. And he seems smart."

"Yeah, and he listed Charlie Sheen as his personal hero. No thanks."

"Look at the other guy. He's cute too." She clicked again and pulled up another profile.

As soon as his link opened, I said, "No."

"You didn't even read it!"

"His screen name is 'I'm4Real.' You can't be real if you use numbers for letters. So, no."

"What if someone disqualified you as a prospect because of your screen name?"

Cue panic. "What is my screen name?"

"Sugar."

My eyes widened in horror.

She grinned. "I'm kidding. I put your initials. That's fine, right?"

"I guess. Let's get this over with. Show me the last one."

She shrugged. "If you didn't like the first two, I don't think the last one is going to do it for you," she said. But she pulled it up anyway.

"Lame profile?" I asked.

"I didn't read it. He's not as cute as the other two."

I opened his profile. His screen name said Harold Crick. "How do you know if he's cute or not?" I couldn't tell much from the picture since it wasn't a close-up, but I caught the glint of glasses, and his dark, floppy hair appealed to me.

"I'm not into guys with glasses," Sandy said, peering over my shoulder. "Besides, what kind of name is Harold Crick? He didn't even put a screen name."

"Yes, he did. Harold Crick is a character." The main character in one of my favorite movies, *Stranger Than Fiction,* as a matter of fact.

"Whatever. Does he say anything good?"

I read through, going as slowly as possible to annoy Sandy. She angled the screen so she could read over my shoulder. It took her all of five seconds to protest. "No way, Jessie. He's a lumberjack."

"He works for the forestry service. That doesn't make him a lumberjack."

"You wanna put money on that?" Sandy challenged me. "I don't know a lot about online dating, but I know you have to read between the lines. Lives within a fifty mile radius, works for the forestry service, and loves the outdoors. This guy is totally holed up in a cabin at the foot of Mt. Rainier, shivering in his moth-eaten flannels and waiting for a pretty lady to come keep him warm." She started singing an off-key version of Monty Python's lumberjack song. "He's a lumberjack—aack."

She ducked to avoid the green throw pillow. "Don't sing. He doesn't sound so bad," I said. "Cool movie choices, cool bands, and he listed some books he's read. I bet Mr. I'm4Real has an impressive comic book collection."

"Yeah, but he's cuter."

"Well, that's more important, then."

"I'm just saying, you should start with someone good-looking right out of the gate."

"But this Harold Crick guy's picture is blurry, so maybe he's cuter."

"Or maybe it's blurry because he's not, and he's trying to fool you."

"You're right," I said. "Online dating is stupid. Thanks for talking me out of it." I pushed the computer aside and made to get off of the couch.

"Wait! Online dating is a great idea. No, really," she said in response to my skeptical expression. "Oprah talked about it in her life class. It's working for people." Sandy missed seeing Oprah on her DVR so much that she periodically signed up for her online seminars.

I said nothing.

She switched to a guilt trip. "When was your last date, Jessie?"

I stubbornly didn't answer.

"Do you even remember?" she pressed.

"LDS guys aren't falling out of trees around here," I said.

"I know that. But you used to go out all the time, and now you never do. You work way too much. You're going to burn out and either quit or get fired, but either way I'll have to hire someone new. It's so much extra work for me." She tried to look pitiful. "If you won't do it for you, can't you do it as a favor to me? You know, have a little fun so I don't have to do extra paperwork?"

"That's the lamest reason I've ever heard," I said.

She continued to look pitiful.

I wasn't fooled. This was not about paperwork. This was about her campaign to reform my love life. And if I didn't give in now, she'd come up with something new and potentially more embarrassing. Barely believing I was about to speak the next words coming out of my mouth, I sighed. "Where's Harold Crick?"

Chapter 2

I TRIED TO JUGGLE A BULGING sack of Chinese takeout and my overflowing workbag, while I fumbled with the lock on the front door, when the knob suddenly twisted and the door flew open. Sandy stood there, obviously on her way out. She groaned. "Let me guess; you're spending the evening getting caught up with work."

"I have a big deadline. I can't miss it." The end of my first project as a manager loomed, all headache-making. I hadn't been gunning for my recent promotion to begin with, but I wasn't about to embarrass myself now that I had it.

"Play with your spreadsheets tomorrow. Come out with us tonight. I'm meeting some people at The Factory. Remember your resolution," she chided.

"Ask me next week when my deadline is over. I've got balance sheets coming out of my ears right now." I shook my head again. As much as taking a break from my crazy hours tempted me, I said, "I just can't." Not without regret though.

"You're never going to meet Prince Charming holed up in here."

"I'm not looking for Prince Charming. Just a nice guy, and I don't think my kind of nice guy is going to be clubbing at one a.m. But dance with a hot stranger for me."

Sandy gave up, tucked a tiny silver purse that couldn't have held more than her ID under her arm, and gave her reflection a once-over in the foyer mirror. "Any hot strangers I find are all mine," she said. "How do I look?" She had a killer body and an arresting face. Looking at her wild red hair, I decided for the umpteenth time that there was never a more misnamed Sandy.

I'm not Alpo, but it's hard to look good next to her. I have my mom's light green eyes and dark brown hair like my dad. My sisters have all that plus perfect Kate Middleton complexions, but I am cursed with nose freckles. Seven of them. I pretend they're endearing, but they're so not. Grandpa Ray used to say I was pretty as a picture when I complained about them and that my freckles were angel kisses. I believed him until I turned eight and he told me Easter eggs came from bright pink chickens. I took everything he said with a healthy dose of skepticism after that.

I took in Sandy's long-sleeved teal wrap dress and silver stilettos then answered her question. "How do you look? Honestly, you look like sin on four-inch heels, and yet I could wear that whole outfit to church. How do you do that?"

"It's a gift."

I shook my head and closed the door behind her.

An hour later, I wished I'd accepted her invitation. After trying to reconcile the same financial statement countless times and picking at my congealing sweet and sour chicken, the numbers on the computer screen refused to make sense. Maybe I was tired, but I felt that way about work too often lately. I majored in accounting in college because I'm practical, not because I love it. Pragmatism is a curse that ranks right up there with freckles. I knew I could make good money in accounting, but I also figured that two years out of college when I sat rocking my first baby and staring out at a white picket fence it would be easy to work from home doing people's taxes. Now, three years out of college, I had the job but no one I wanted to share a white picket fence or babies with. Just me and my balance sheets. Good times.

"Okay, Jessie. Get a grip. This is easy. Think," I lectured myself—because that's not weird to do out loud when you're alone. The screen blurred with nonsense. I gave up after another minute, in need of a brain break. Deciding to catch up on some e-mails, I winced to find eleven messages waiting in my in-box. Yikes. Two from my sister in Virginia, a couple from college friends, an ad for a new colon cleanser, and an announcement about an upcoming ward ice cream social (Really? People still did those?), and then I paused. A notice from Lookup reading, "Harold Crick has sent you a message" leaped from the screen.

Interesting. Taking the path of least resistance with Sandy, I had sent Harold Crick a wave, an icon which supposedly landed in his Lookup inbox to let him know I said hello. But apparently, instead of waving back, he'd sent a full-on message in return.

He probably couldn't spell. Or worse, he probably wrote in all caps. I opened the link to find out.

To: JKT
From: Harold Crick
Hello, JKT. I wonder what that stands for? Just Killing Time, maybe? Are you the Junk King of Tacoma? Or maybe you're depressingly positive, and it means Just Keep Trying. Tell me more. . . . . . . Please?

He signed it "Ben."

Ben. That didn't sound like a lumberjack. Lumberjacks were named Big Red or Moose. Ben sounded like a guy who worked for the Forest Service and didn't wear too much flannel. Ben also sounded funny. The Junk King of Tacoma. I typed a reply before I could second-guess myself out of it.

To: Harold Crick
From: JKT
Hi, Ben. JKT stands for Jasper Killed Terence. Those were my Chinese fighting fish. Terence is obviously gone now, but Jasper died soon after from loneliness. Very sad. Good guesses though.

I smiled to myself and picked up my chicken, choking down the last jellied bites. An unfamiliar "ping" from the computer startled me. I looked up to see an Instant Message Request from Lookup. It was Ben.

Why was he home on a Friday night? Um, why was I? Oh, wait. I was pathetic.

And in no position to judge.

I accepted the IM request and read his reply.

HC: Chinese fighting fish? I felt sorry for you until I remembered your profile says you don't have any pets. So no Jasper and Terence. Okay. I'm going to go with Jacobus Kapteyn Telescope. A forty-ton telescope with CCD imaging? I'm impressed. You must have some serious astronomy chops.

I sat back with a furrowed brow. Jacobus what? Was he nerding out on me? Then I relaxed and reached for the keyboard.

JKT: You totally Googled that.

HC: Guilty. Nothing gets by you accountants. But if Google can't crack it, what hope do I have? Can I get a hint?

JKT: How do you know I'm an accountant?

HC: I'd claim brilliance, but your profile said so.

JKT: Right. Sorry. Stupid question.

HC: So . . . your screen name?

JKT: I guess you've earned it. JKT are my initials.

HC: Jacinda? Jahzara? Jezebel?

JKT: No! My mother loved me. Guess again.

HC: January? Jasmine? Juniper?

JKT: Nope. Think June Cleaver, not hippie. I'm Jessie.

HC: Hi, Jessie. Nice to meet you. So what drove you, um, I mean *brought* you to this site?

I admitted the embarrassing truth.

JKT: My roommate signed me up.

HC: Seriously?

JKT: Yep.

HC: Did you kill her?

JKT: Still trying to figure out how to do it without leaving any evidence linking me to the crime.

HC: You're smart. I don't think I'd have thought it through that far. But you're going along with the online thing?

JKT: For now.

HC: What changed your mind?

JKT: The guys in my singles group scare me.

HC: I don't know how to spell the sound I just made. What's halfway between a snort and a laugh?

JKT: You lorted? Sounds like a personal problem.

HC: I did an unambiguous snort this time.

JKT: To answer your question, the last guy who asked me on a date had a daughter in Mia Maids. I'm only 25. No thank you. What about you? How can you live in the Seattle area and we haven't met yet? Are you new around here?

HC: Yes and no. I grew up here, but my family moved to Idaho during my mission. I spent a few years in Arizona doing postgrad stuff and working, but I got a work contract here a few months ago. I've been laying pretty low as far as the singles go. And I've sort of been ducking matchmakers in my family ward since I moved back. That left the Internet, aka the Final Frontier in the LDS social wilderness.

JKT: Oh, yeah. Ward matchmakers. Two bad experiences almost put me off of dating for good. Maybe this website is a first step toward healing.

HC: Only two bad experiences? My ward matchmakers must be overachievers.

I laughed. Again. This *so* beat work. Speaking of which . . . I glanced at the time. Almost eleven thirty. How had that happened?

JKT: Thanks for making me laugh, but I should go. It's almost pumpkin time, and I need to get some sleep.

HC: No problem. Good night.

Smiling, I shut the computer down and headed for bed. I would have to get up early to catch up on work, but for once, I didn't mind. The look on Sandy's face would totally be worth it when I told her I'd spent the night with the lumberjack.

Chapter 3

"Why are you up already?"

I looked up from my latest spreadsheet to find my disheveled and grumpy roommate standing in front of me wearing ratty old sweats with "Go, Banana Slugs!" emblazoned across her chest.

"Good morning, sunshine. Nice pajamas," I said.

"I got in late last night, so I grabbed the first thing I could find."

Considering the chaos of her room, I could understand how she'd ended up in a shirt dedicated to homeless snails.

"It's lunch time," I said. "A better question is why are *you* barely getting up?"

"I got in late," she repeated then thought for a moment. "Wait, is two a.m. late or early?"

"It's crazy."

"You're just jealous because you didn't meet *him*," she said.

"Who him?"

"Him. Mr. Right. The one you said couldn't be found in a club. But I found him. Tall, blond. Think Brad Pitt."

"Okay, is this like creepy *Interview with a Vampire* Brad Pitt? Or old guy *Benjamin Button* Brad Pitt?"

"Yuck. No, more like *Ocean's Eleven* Brad Pitt. Or maybe *Troy*."

"I saw the posters for that. Your guy rocked a toga and sandals?"

She glared at me. "Yeah, you know my type so well. A guy in a sheet in the middle of winter made a style statement I couldn't resist."

"Was the statement, 'I can't afford pants'?"

"Laugh it up, Jessie. Even you can't get to me today. He's perfect. Smart, good looking, well dressed. In an expensive suit. And he was a total gentleman."

"Well, good. He sounds nice," I said.

A beat of silence passed.

"That's it?" Sandy asked suspiciously.

"Uh . . . I'm glad he wasn't wearing a toga?"

"No, I mean . . . no lecture? You're supposed to tell me how I can't meet a guy with my standards in a club." She looked at me in disbelief. "You always give me that speech."

True. Sandy wasn't active in church, but she walked the line on most stuff.

"I don't give speeches. Only unsolicited advice. And it's only payback for your nagging. Besides, I mean it. He sounds nice." I turned back to my spreadsheet. After a moment, she padded over to the kitchen and began foraging for breakfast, probably in the form of unnaturally textured low fat egg substitutes. She has an unhealthy obsession with health food. I settled in to study another column of numbers when the fridge door slammed and Sandy's feet raced back across the wood floor.

"Something's wrong!" she burst out.

"With the fridge?" I asked, confused.

"No. Something's wrong with *you*. Cough it up. Why are you so mellow this morning?"

I studied her for a minute and grinned. "It's the lumberjack."

"What about him?"

"He e-mailed me back."

She looked at me blankly. "Wait. One e-mail de-stressed you and turned you back into a regular girl?"

"Well . . . maybe it was more than one e-mail."

Sandy cocked her head. "Tell me."

"We ended up IM-ing a few times last night. He's funny. I didn't even get all my work done."

"I love this guy already!"

"What about your antilumberjack prejudices? You're in favor of them now?" I teased.

"No, but the fact that he actually distracted you from your work for an evening means I'm totally on his team. Did you make a date?"

I shrugged nonchalantly. "No, we just talked. I don't even know him."

"Yeah, but you want to know him. So what's the next step? Are you going to e-mail him again?"

"I guess."

"That's the kind of thing that's pretty easy to know." She studied me. "You're doing the Jason thing again."

I winced at the mention of my first boyfriend. "Whatever. No, I'm not."

"I don't believe you. You had a great conversation with a funny, interesting guy, and suddenly you're not sure again. That's got Jason written all over it. Who needs Seattle rain when you've got his cloud hanging over your head?"

"Who needs Broadway when I've got a live-in drama queen?"

Sandy looked at me and said nothing.

"I've got to work on my comebacks," I muttered. She walked off toward the kitchen again as I called after her. "This has nothing to do with Jason!"

She ignored me, passing me on the way back to her bedroom with a bowl of granola in her hands. "You still have a Jason problem," she said. And she shut her door behind her with a decisive click.

I sniffed and turned back to my desk, but before long, I gave up and threw the file down. Sandy was right. I did have a Jason problem. I was so over not being over him.

I needed some heavy artillery.

I pulled up the IM log with Ben on my computer and reread it. Even as I smiled over the conversation from the night before, I could feel the Jason shadow hovering. Stupid shadow. Really stupid Jason. The relationship had ended four years ago. It shouldn't still be getting in my way. I pushed away from the desk, too distracted to get any work done.

I stood in the middle of the living room, looking around for a minute, taking it all in. A soft sand tone covered walls, and shots of apple green pillows and throws brightened the brown sofa and oversized arm chair. The chair sat under a wide window with a small table beside it, a pile of books I meant to get to stacked on top. The whole room felt bright without being overwhelming, and the green made me happy on the frequent Seattle rainy days.

I'd saved my signing bonus from Macrosystems, plus hoarded my generous salary and lived cheaply for two years to buy it. Sandy and I used to share an apartment with two other girls, but when one got married and the other moved the year before, I took an uncharacteristic risk and bought a condo while the slumping real estate market held prices down. With Sandy paying rent, I could afford the modest townhouse in Capitol Hill, the zip-code magnet for aspiring Seattle hipsters. It wasn't the cozy cottage I'd dreamed of in high school, but it felt like home.

I wanted to believe there comes a point when a string of accomplishments, like owning my own place, would sort of tip the success and failure scales back to even. Right now, though, I still saw Jason as a black mark on the record of Things I've Done in My Life. Education? Great job? Home? Promotion? Check. Healthy relationship? Not so much.

It wasn't like I hadn't tried to put it behind me. After our breakup, I changed colleges, moved to two different states, and dated dozens of guys in my quest to move on. Well, dozens at BYU and a few here before I ran through the limited options in the Seattle dating pool. Nothing stuck. I read in a magazine once that the average recovery time from a breakup is twice the length of the relationship. I hoped—no, *prayed*—it wasn't true, or I was in real trouble. I'd met Jason in Primary, for pity's sake, and we'd started dating when we were seventeen. For four years. I was not on board for an eight-year recovery.

An unexpected whisper in my ear made me jump. "Jjjaaasssooonn," Sandy hissed in a ghostly voice. I shot her a dirty look.

"I knew it," she said. "You have that lost puppy look on your face. He's the only thing that does it."

"That's—" I began to protest.

"Ridiculous?" she challenged me.

"No. Sad. I'm so lame."

"You're not lame. More like emotionally crippled."

"Thanks. That helps. You have a special touch."

"I wasn't finished," Sandy said, unperturbed by my sarcasm. "I'm staging an intervention. Come on." She grabbed my wrist and pulled me down the hall.

"Wait, no. I can quit on my own. And this can't be an intervention. You have to have more people than this."

"You're right. I should conference call your mom and sisters. Good plan."

"No! I surrender. Don't sic them on me. One is a good number for an intervention." I'm the youngest of four children, all girls, all convinced they know better than I do how to run my life. Dante couldn't imagine a circle of hell lower than the one where they and Sandy gang up on me over my relationship issues.

"I thought so. We're going to take care of this, starting now," Sandy declared as she threw open my bedroom door and dragged me inside. "Where is it?"

"Where is what?" I asked, confused. Trying to figure out what she wanted, I scanned the double bed centered against one wall, topped by a down comforter in a soft cream duvet. A few blue and chocolate brown throw pillows lay on top, reflecting the same colors in a simple window valance and some scattered area rugs on the wood floor. Two bookshelves full of my favorite books, photos, and CDs lined the opposite wall. "What am I looking for?"

"The box. Full of Jason stuff. Where is it?"

I jerked my arm away. "How do you know about the box?"

She shrugged off my glare. "We all have that guy, Jess. The one whose pictures we can't throw away. The more toxic the relationship, the longer you hold on to the box, so you for sure have one full of his stuff. Get it out. Every last bit of it."

Our stare down lasted for a full ten seconds before I glanced away. "It's not a big deal. I never even look at it."

"And why would you when it's all burned into your steel trap of a brain? That box is a pit of bad feng shui, and you need to get it out of here."

Now I rolled my eyes. "Feng shui?"

"You mock, but it works. I wasn't sleeping well, so I changed the direction my bed faces, and now I have good dreams."

"Wow. How did they ever penetrate the dirty laundry fortress at your footboard?"

Her eyes narrowed. "I'm counting to three, and then I'm calling your mom. Move it."

I trudged to the closet and reached into the back. I pulled out a battered shoebox and tossed it on the bed. "See, it's even dusty. I told you I don't look at it."

She ignored me, grabbed it, and marched out of the room while I followed like a lemming until I figured out her destination. I hustled to jump in front of the fireplace. "You can't burn all that! It's my personal history."

"Oh, it's history all right. But I'm not going to burn it. You are." Dropping the box at my feet, she headed back to the kitchen. "Stay there," she called over her shoulder. "I'm not done with you yet." She returned with the fireplace matches and my phone. Handing me the matches, she pretended to study the phone. "Let's see, your mom's speed dial number is one, right?"

"No," I gritted out through clenched teeth. "That's 911, but you'd better hit it because I'm going to kill you."

She held the phone out of reach, unfazed. "So your mom is on two. Do I have to count to three again?"

When I glared, she softened. "It's for the best, Jessie. You have to exorcise the bad Jason juju if you're ever going to get anywhere in your relationships." She sighed when my expression didn't change. "Think of it this way. Does he deserve even a corner of your closet?"

I blinked. Then I did it again. And then I was blinking back tears. "I've worked so hard to be done with him. Why can't I get rid of this box?"

She took my wrist again, only this time she led me to the sofa. "Come on; sit down. We're not getting through this without chocolate." Her phone blared "Crazy Train" by Ozzy Osbourne, the ringtone she used for her mom. I used to think it was mean until I met her mom and realized it was merely accurate.

"Go ahead and get it," I told Sandy.

"Nah. She's probably having another meltdown."

"Well, so am I."

"Yeah, but this is your first. This won't even be her first this week. She'll have another one tomorrow, and I'll talk to her then."

She disappeared for a moment, and thirty seconds later I found myself holding a carton of fudge ripple and a giant serving spoon. "This can't be good," I said. The bigger the spoon, the worse the problem. I took it and asked, "Am I this messed up?"

"Start eating, sister. We've got years to untangle."

I grumbled but dug into the ice cream while she retrieved the box and yanked the lid off. She riffled through the items, forming them into a heap on the sofa cushion. Movie tickets, a concert stub, mementos from hiking trips. While she examined a Kit Kat wrapper, "Crazy Train" went off again, but she sent it to voicemail.

I picked up a photo from a barbecue with my family and the Stewarts, Jason's family, sending waves of memories washing over me. My parents had moved into our ward on the California central coast before I was born, and the Stewarts had immediately befriended them. Jason had always been one of my buddies growing up—until somewhere along the line he'd decided he wanted to date me and made me realize I liked the idea.

I sorted out a couple dried-up corsages from high school dances, feeling silly for keeping the long-dead carnations.

Sandy flipped through my high school graduation pictures. "I don't get it," she said. "Why didn't it work? As girls go, you pretty much rock. What else did he want?"

"If I knew the answer to that, do you think I would be so emotionally stunted?" I asked. Sandy shook her head and almost sent her ringing phone to voicemail for the third time when I stopped her. "I'll be okay. The ice cream's working. Go see what your mom wants." She hesitated, scowling at her phone. "It's fine, I promise," I reassured her, waving the nearly empty ice cream carton as proof. She sighed but grabbed her phone and headed for her room.

"I'll listen as fast as I can," she called over her shoulder.

I picked up the graduation pictures she left behind. It felt like seventy years, not seven, since I had smiled so hopefully into the camera, sure I knew what would come next. I had always had a clear direction for my life, even as a kid. My sisters teased me about what they called "the plan," as if it loomed in front of me in capital letters. Because of my dad's teaching position at the nearby university in our town, all of us got half tuition, so I would earn a scholarship for the rest. I'd graduate without debt, get married, and pursue a career until I had kids.

As our relationship evolved, my plan became our plan, and I followed it exactly. I got the scholarship, sent Jason off on his mission to Italy, and studied hard while I waited. We wrote every week. At first. But somewhere along the line, his letters grew farther apart, and so did we. He explained that he was immersed in the work and apologized for not writing more. But the letters, previously full of the challenges and rewards of missionary life, grew terse as the months passed.

I stuck it out, sure it would all fall into place when he got back. It didn't. There was nothing in "the plan" about the Jason who stepped off the plane. He seemed the same at first. We hung out with the same people again, did all our old favorite things, spent time with each other's families. Secretly though, in my stomach, where I couldn't ignore it, a black pit yawned wider by the week, and I couldn't pinpoint the problem. I kept a good face on it, but the perfect future I'd envisioned for four years slowly crumbled, and I scrambled to pick up the falling pieces by myself. Jason acted like his old self in groups but doggedly avoided time alone with me. Our conversations stayed superficial, and he subtly changed topics whenever the future came up.

I knew missionaries sometimes had a hard time adjusting after returning home, and I tried to give him the time he needed. But when he finally shook himself out of his funk, he shook me to the core in the process.

Digging through the box, I found the smooth rock I wanted. Our last conversation replayed with painful clarity. We were hanging out at an institute bonfire on the beach when Jason surprised me by suggesting a walk along the water. It wasn't at all like him anymore to try to get me alone. We headed down the shoreline, away from the chatter and laughter of the activity. The silence weighed on me so I broke it. "The sunset's pretty."

"It's always pretty."

"Is that a bad thing?"

He shrugged. "What could be bad about a pretty sunset?"

I stopped and turned to face him full on. "I don't know, Jason. Why don't you tell me because something about it isn't sitting right with you."

"It's the same sunset it always is, Jess. What do you want me to say about it?" He stared off into the distance as if he could see past the horizon.

I watched him for a few moments. "What's wrong with you? I thought best friends told each other everything. You haven't *really* talked to me since you got home."

His face tightened, and his shoulders tensed. I would scream if he shrugged again. But he stopped himself and drew a deep breath, studying the sand for a few nerve-wracking seconds and then looking up to meet my eyes. My breath caught at the misery in his. "What's wrong?" I whispered.

He didn't answer for a moment. Instead, he stooped down and picked up a stone from the edge of the wet sand, took my palm, and placed the rock in it. It was a pretty cream color, worn smooth, and glowing with a faint gold tinge from the sunset. "What do you see?" he asked me.

This was an old game. Since we were kids, he'd always made a big production of searching the sand and proclaiming he had found the prettiest rock or shell and then presenting it to me. "It's a rock," I said. He looked at me searchingly, and my smile faltered. I wasn't sure what he wanted. "It's pretty. I . . . like the color."

He shoved his fingers through his hair and turned back to the horizon. The sun dipped low now, and a deep purple crept in, signaling nightfall. "I've changed, Jessie. It started on my mission, but I didn't realize how much until I came home." He took the stone back and turned it over and over. "Before I left, I would have thought this was a pretty rock too. But now all I see is that it's part of something bigger that's been worn down. And it's because it stays in one place and lets the sea move all around it."

"What are you trying to say?" I asked, fearing I already knew.

"I never really thought about what I wanted before. Go on a mission, finish school, work for my dad, get married, have kids. It all sounded good. You and I, the perfect fit. Why not?"

"Wow. Even for a backhanded compliment, that stinks," I said.

Jason finally turned to look at me again. "I do love you, Jessie. You've been a part of my whole life, but . . ."

My stomach dropped. "But what?"

"But this is not what I want. I'm so sorry," he finished. Misery spilled into his voice.

I stiffened. "You're sorry?" He glanced away again. I studied him, trying to find some clue, some reason for this change written on his face. "So what do you want? You say you know it's not this. What is it, then?"

"I know I don't want you to hate me, and I don't know how to give you an answer that won't make you do that." His eyes pleaded with me to understand something he couldn't explain.

"Try. You owe me that."

"I do want marriage and family and all of those things. Soon." He paused. "But with someone else."

My breath stopped. Maybe even time stopped before I strangled out a question. "Who?"

"Jessie . . ."

"Who?" I almost shouted.

"I never meant for this to happen . . . I'm not sure it even will happen," he said.

"*This* is . . ." I had no words. I couldn't even think. I turned around and walked back up the beach, trying to leave him behind. He ran to catch up and blocked my path.

"Jessie, I want you to know I haven't done anything yet." He lifted my chin. I slapped his hand away and stepped around him. He blocked me again, this time holding me in place with his hands on my shoulders. "I'm about to take the biggest risk of my life by letting you walk away. But I have to."

I looked at him, stone-faced.

"A sister serving in the mission with me. I never crossed a line or broke any rules, but I started having feelings for her. I tried to stop it. I requested a transfer, but it didn't get her out of my mind. We e-mailed after I got home. I told myself it was so I could keep track of the mission, but . . ." He stopped again and swallowed. The pain on his face forced me to brace for the worst. "She got home two months ago. When I told her about you, it tore her up. She shut me out, and I realized how bad I had it for her. I have to make it right with her, convince her to give me a chance. I have to know where it's going to go."

I stared at him, trying to see in his face the Jason I had grown up with, had loved for four years. But this new Jason wasn't anyone I knew. Stepping away from him for the last time, I took the stone from him and tossed it up once before catching it and sliding it into my pocket. I walked away again.

"Jessie!" he called after me. But I didn't turn around. There was nothing left to say.

"Come in, Jessie. Over."

I snapped out of the painful memory to find Sandy waving a hand in front of my face. "There you are, good buddy," she said.

"Are you speaking trucker?" I asked.

"Ten-four. I want a trucker hat."

"You can't have one."

"Why not?"

"Because I'm saving you from a trend Ashton Kutcher killed five years ago."

"Fair enough," she said. "What's this? It looks personal."

"It's *all* personal. You have boundaries *now*?" I asked, but I took the card from her hand, flipping it open to see Jason's handwriting. More than anything else in the box, the familiar slants and angles of his cursive conjured him like he was almost there in the room. "He sent this to me about six months after we broke up." I scanned the familiar lines, but I didn't need to. I remembered them. He'd apologized again for handling everything so poorly and told me about his recent engagement to his sister missionary. He'd said some nice things to me and told me he knew I'd soon find the person I was truly meant to be with.

Four years later, it turned out he was wrong. But the bitterness I'd read that card with hundreds of times in the first few months after I got it . . . failed to materialize.

I picked up the rock from that awful night on the beach and turned it over and over in my hand. It wasn't as pretty as I remembered it. And the dried-up carnation was just an old, dead flower. And the dozens of scraps of paper? Clutter. Worse, it was emotional clutter.

"I want to show you something. It's arts and crafts night," I said.

Sandy snorted. We both hate crafts. Not doing them together is another way we've bonded. I waved the rock at her.

"What are we doing with it?" she asked. "Stoning Jason's pictures with it? Let the healing begin."

"No. I told you it's craft time. I need a Sharpie."

She jumped up and grabbed one from the junk drawer in the kitchen. "Make it quick, sister. You know my craft allergy drove me from Relief Society," she said as she handed it to me.

"No, I didn't realize that. I thought it was existential angst."

"And that."

I took the marker and carefully printed across the top of the stone. When I finished, Sandy read it and smiled. "Perfect," she announced. She walked to the fireplace and set it on top of the mantle. "It looks good right here."

"You should start a fire while you're up," I said, pointing to the pile of papers she had made on the sofa. "I've got the kindling."

She whooped. "She's back!"

I smiled, but I could only hope she was right. I'd hung on to that box for a long time. I wasn't so sure it was as easy to banish those memories as sending them all up in smoke.

Chapter 4

So far, Monday stank—bad. An overturned trash can, courtesy of a neighborhood dog, made me almost twenty minutes late to work after I cleaned it up. Being late meant I had no prep time for my weekly managers' meeting. After listening to Craig, another project manager, drone on about his team's progress, I had nothing interesting to contribute when he asked, "What about your team?" except to answer, "Our spreadsheets are almost done." I sat back in my chair and doodled, hoping it looked like I was taking notes on the riveting discussion about the recent change in office supply vendors Craig had initiated. Mmm, office supplies. Heady stuff.

Bettina Langley tapped my notepad and mouthed, "Gotcha." I had drawn a mini-Craig with a giant head. Since I'm no artist, only the oversized Starbucks mug in my cartoon's hand could have given me away. I never saw him without it. He probably had pure coffee coursing through his veins. He sent his assistant to the corner kiosk at least four times a day for some drink with several words I didn't even know in the title. No big deal, except I'm pretty sure he expended the extra caffeinated energy on plots to embarrass me. He'd taken his bump to being only the second youngest person on the management team with a noticeable lack of grace.

"His head's not *that* big," Bettina whispered.

"Well, not literally," I whispered back.

Craig smiled, all toothy and friendly. "Care to share with the rest of us?"

"Yes, I would, Craig. I was telling Bettina how much I enjoy our new graph paper—so much more than the old stuff," I said, referring to the fruits of his recent office supply cost-saving measures. "Thank you for taking the time to make it happen."

It was Bettina's turn to cough.

Craig looked like he doubted my sincerity. "That one small change is saving more than three hundred dollars a year. We should all be looking for these kinds of cost-cutting measures," he said.

"Mmm, you are so right. I wonder, how long did it take to find that particular shortcut? And how much did we pay hourly for your assistant to compare the hundreds of supplies we use?" I asked. I saw Dennis Court, the department head, suppress a smile.

Craig flushed. "It's a long-term savings strategy. These things add up."

"So does paying an assistant to shop around every time the prices change," Dennis interjected. "Payroll eats into the profits. Miss Taylor, don't you have a contact in human resources?"

"Yes."

"Why don't you have your team transition to an internal payroll audit when you complete your current project? See if you can find some additional cost saving opportunities."

"Sure. We'll get right on it." I smiled at my boss. Could my day be turning around?

After the meeting, I went back to my office and checked my e-mail to find a message waiting for me from Lookup. Ben again. The subject line read "Membership Offer, Limited Time Only," causing my eyebrow to creep up in confusion. Was he spamming me?

To: JKT
From: HC

Good Morning. I'm starting a new club. I'm going to be the president, and you can be the vice president. It's called the League Against Monday E*******, or LAME for short. I don't know what the E stands for yet, but I need it or I won't have an acronym. Clubs need their initials to spell a word, or they're not legitimate. The membership requirements are strict though. If you don't like Mondays, you're in. What do you say?

I hit reply.

To: HC
From: JKT

Too bad you didn't catch me an hour ago when I thought I hated Mondays too. Maybe you could call your club the League Against Monday (Except when it's good), and then I can join. And you'll have your E all taken care of too. Having a bad day?

To: JKT
From: HC
I've had better. It's no big deal, just a case of everything going wrong. I've learned it can't go on forever. That's an actual law of physics.

To: HC
From: JKT
No one likes a frowny face. Change it for a smile. Make the world a better place by smiling all the while. I think Gandhi said that. Him or Einstein. They said all the cool stuff.

To: JKT
From: HC
Thanks, Sister Taylor. So . . . to be totally honest, I just experienced a long, awkward pause. Uh . . . how would you feel about exchanging actual e-mail addresses? Also being honest, that should be read with me sounding smooth and suave because that's how I wrote it.

I thought about it for a minute. Why not? I wasn't getting a psycho vibe from him, but granted, it was e-mail. I've been sensitive to that ever since one of my BYU dates showed up dressed in a full Harry Potter costume for a midnight screening he invited me to. Kind of funny when you're sixteen, sad when you're twenty-four.

To: HC
From: JKT
Sure. But now I have to go. I'm smiling, so I think Craig the Snitch figured out this isn't work. We don't smile about spreadsheets here at Macrosystems. I'm glaring at my computer now to throw Big Brother off the scent. But I'm on the company dime so I guess I better do company stuff.

I typed out my e-mail address, sent the message, and logged out. Craig eyed me suspiciously through the window, so I waved and smiled at him. He retreated down the hall. I sighed and hit the desk intercom. "Katie," I called to my assistant. "Can you get Lauren and Mike in here? And tell them to bring their laptops. It's going to be a long morning."

* * *

The day ended up stretching way past five again, and I collapsed on the sofa when I got home. I had worked through dinner, and hunger was making me stupid. In a stupor, I watched Sandy do a yoga DVD. After a particularly bizarre contortion, I asked, "What's this one called? Drunken fish? Cranky panda?"

She assumed a serene cross-legged pose and answered, "You are a big, ugly rock in my emotional river, and I'm going to flow around you. And I'm also not going to help you with your payroll stuff now because you're mean."

"What? I'm showing a sincere interest in your meditation mumbo jumbo."

"Yeah, calling it mumbo jumbo really makes your point."

"Fine. I have stuff to do anyway," I said and bounced off of the sofa, a sudden spurt of energy speeding me toward my laptop.

Sandy cocked her head. "What do you have to do that could possibly be more fun than getting on my nerves?"

"Oh, answering some e-mails and stuff. And eating."

"Uh-huh. You only do that when the Internet is about to collapse under the weight of your unopened messages. You're checking on the lumberjack."

"Your mind always goes from A to Z without stopping along the way."

"Not true. I did stop. At *B* for *Ben*."

"Okay, you caught me." After a hesitation, I confessed, "I gave him my actual e-mail address."

"Well, you're practically married now. You move fast."

"Be nice. It was a big step."

"Only because you're the most commitment-phobic woman in Seattle, Jess. But I'm glad you at least gave him that much. My little girl is growing up." She said the last part with her face in her lap, arms stretched straight up behind her.

"Ha ha. And I'm not commitment phobic."

"You are too. You don't even own a pet."

"I have plants."

She straightened. "You've killed three ficuses in a row."

"Which is a great example of why I shouldn't get a pet."

"You're a plant-killing commitment phobe. That makes you a Lifetime movie waiting to happen. Poor Jessie."

"Who do you think will play us in the movie?" I pretended to think. "Ooh, I know. For me, they'll get Olivia Munn and for you, Kathy Griffin."

"Evil. All redheads are not created equal."

I smiled and turned on the computer. Sure enough, a message waited from ben_bratton@datalock.com.

To: JTaylor@earthnet.net

The laws of physics win. Everything's all right again. I'm disbanding my LAME club. I hope your day stayed good. You'll have to tell me more about Craig the Snitch. I think I work with him too, only we call him Tina the Tattler, and he's a she. Oh, and she doesn't work in your office; she works in mine. But I guess every office has one.

To: ben_bratton@datalock.com.

I'm sorry your club didn't work out. Maybe tomorrow you can start Tuesdays We Irritate Tina. TWIT. Why does your e-mail say Datalock? I thought you work for the Forest Service.

It didn't take long for his reply to come back. It felt good to know I wasn't the only one developing a codependent relationship with my e-mail server. Then again, he could also be a workaholic who was always at his desk. I knew about that too.

To: JTaylor@earthnet.net

I guess it's better to say I work with the Forest Service rather than for them. I'm consulting on a data project they have so I've been on a contract with them for a few months.

To: ben_bratton@datalock.com

So you're not a lumberjack?

To: JTaylor@earthnet.net

Hypothetically speaking, is a burly lumberjack or a wiry computer nerd more likely to get a date with, oh, say . . . you?

To: ben_bratton@datalock.com
Does the computer nerd have a secret superhero outfit with a cape?

To: JTaylor@earthnet.net
Yes?

To: ben_bratton@datalock.com
Then I pick the lumberjack.

To: JTaylor@earthnet.net
Ouch. My mom always said to be myself. The truth is, I don't have a superhero costume. Sometimes I tuck a towel into my collar like a cape when I'm home alone to make me feel more important, but my only super power is amazing data analysis. Is it enough?

To: ben_Bratton@datalock.com
It's enough. I'm more of a Clark Kent fan anyway. But I'm confused. I thought your profile said you were looking for new friends, not dates.

To: JTaylor@earthnet.net
True, but that only applies to girls I don't know who might be cyber stalkers.

To: ben_bratton@datalock.com
You mean girls you don't know . . . like me?

To: JTaylor@earthnet.net
Of course I know you. I know your favorite color is . . . um. Wait. You love to eat . . . yeah. You like to listen to . . . huh. You're right. I don't know you at all. That's gotta change. I'm going to need more of your data.

To: ben_bratton@datalock.com
What can I tell you? Blue. Chicken enchiladas. The Arcade Fire when it's raining, Jack Johnson when it's not. Does that help?

To: JTaylor@earthnet.net
I'm getting an input error. I need more data. Like a seven digit number starting with your area code.

I burst out laughing. He was definitely funny. And unexpected.

"Well, that's not work. And yet it's the computer. It must be the lumberjack," Sandy deduced as she entered the kitchen.

"You're so wrong."

"It's not Ben?"

"No, it's Ben. He's not a lumberjack. He does computer stuff for the Forest Service."

"And that's funny?"

"Yep. Data analysis is hilarious. You have no idea."

"Seriously, what's funny?"

"He wants some data input."

"Why is that funny? You can tell me to mind my own business if you don't want me to know what's going on, you know."

"Will it work?"

"No."

"I didn't think so. Ben's asking for my phone number. It's the way he did it that was funny."

"Why are you talking to me then, woman? Type it in!"

"Really? You don't think it's kind of soon to be giving my number out?"

"No, I don't. I think it's premature to name your future mini Bens and Jessies, but I definitely don't think it's too soon to spill your digits."

"But we just met."

"No, you haven't met. And you never will if you don't give him a phone number."

"What if he turns out to be crazy and calls me at all hours of the night?"

"What do I care? It's your cell phone." Sandy smirked when I glared. "You're totally overthinking this. This sounds like a stable guy with a good job and a sense of humor, and he's a Mormon. Does any of that scream stalker? Give him your number."

"Okay, I will. But not because you told me to."

"Of course not. You thought of this all by yourself."

"Yes, I did," I said. "Bossy pants."

Sandy did not look repentant. "Sticks and stones, blah, blah. Give him the number."

I sent off another e-mail.

To: ben_bratton@datalock.com
I believe in solutions too. My number is (206) 555-5683.

"I hope you're right," I muttered to Sandy.

"Who cares if I'm right? Let's hope he's Mr. Right."

"So far he's just some guy," I retorted.

"As long as you remember he's not Jason Stewart, that should be more than enough."

"Jason who?"

Sandy smiled. My e-mail alert dinged again.

To: JTaylor@earthnet.net

That's the piece of data I needed. Unfortunately, I also just got a call from work. Apparently the morning's problems have made a repeat appearance, and I need to take care of them. But I'll call you. Soon. Good night.

Well. That would teach me to get all worked up about giving my number out. At least I could be pretty sure he wasn't a psycho. He definitely wasn't in a rush to ring my phone off the hook. But I understood better than anybody how work could creep out of the office and pounce when no one was looking. I wondered how long it would take for him to get out from under it all. Looking at my own pile of payroll records, I had a bad feeling I knew how long it could be.

Chapter 5

Seventeen hours. Not that I counted how many it took before Ben called. But when my cell phone rang midmorning on Tuesday with an unfamiliar number, I had a hunch as to who it was. I swiveled my office chair to face the outside window and answered.

"This is Jessie."

"Hi, Jessie. This is Ben." He sounded warm and confident.

"Ben . . . Ben. You mean Ben of bathroom towel-cape fame?"

"No, this is Ben, president of the TWITs." He sounded pretentious, and I smiled at his playfulness.

"The president? I feel so honored."

"Normally I have my assistant call to invite new members, but she said you were a potentially *big* TWIT, so I thought I'd better call you myself." I could hear a smile in his voice.

"Wow. Quite a club. But I have a question. Is tweeting required to be a TWIT? Because I can't handle one more social network."

"No tweeting. That's for hipsters. We take ourselves too seriously for that."

"Well, I'm impressed with your member services so far."

"Oh, it gets better. It's customary for us to treat new members to lunch in the downtown Seattle bistro of their choice."

"Really? How do most of your new members feel about that?"

"I don't know. It's a new custom. I started this club yesterday."

"I think I remember reading that somewhere."

He laughed. "I'll give our PR department a raise. How'd they do selling you on lunch?"

I hesitated for a minute and then answered, "That's tempting, but I can't."

"I see," Ben said, followed by a long pause. "Is this because you think my club is stupid?"

"No," I said, laughing. "I have a lunch meeting today." After a long breath, I took the plunge. "But Thursday looks good."

"Hmm. Yeah, Thursday works for me. Do you have a preference, or should I pick a place?"

I frantically wracked my brain for a moment. I wanted to pick somewhere that sent the right message. Noodle Ranch? No. Great food but not a first date kind of place. Chez Shea? Candlelit tables would be too over the top. Finally I asked, "Do you know Trattoria Fredo?" It would be cozy without screaming romance and quiet enough to have a conversation without yelling.

"Near Pioneer Square?"

"That's it. Sound okay?"

"Sounds perfect. I'll meet you there Thursday at noon?"

"Yeah, Thursday." Stupid Wednesdays, always getting in the way.

Silence hummed on the line for a moment. I wondered if he was trying to figure what to say next too. I needed to get back to work, but I didn't want to hang up yet. When the quiet verged on uncomfortable, Ben spoke again."We should work out a signal to be sure we recognize each other. Maybe I could wear a purple polka dot tie, and you could wear a big floppy hat."

"That's a good idea. Or we could double check each other's pictures before then."

"Yeah, that was my backup plan." He hesitated. "Except I look kind of different from my picture."

Uh oh. Had he gained fifty pounds or shaved his head or something? I had a bad feeling about this. But it's not like I could ask him how he looked different because I didn't want to come off sounding like it mattered. I went with a noncommittal, "Oh, really?"

"Yeah, that's an old picture. But it's the only digital shot I had when I filled out the profile questionnaire. Kinda lame, I know. So maybe one of us should still wear a giant hat."

"I'd totally do it if it weren't for the dress code here at work. It says to wear collared shirts and business appropriate trousers. No giant hats are allowed. Sorry."

"No, you're not. And I never wear trousers."

"Excuse me?"

"I only wear pants."

Ah. "That's better than slacks."

"It's not a high bar."

I noticed Craig lurking near my door. "Craig alert. I have to go rescue my assistant from him. But I'll see you Thursday?"

"It's a date."

* * *

"Help! I have a date!" I called to Sandy as soon as I walked through the front door after work.

She whooped. "Yes! You've joined the living."

"You are such an exaggerator. You keep forgetting all the dates I went on when I moved here."

"No, I don't. But they don't make up for not going out at all for the last year."

"It hasn't been that long."

"Name the last time you went out."

"Six months ago. I went out with that Blake guy."

"I quit listening after you said 'six months ago' and made my point for me."

"So are you going to help me?" I demanded.

"Do what?"

"Get ready for my date."

"Sure. When and where?

"Aren't you going to ask who it's with?"

"No, because I already know it's Ben."

"Wrong." I said. She looked at me in surprise. "It's with Craig," I added.

Her look changed to disbelief for a moment, and we both burst out laughing. "It's a double date," I told her. "You get to go out with his ego."

"Yeah right. There's not enough room for both of us. Seriously, it's Ben, right?"

"It is. We're going to meet at Trattoria Fredo for lunch on Thursday."

She sighed and shook her head. Now I was the surprised one. "Aren't you excited? You've been bugging me about dating for . . ." I pretended to glance down at my watch, "ever. You got your way. This usually makes you happy."

"I'm happy you're going. But I'm saving the celebration for an actual date. Lunch is you sticking one toe in."

"Don't I get anything for that?" I asked.

"Yes." She leaned over and patted me on the back.

"I'd settle for wardrobe advice instead."

"Come on, then." She dragged me toward her bedroom. "We'd better look in my closet."

"What's wrong with mine? I've got plenty of suits in there."

"Exactly," she retorted.

I happen to like my suits. I have some nice ones. A few black ones, a few gray ones, a few navy ones. Hmm.

A few too many suits. Good thing Sandy had a whole other closet for me to shop in.

She threw open the closet door and waded through the piles on the floor. It appeared to be mostly towels, more than I ever thought one person could need. Unless that one person is someone who hates doing laundry as much as Sandy does. I have personally seen her drive to the store to buy new underwear because she didn't feel like doing a load of wash. And no, the argument that it takes more time to go to the store doesn't work.

She yanked a dress off the hanger and threw it at me. "Try it," she ordered.

"No way," I said. "I'm not wearing pink to work."

"Even men wear pink work shirts now, Jessie. Get with the program. And put it on." I left her whipping through her rack of hangers and pulling more things out. I put the dress on in front of my mirror and grimaced. Cute dress, but if I wore it to work, I'd get double takes all day long, and I didn't want to deal with it. Sandy walked in with a pile of more clothes over her arm and looked me over.

"Looks good, but it's all wrong for work," she said. She laid the clothes on my bed and dug through them, muttering. A moment later, she straightened with a brown skirt in her hand. "Try this."

"Really? It looks kind of conservative. I thought you said I dress that way too much already."

She grinned. "Try it on. I'm going to find some things to match it." She took off for her room again, intent on her mission. I shrugged at my reflection and slipped the pink dress off and put the skirt on.

Whoa.

The deceptively simple cut and the deep shade of chocolate managed to look both sexy and classy. I checked the label. It was from an up and coming designer who had recently been featured on the local news for opening a boutique at Pine Street and Fifth Avenue, the trend hub for fashion-conscious Seattle women. It fit amazingly. I stared in surprise. The pencil cut skirt found and accentuated my invisible curves without being indecent. Quite a trick, that. The finding my curves part, I mean. Sandy and I wear the same size, but we're not even close to the same shape. My Grandma Jean would have called Sandy "womanly." She was built for dresses. I, on the other hand, could wear any pair of pants in the mall because I had no hips to interfere with the fit. Sandy insisted it wasn't fair because she had to buy more expensive pants, but I'm pretty sure her hips didn't make her pay more than two hundred dollars for her Hudson jeans. She just loved to shop. But I'd lost that argument so many times I didn't even bother making it anymore. She definitely doesn't think like an accountant.

Still, I had to give it to her. If paying extra meant I looked like an actual girl in a skirt, I might rethink my shopping strategy. I reached into my own closet and grabbed a new Gap shirt, a white cap-sleeved shell, to see how it looked with the skirt, but I frowned at the result. Boring again. Sandy popped back in. "Perfect."

I raised an eyebrow at her.

"With this," she clarified, and tossed me a pink cardigan.

I pulled the thin material over the blouse and buttoned it in the middle.

"Would you look at that," she teased me. "It's a waist."

And that wasn't all. The color did good things for my complexion, and the thin knit of the sweater looked feminine but work appropriate. "It's so soft," I said, rubbing the three-quarter-length sleeve unconsciously.

"It'd better be. That's pure Tibetan cashmere."

I tugged it off. "I'm not wearing it."

"You have to! It looks so good on you."

"We're eating Italian. What if I spill marinara sauce on it before I can give it back to you? I guess I could hide it in one of your laundry piles. That way you'd never find it," I mused.

"Ha, ha. Get their artisan meat plate with a side of cheese instead of pasta and you'll be fine."

"Is it easier to clean out of cashmere?"

"No, but it's harder to spill. Try these," she said and held up a pair of BCBG boots. The gorgeous deep brown leather ended in her signature four-inch heels.

"Those are your favorite boots!"

"Yeah, well, for some unexplainable reason, you're my favorite roommate. Go ahead and try them."

"No way. I'll cry if something bad happens to your sweater, but I'll lose the will to live if I screw up the boots too. Besides, I'd be almost six feet tall in those. What if he's one of those guys who lies about his height?"

Sandy cocked her head and looked me over for a minute. "You're right. You'd probably break your neck trying to walk in these." She put them down and rooted through my shoe collection. I have a lot of great shoes; they just have lower heels than hers. She pulled out a brown pair with a slightly pointed toe and an ankle strap. "These will work. Wear your hair down and some lip gloss, and you'll be good to go."

Much like her belief in Oprah, Sandy also believed lip gloss could cure most of the world's ills. I had a quick mental flash of her hawking her own line of lip gloss in an infomercial some day. "Fixes thin lips, weak chins, and poverty," she'd say as she waved some of the wonder goo around.

I'd learned not to question her in matters of style though. It was like having the fashion police right across the hall. I looked over my reflection in the mirror once more. The girl I saw looked chic and fresh. I liked it. "You're good at this clothes thing," I said.

She lifted a dismissive shoulder and smiled. "You're the one wearing them. Don't sell yourself short." She paused to consider the total effect for a moment. "You look Jennifer Garner-esque."

I straightened my posture and looked down my nose at her. "You're right. I'm fabulous." And then I rubbed feverishly at my freckles. "If only I could do something about these."

Sandy walked out, laughing. "Keep rubbing them," she called over her shoulder. "That's supposed to work real well."

I leaned toward the mirror and glared at the seven offending freckles. "Is it wrong to pray for your freckles to go away?"

An emphatic yes echoed down the hall.

"What about for my roommate to go away?" I asked and ducked as a pillow came flying through the doorway.

Once I heard her door shut, I reached for my jewelry box. Time to figure out my accessories. As I sorted through my meager jewelry collection, I examined my nerves over this date with Ben. True, I hadn't been on a date in more than six months, but I had gone on several before the pool had dried up. I wasn't a novice. So why was I so nervous?

Chapter 6

I COULD SEE KATIE'S FOREHEAD over the stack, but that was about all. The towering mound of paperwork separated us.

"This is ridiculous," I said.

"Is it for real?" she asked, walking around to my side of the desk.

"The view doesn't improve," I told her. Craig had made his next move. In the past, I'd ignored a story or two about people he'd stepped on in his climb to management, but the whispers came back to me. I wished I could explain to him that I never asked for my promotion, but I suspected it would only inflame him more. And he felt plenty mad already based on the mountain on my desk.

It had appeared this morning when his assistant had trailed him into my office, pushing a cart overflowing with stacks of paper.

"Good morning, Jessie," he'd said, friendly as ever. "I enjoyed your input at the manager's meeting on Monday." Nuts. "The more I thought about it, the more I realized you're right. There *is* an opportunity to save money on payroll. It made so much sense that I'd like to offer my assistance. So I had Brad here," he gestured to his uncomfortable-looking assistant, "pull some preliminary records for you to look through. Consider it a goodwill gesture."

I'd waited warily for the punch line, and he'd delivered. "Of course, if you don't think you guys can get to it, I'd be glad to let Dennis know we're ready to step in if you need us."

So Craig wanted to usurp the payroll project. My temper bubbled, but I kept it on a low simmer and returned his smile. "That's nice of you, Craig. Really nice. I'll let you know if we need your help," I'd said and begun unloading the papers from his cart.

It totally threw him. He didn't need to know I only called his bluff so I could buy myself some time while I figured out what to do. He didn't know how good my human resources contact was, but until I could talk to Sandy, I didn't either, so I needed to keep him guessing.

"Yes, well," he'd said, as I kept transferring the stacks. He tried to inject some nonchalance into his voice. "You let me know what I can do."

Oh, I had several suggestions for that. "You bet," I'd said. He'd left with Brad trailing obediently after him.

Now, three hours later, I cursed myself for not thinking faster on my feet. I'd been trying to get Sandy on the phone all morning, but she had a staff development session until noon. That left me with Mt. Paper until she or I had a better idea.

"Well played, Craig," I mumbled under my breath.

"Excuse me?" Katie asked.

"Nothing. Thinking out loud," I said. "Why don't you go ahead and take off early for lunch?" She smiled gratefully and left.

I eased back into my chair and surveyed the mess. I didn't know why I'd let Craig suck me into his petty power struggles. He thought I was as ambitious as he was because Dennis promoted me so quickly. But I couldn't have care less about the promotion. I worked extra hours because I got absorbed in a problem and was compulsive enough that I couldn't leave it alone until I'd figured it out. Add in the fact that I never had anywhere else to be anyway, and it translated into a lot of overtime. I caught a few people's attention. My department head, Dennis, asked me to pinch hit when my boss periodically went down to our Southern California office. When she got promoted, they offered me her old job. I liked having a reputation as a hard worker, but truthfully, I spent the same amount of energy on the Sunday crossword. I didn't have a passion for my job as much as I had a need to see things through.

Yet somehow, despite not caring about office politics, I'd ended up in some sort of turf war with Craig. For him, it was a power struggle, but for me, it was that I hated to be pushed. I always push back whether it's the smart thing to do or not. I glowered at the paper pile and fumbled for a solution. I would push this back to Craig one last time and then abandon the fight. But only after every scrap disappeared from my office.

My phone rang. Sandy's extension flashed on the caller ID. At last. I grabbed it and said, "I'm drowning."

"On dry land? How original of you."

"No, in paper. Craig decided to help me with the payroll audit, and now I've got thousands of sheets to go through."

"Why?"

"Because I have to find some cost savings, so I've got months of log sheets to check for patterns."

"No, I mean why would you go through the paper to find that out? HR is ground zero for gossip. I know who's fifteen minutes late and always claiming they're on time, I know who's overworking their assistants, and I know which departments have the lowest morale and worst attendance."

"That's perfect! I don't know if I owe you more for this or for loaning me your skirt."

"Definitely the skirt. Do you know how hard it is to find a size six on sale in such an obnoxiously healthy city? They always fly off the racks first."

I caught sight of my nemesis. "Thanks again, Sandy. I've got to go," I whispered.

"Craig?" she whispered back.

"Why are *you* whispering?" I asked in a normal voice.

"To make you feel better about acting crazy."

"Thanks for that too. I'll see you at home." I hung up the phone and called Katie in on the intercom then surveyed Mt. Paper thoughtfully. "You think you can find us a cart?"

"Is this going to make Craig mad?"

"Probably."

"Then I can definitely find a cart." And she headed off. Having an assistant who knows where everything is kept is the first rule to succeeding in business. Sure enough, Katie came cruising back a few minutes later with a media cart in front of her.

"Perfect. Let's load it up."

When we had returned the stacks to the cart, I turned to Katie. "Ready to rattle his cage?"

"Yes, please."

"Let's push."

We made slow progress down to Craig's office and rolled right through his open door.

"What are you doing?" he asked. After taking in the cart, he added, "Did you give up?"

"No. But I have a wager for you, since I know how much you love competition."

"I didn't think you were the betting kind, Jessie."

"Only when it's a sure thing."

"I'll bite. What are the terms?"

"Whoever saves the most payroll hours by noon tomorrow wins. The loser forfeits their assistant to the winner for three working days." Brad looked hopeful, but Katie looked faintly sick. I winked so Craig couldn't see. No way would I lose this. For one, Brad didn't love working for Craig, and he wouldn't knock himself out trying to find a solution. And Craig actually thought the answer would be in the mound newly transferred to his desk.

I could almost see the cogs churning in his brain, calculating the odds of losing Brad temporarily versus beating me and overworking Katie for a few days.

"I'll take that bet. This should be embarrassingly easy."

"Oh, I hope so, Craig." His smile slipped, and I turned and walked out of his office. Katie scampered after me.

"Now I'm scared," she said.

"Don't think for a second I'd throw you under the bus. Trust me," I said and headed to my desk to call Sandy. Katie veered sharply toward the cubicles to tell Lauren and Mike about the brewing drama.

I closed my door with a smile, then reached for the phone and punched in Sandy's extension. I had a wager to win.

Chapter 7

THE DAY OF MY LUNCH with Ben started out badly. I ducked into the restroom at work and leaned against the door. My Thursday already needed a reboot. Big time. This did not bode well for lunch. I checked to make sure I had the bathroom to myself before I faced the mirror. I figured I had cilantro from my breakfast omelet in my teeth or a roller in my hair.

But . . . everything looked fine. I leaned back in irritation. I dug my cell phone out of my handbag and called Sandy.

"Yeah?"

"This was a bad idea."

"Are you okay?" She sounded alarmed.

"Everybody stared at me."

"Where are you?"

"In the fifth floor bathroom." A weird noise came over the line. "Are you laughing at me? Because I will kill you."

"Um, no." She took a deep breath. "So you're wearing your lunch date outfit?"

"Yes."

"Did you leave your hair down?"

"Yes."

"And you have on lip gloss?"

"Yes! I said I would."

"Well, there's the problem."

"I should take the lip gloss off?" I asked in confusion.

"No, you should take a closer look at yourself. Since I didn't see you before I took off this morning, you'll have to tell me. Do you look good?"

I studied my reflection again. It was me, just . . . shinier. "Yes."

"And has anyone laughed?"

"No."

"That rules out your skirt being tucked into your underwear or a run in your stockings." I craned my neck over my shoulder to verify that I was still keeping Victoria's secret. I was.

"You probably look like Sunday Jessie. Your office isn't used to Sunday Jessie. Give them a few minutes to acclimate. I bet you look great, so don't worry about it, okay?"

"I feel like an idiot," I complained.

"You're going to be fine. Maybe pull your hair back and wipe the lip gloss off until lunch. You'll feel better. But remember they're looking at you because you look *good*," she said. "I have to go, but I want a full report after lunch."

I hung up the phone. How ridiculous. I always wore makeup to work, but I kept it toned down and paired it with basic suits to maintain some professionalism. Sandy could show up in a bright yellow blouse and zebra print heels and be taken seriously because she came off as sophisticated. Not me. It disconcerted me that MAC lip gloss could cause an outbreak of sidelong glances. Then again, if this was all it took, maybe I *was* too buttoned down. I'd have to remember to wear skirts and lip gloss on alternating days in the future. Clearly, my workmates weren't ready for the two together.

Taking Sandy's advice, I blotted the lip gloss, whipped my hair into a low ponytail, and took the pink sweater off for good measure. It fit neatly into my handbag. The office would have to deal with my skirt, but hopefully that by itself wouldn't completely blow their minds. Sheesh, they acted like Dennis Court had shown up wearing it.

I headed back into my office. Some of the cube dwellers outside my door had apparently invited their friends to gawk because they all looked vaguely disappointed when I came back looking like my old self. They wandered off in search of juicier office drama. Buzzards. They earned the nickname for their relentless pursuit of the latest buzz. I shoved my purse in my desk drawer and pulled up the payroll project. By the time I finished tracking down some of the leads from Sandy, people would forget about the lip gloss, and everything would be back to normal.

Three hours and a dozen phone calls later, I teetered on the cusp of victory in the Craig Payroll Smackdown. I had spent all morning confirming Sandy's information, which proved to be golden. After each phone call, Katie cross-checked the data with the payroll records, and a plan to save emerged. If they adopted our proposal, the company would pocket a nice chunk of change. It surprised me how much, actually. I hoped it impressed Dennis too. If so, maybe I could get away with a slightly longer lunch today. I glanced at the clock.

Craig and I had agreed to present our findings together and leave the wager out of it. That might not come across as . . . grown-up. I filled in the final spreadsheet and hit print, watching without much enthusiasm as the paper landed in the tray. I doubted Craig could beat me. I should be elated, but I only felt relief at finishing. Pride was a stupid reason to overwork myself, and yet I kept falling for it.

Good old Jessie "All or Nothing" Taylor, my dad used to tease me. My sister Breanna says it gets in the way of my relationships. "You can date a guy for fun," she always lectures me. "It doesn't have to be either marriage material or nothing. There is an in-between." I know Breanna loves her life, but I'm pretty sure her constant needling to go on "just for fun" dates has something to do with living vicariously through me. Kind of like why I watch *The Bachelor*. My mom thinks my all-or-nothing tendencies are messing me up because the "all" is work and the "nothing" is my social life. I'm not great with balance. I stay so focused that I don't always notice other things going on around me.

Until today. In fact, this whole week my mind had wandered to this lunch, sifting through the possibilities. I imagined a good meal with great conversation and plans for another date. Then I imagined a disaster, where I ruined Sandy's sweater, couldn't think of anything to say, and turned out to have something unsightly clinging to my nose the entire meal. Maybe worst of all was the scene where the lunch is perfectly ordinary, Ben turns out to be a nice, boring guy, and we have a pleasant, boring conversation, and I regret putting myself through the torture of wearing a skirt to the office because he doesn't notice anyway.

The intercom on my desk intruded. "Dennis Court's assistant called. He's waiting for you," Katie said.

"Thanks," I answered. I collected my report from the desk printer and was shuffling the last piece into place when Craig poked his head around the door.

"Are you ready?" he asked, challenge clear in his voice.

"Of course," I answered. I grabbed my file folder and followed him into Dennis's office, ready for my last hurdle before lunch. I could almost hear a ticking clock in my head, counting down the minutes until I could leave, meet Ben, and be done with Craig. All great motives to get this going. Luckily, Craig wasted no time. As soon as Dennis greeted us, Craig laid down his report.

"When I realized what a good point Jessie made about payroll savings on Monday, I couldn't wait to help her with the project," he said.

Dennis raised an eyebrow at me. He knew Craig rarely played nice without a reason.

"I've been working hard for the last two days," he continued, "and in my preliminary audit, I found over fifty hours we could cut every month without impacting productivity." He pushed the report toward Dennis triumphantly. Oh boy. I hadn't counted on him finding only fifty.

Dennis looked the report over and nodded his head occasionally. Craig grew more smug with each nod. Finally, Dennis turned to me. "Ms. Taylor, I assigned this project to you. I assume you have something to report as well?"

"Yes, I do." I tried not to look uncomfortable as I pushed the spreadsheets over to him. "My team worked hard too." I almost felt like apologizing to Craig. Dennis leafed to the summary page and looked startled. He flipped back to the beginning and read more closely, his eyebrows climbing even higher than before. Craig tried to smother a smile, turning it into fake concern.

"You're sure these numbers are right?" Dennis asked.

"I'm positive. I confirmed it all this morning. A few key changes will save us almost seventy hours a week as soon as we implement them." I didn't dare look at Craig. No way would he take this well.

"That's not possible!" he burst out.

I was afraid of that.

He took a moment to collect himself. "I checked hundreds of payroll records, and this is the best solution. Those numbers won't do anything else. You should double check your facts."

"I'm sure this is accurate, Jessie," Dennis said. He looked intrigued rather than surprised now. "I'm curious though. How did you make it work?"

"I skipped the payroll records." A vein throbbed in Craig's forehead when I said that. I'd never seen his head do that before, and I tried not to stare. "I went straight to the department heads and project managers and asked if they could participate in reducing operating costs. No one wants to be seen as inefficient. They tripped all over themselves to shave off time from their departments. We should have more money for hiring additional software developers now." That really got Craig's attention. The programmers drove profit for the company. He knew I had scored with Dennis. He didn't lose his cool again though.

Instead, he said, "That's excellent work, Jessie. I'm proud of you."

Ugh. I forced a smile. He wanted to come off all professional and magnanimous, mentoring the rookie in front of the boss. I said nothing and waited for Dennis, not liking the gleam in my boss's eye.

"It seems healthy competition brings out the best in both of you," he said. "I'm keeping both of your teams on this project to see what more auditing turns up. If this is what you can do in three days, I'd love to see what you come up with in the next three weeks."

What? No!

Dennis picked up his phone and dismissed us both. "Now, if you'll excuse me, I need to take a conference call."

I did not expect this outcome. More time with Craig and his ego? That stank. I headed for my office to stew in peace for a few minutes, but Craig stopped me with a hand on my arm. "Looks like we'll be working together closely. I hope it's not too much pressure for you," he said. The faintest hint of a threat laced his voice.

"Not at all, Craig. I'm just worried about you," I said and removed his hand from my arm. "I hope you can hold up your end of things without Brad for three days." I walked away; I love a silver lining. Craig would be eating humble pie for lunch, and I was on my way to much better company. I hoped.

Chapter 8

I STOOD ON YESLER WAY, glossed, spiffed, and shined. One more block straight down and I would be in front of Trattoria Fredo. I like Trattoria Fredo, so I felt bad for my stomach's behavior. The craziness in there went far beyond butterflies. Maybe more like acrobatic hedgehogs. Mean-spirited, dive-bombing hedgehogs. No way could I eat.

Get it together, Jessie, I admonished myself. I reached deep down inside, searching for my inner confident, modern woman. Nope, not there. I checked my reflection in the window of a nearby café. When I saw my anxious expression, I smiled. This was silly. This was lunch—not even a real date. I looked good in my skirt and wore rocking lip gloss—even my winter-lined, dark-denim peacoat looked sharp. Ultimately, this was just a guy. I might not turn heads the way Sandy did in any room, but I could hold my own in a conversation. Rumor has it, I'm kind of funny too. I started that rumor, but it didn't make it less true. At the very least, I would get tasty food and a good story out of the whole situation. I set off toward the restaurant again with a bounce in my step.

I slipped inside the door to check the place out. Several business types sat in pairs or groups, and they all looked older than twenty-seven—Ben's age, according to his profile. Finally, I noticed a lone guy sitting at the bar, nursing a soda and picking at a plate of garlic bread. Working my way over, I honed in on the black frames of his glasses and his dark hair. I studied him while I held the advantage of being undetected. No white socks with dark pants, no sports jersey. Even overly feminine highlights in his hair might send me skittering back to the safety of my Macrosystems cave. But he wore unobjectionable khakis, brown loafers, and a navy polo. And no highlights.

I took a deep breath and slid into the seat next to him.

"Hi," I said.

He looked surprised. "Hi."

"So this is kind of weird, right?"

"Uh, sure. Kind of," he fidgeted. His voice sounded more anxious than it did on the phone. I had checked his profile picture again before leaving work, but since it wasn't a close up, I couldn't get a real sense of the details. Seeing him in person, I realized I had managed to fill them in using my imagination, and he differed from my mental picture in subtle ways. He had a rounder jaw and shorter, straighter hair than I had expected. He wasn't bad looking. If anything, his looks put him on the pleasant side of plain. He reminded me of one of Jason's high school buddies who came off as exceedingly average until he opened his mouth and became cuter because of his personality.

Trying to break the ice, I said, "So . . . I'm Jessie," and tried not to wince at my mastery of the obvious.

"Hi, Jessie," he said.

I tried a joke. "Glad to see you wore pants."

He furrowed his brow in confusion.

"You know, instead of trousers."

"Right," he said.

"Which are still better than slacks," a voice said from behind me.

I jumped and spun on my barstool to see a tall, dark-haired guy standing there with his hand outstretched to shake.

A sinking feeling unfolded in the pit of my stomach and deepened when he said, "Hi, I'm Ben."

Oh no.

I looked at the random stranger sitting next to me. "Who are you?" I blurted helplessly, my embarrassment making me stupid.

"I'm Jeff."

I closed my eyes for a brief moment. "Sorry to bother you. I thought you were *him*," and I jerked my thumb over my shoulder in the direction of the real Ben.

Jeff shrugged. "No problem," he said and turned back to his garlic bread.

I turned to face Ben again and found him standing there, looking amused.

"You *are* Jessie, right?" he asked, faint hesitation in his voice.

"Yes. You're the *real* Ben?" I asked with a glare at the hapless Jeff.

"I am." He paused and looked unsure about what to do next. Finally, he nodded to a table and said, "Window seat okay?"

"Sure," I said as coolly as possible, trying to recover my dignity.

When I stood to follow him, he measured every inch of the six feet plus he had claimed in his profile. He had blue eyes, and his dark, wavy hair looked significantly less floppy than in his picture. Also, no glasses. Without them, his sculpted cheekbones stood out, balancing a strong jaw. Oh yeah. This looked much more like my mental picture.

He held my chair out for me, and I slid into it, trying not to slouch under my crushing humiliation.

"So, you look suspicious. It really is me," he said.

"I don't believe you. The Ben in my computer has glasses."

He looked sheepish. "That's one of the differences from my picture, I guess. It's from grad school, but like I said, it's the only photo I had when I joined Lookup, so I used it. I can afford regular haircuts now, and I've had laser eye surgery since then." He smiled. "It cost less than replacing my glasses every time I broke them."

"Oh, you're accident prone," I said and made an exaggerated show of moving the flower vase and glass salt shakers on the table out of his immediate reach.

"The vase is safe. But if I told you about all the crazy ways I've destroyed my glasses over the years, you'd never believe me."

"Well, to be honest, I'd probably feel better if we could even the score," I grumbled. "You can tell me your most spectacular spectacle deaths, but maybe make them all be your fault so you come off looking kind of like a dork, and maybe I can forget about how I tried to pick up on a total stranger at a bar."

He grinned. "I will possibly owe you forever for that. I'm so much less nervous now."

I ignored that. "About your glasses . . ."

"Um, crushed by a horse, run over by a train, drowned in the Mediterranean, melted in hot lava, and snapped in half by an elephant."

My jaw dropped slightly. "Are we talking about your glasses or an Indiana Jones movie?"

He laughed. "Those are all true stories."

"Wow." I paused for a moment. "I'm sad your glasses have a more exciting life than I do."

"Don't be. The elephant was in a zoo, the horse was at a ward Halloween hayride, and the train was the monorail stop at Seattle Center."

"Leaving merely the Mediterranean and an active volcano. How lame," I teased him.

"Okay, those were pretty cool."

A server appeared at the table to take our drink orders. I stuck with water, but Ben skipped the fountain sodas and ordered a microbrew root beer. "Are you a root beer expert?" I asked.

"No, more like a root beer junkie. My older brother hooked me on it after he brought back this stuff called Old Dominion from his mission in Virginia."

"And all this time I've been thinking A&W was the good stuff," I said.

"You can't argue with a classic. Besides, I should confess something."

"What's that?"

"I worry that servers who get a nondrinking table are bummed when no one orders alcohol because they think they're going to get a weak tip. I feel better when I order expensive root beer."

That made me laugh. "I order appetizers for the same reason."

"Now there's a plan." He reached for his menu and scanned the list of starters. Little did he know he faced Sandy's first test for dates involving food. Her theory is that guys who don't like spicy foods are bad kissers. I waited for his selection with interest. "I think the artichoke fritti sounds good," he said. It came with a spicy aioli. Score.

"Sounds perfect," I said.

We discussed the rest of the menu options while we waited for the server to come back with the antipasti. Ben settled on the pesto ravioli, and I succumbed to the chicken fettuccine Alfredo. I couldn't resist a good cream sauce.

Our food arrived quickly, and the last traces of my embarrassment over the identity mix-up evaporated with the clouds of savory steam. Bye-bye hedgehogs, hello hunger pangs. I practically wiggled with happiness with the first bite of Alfredo. Heavenly. I savored it for a minute and then focused on Ben again. "I hope yours is at least half as good as mine," I said.

"It's pretty awesome. Great lunch choice."

"How does it compare to the food in Italy?" I asked. He had listed it as one of the places he had traveled in his profile.

"It kind of depends on which part of Italy we're talking about. The food in Rome was good, but the food in Florence . . . talk about amazing."

"I've heard that," I replied. "It's on my list of places to go. I'm planning a world food tour, where all I do is eat amazing food and shop."

"I'm with you on the food, but I'm not too big on shopping," he said.

"It's good planning. If I spend the whole vacation eating, I'll have to buy clothes to fit as I grow."

He gave me an admiring look. "That is a good plan. I hope you never use your talents for evil."

"No worries. It's against my religion."

"Oh, right. Mine too. Hey, can we skip France on the tour? I spent three days in Paris, and I think French food might be overrated."

"You're so right. I hear it's better when you get out of Paris, but when I visited there after high school, we never left the city, and I would have starved without the crepe stands."

"Tell me about it," he agreed. "I think . . ." and then he trailed off, staring at my chin.

Uh-oh.

"Um, you have something right here," he said, pointing to his own chin.

I snatched my napkin and took a swipe at it.

"Did I get it?" I asked, mortified that I even had to.

"No, it's more on the left," he clarified with a small wave.

I swiped again, but he immediately shook his head and said, "I meant your other left." He reached over with his own napkin to help while I wondered if humiliation could literally petrify me. Just then his elbow brushed against the vase on the table and sent it flying off the edge. It crashed to the floor with a cringe-worthy shatter. He froze too. That freed me to move, and I grabbed the napkin from his hand that had been en route to me. I did a full side-to-side swipe of my chin and returned the linen to the table. I made a split-second decision between slinking out and never showing my face in public ever again or rolling with the punches.

"So you lied about being a klutz?" I asked, as our server scurried over to handle the mess.

That startled a laugh from him, and the next half hour disappeared in a blink as we swapped embarrassing moment stories. I didn't realize how fast it went until the waiter appeared with a dessert menu and I snuck a glance at my watch.

"What do you think? They have great pie," Ben said.

"I like pie." More to the point though, I liked spending time with Ben. Unfortunately, my job intruded. "The desserts look awesome," I answered. "But I have to get back."

"Oh, right," he said, looking vaguely disappointed . . . a good sign? "Let me get the check." He handed the server some bills and sat back while he waited for the change. "I hate to tell you this, but . . ."

My stomach clenched.

"I don't think you're going to make it as a TWIT," he finished.

"I'm crushed," I said, relieved to know I didn't have anything clinging to my nose or more food decorating my face.

"Yeah. Sorry about that. You're kinda normal."

"It's a curse."

"Well, I'm on a twelve-step program to quit clubs anyway. I resign from the TWITs. I have a new plan."

"Oh, do tell," I encouraged him.

"I thought I might ask you out again—no clubs involved. What do you think?"

"Hmm." I pretended to mull it over while doing a victory dance inside. "A chance to get to know the man behind the title. Tempting."

"I've got all kinds of hidden talents you don't know about yet."

"Like what?"

"Like dope mime skills."

"Seriously?"

"No."

"Thank goodness. And I'm not a big fan of clowns either," I confessed. "Is that un-American?"

"Do you like hot dogs and baseball?" he asked.

"Only if the hot dogs are grilled and the games are live. I can't watch it on TV."

"I guess I know what to plan for our next date," he said.

"There's no baseball in January," I protested.

"There is if you want it."

"This I gotta see."

"So it's a date?"

"Yes," I answered. "I guess it is."

"Cool. Let's plan for this weekend. I'll call you tomorrow, and we'll firm up the details. Work for you?"

"Work." Dang. How did I lose track of time again? "I have to go. But yeah, call me tomorrow. We'll figure it out." I hurried to grab my handbag and slid out of the booth. Ben jumped up to walk me out. On the sidewalk, I turned and said, "It was nice to meet you." So lame! I gave him a dorky good-bye wave and set off for the Macro cave before I could try to shake his hand or something equally dumb, trying to hurry so I could outrun my lameness and get back in decent time.

"Hey."

I turned at his soft call.

"I'm glad you came," he said with a small smile. Then he stuck his hands in his pockets and strolled off the other way.

I watched for a moment. Nice walk. And then I sped off again toward my office. Time to see what kind of havoc Craig had wreaked in my absence.

Chapter 9

He was the Master of Disaster, for sure. And to give Craig credit, he rallied quickly. I had been gone from the office for fewer than two hours, and he still managed to turn it upside down.

As soon as I walked in, Katie rushed up to me, breathless, her bangs in spiky disarray, and pointed toward my office. "In there, in there!" I shut the door behind her and watched in alarm as she clutched at a fistful of her hair. That explained the bangs. "I'm toast!" she wailed.

Okay, then.

"Calm down," I said. "Tell me what's wrong."

"Craig is going to tell Mr. Court I've been stealing office supplies, and I'm going to get fired."

"Why would he tell Dennis that?"

"Well . . ." she hedged.

"Katie! You didn't actually steal anything, did you?" I asked, shocked.

"No! But I didn't fill in the log."

That didn't make much more sense. "What log?"

"Craig made everyone fill out a log whenever we took office supplies from the closet during his audit so he could track what we used. It took forever to get a pen, so I skipped it whenever I got stuff. I never stole any of it. It's all right here in our pod." I hated that expression for the group of cubicles outside my door. It made me feel like the queen of an alien colony that hatched earnest and underpaid office assistants.

Office assistants who needed defending. Craig had executed an end run around me, threatening me with the loss of an assistant to even the playing field. I considered the options. First, kill Craig. Second, maim and then kill Craig. Third, give him what he wanted.

No way. That would kill *me*.

But I couldn't let Katie take the fall either. She might not have followed procedure, but she hadn't organized an epic supply closet heist. This required drastic action. I jerked open my desk drawer and snatched up every pen, paper clip, and thumbtack I could find. "You're not getting fired, Katie. Tell the rest of the pod to empty every single supply they can find onto your desktop and then get me a yellow legal pad."

That's how Craig found us, counting thumbtacks, like squirrels with a bizarre hoard of nuts, when he sauntered over to gloat a half hour later. I'd embarrassed him by showing him up in front of Dennis, and now he intended to undermine me in return. Ha. Good luck, sucker. I counted louder.

"403, 404. There are 404 tacks. Oh, hi, Craig," I added.

"Well done this morning, Jessie."

"Thanks." I moved on to a pile of paperclips. By the ninth one, he twitched with impatience. The fifteenth undid him. He broke.

"What are you doing?" he asked.

"Counting."

I could almost hear his teeth grinding.

"Right. And why?"

"We need to verify how many office supplies our team has borrowed from the closet. You supported us in our payroll audit, and now we want to support you."

Craig was no dummy. He knew our "support" meant bad news for him. "That's great." He watched for another minute, trying to figure out my game plan, but he couldn't make anything of the counting. Mike droned on behind me over a pile of pencils, "Twenty-three, twenty-four . . ."

"So what form is this help going to take?"

"I heard you're concerned with the numbers from your supply audit. Something about a log book not getting filled out? I felt bad, so I put my whole team on figuring out exactly what we've used in the last two months. We're going to present our findings to Dennis for you, and he can see how much time we invested for you in counting everything. Again. Because we believe in returning favors."

Katie snorted and tried to hide it with a cough, but Craig's face darkened. We had him up against a wall, and he knew it. He already looked bad for spending hours on the office supply audit, and this would make him look worse.

"That's incredible you would do that, Jessie. Incredible," he said, smiling. "But it turns out that we've been able to resolve the log sheet discrepancies. Our office supplies are at normal levels, so I'm sure there's no need to worry."

"I'm sure you're right," I agreed. "Could you send Brad over? We lost some time on this, and I'd love to get caught back up. Might as well start his three days now."

He clenched his jaw in irritation. "I'll send him. Happy to do it. I'm sure he'll only be a time suck though."

"I'll risk it. Thanks, Craig." I watched with satisfaction as he walked away.

Katie turned to me wide-eyed. "Wow, we have 404 thumbtacks?"

"I have no idea. I made it up."

"Oh man," Mike said. "I only made up twenty-seven pencils."

"That's why I'm the boss," I said, grinning. I swept my supplies up and headed back toward my own desk. "Pizza's on Katie next time," I called over my shoulder. Pizza was the traditional bribe when our team had to stay late.

My ploy had only taken a half hour, but I didn't have an extra thirty minutes lying around, especially when I looked at the backlog of work on my desk. Even with Craig's team now helping on the payroll project, it would only get worse. Not only would I have to bust my tail to get it done by the deadline, but I would also have to work harder to make sure we outpaced Craig.

To make sure *I* outpaced Craig, if I were being honest with myself. This wasn't my team's fight, although they would follow me wherever I went. Pizza and working beside them had bought me a lot of good will. But they didn't care about beating Craig. Only I did. It was that hating to be pushed thing. I'd gotten so used to being the best at things that it'd become a bad habit.

I shoved away the stack of papers in front of me in frustration. This wasn't how I wanted to invest all my energy. Sandy's lectures on work/life balance occupied an annoying chunk of my mental real estate lately. Maybe she'd made some good points. Okay, she had. I would give Ben more of my time, but I wouldn't be taking the Sandy Burke approach of throwing myself into a sizzle-then-fizzle romance.

Throwing myself into exploring things with Ben? No way. All or nothing had failed me with Jason, and I had learned from my mistakes. Time to try the middle ground. I'd eaten one lunch with Ben. That didn't equal a relationship. I had no reason to neglect my job for something that might not pan out. As long as I stayed open to dating, like I promised Sandy, I could find the balance between excelling at work and having a bit of romance on the side.

Right?

I straightened up and grabbed for the papers I'd pushed away. Right. I could do this. Let Ben set the pace, and I would follow. I had work to do.

Chapter 10

"RING, STUPID PHONE, RING!"

I shifted my laptop so I could watch Sandy. She stood, hands on hips, glaring at her cell phone lying on the counter. Sandy pleading for a phone call instead of ducking one? This was new. She tapped a manicured nail on the counter next to the phone. French tip, of course.

"Does that work?" I asked.

"The phone?"

"No, yelling at it. I've never thought of that."

She didn't answer. Instead she came to fling herself onto the sofa next to me. "He hasn't called," she grumbled.

"Who?"

"The Brad Pitt look-alike from The Factory. It's been a week, and nothing."

"That's a first. Maybe he lost your number," I suggested.

"Fat chance. I typed it directly into his cell phone."

"Maybe he lost his cell phone."

"Or maybe he doesn't want to call me." Good old Sandy, the angry pragmatist.

"We should burn your cell phone to help you move past it," I said.

She ignored me. "I don't get it," she said instead. "I thought we had a connection. I'm hot, he's hot. What's the problem?"

"Sitting around being hot for hours at a time might get old. Did you talk?"

"Yes, we talked." She pouted for another minute. "That's what's bugging me. We talked all night. About sports and work and movies and music. No awkward pauses where I had to redirect his eyes above my chest. He was smart; I was funny; it flowed. So why wouldn't he call?"

That did seem odd. I'd never known anyone to resist Sandy's charm once she set her sights on him. She left a slew of broken hearts and busted egos in her wake, but she never intentionally acted cruel. I could tell from her face she had figured out that careless could sting too.

I tried to think of a way to comfort her. "There are a million good reasons he might not have called."

"Name one," she challenged me.

"He broke his dialing thumb." That earned a reluctant smile. I tried another one. "You accidentally typed in the wrong number, and he's been calling an insurance office day and night asking for you." Another smile. "Or probably, he's an idiot," I concluded.

"Ding, ding, ding. We have a winner," she said.

"I'll get the chocolate," I replied.

"Don't worry about it. It's not a big deal." She listlessly waved me away from the kitchen.

"I know. I just want chocolate." I headed into the kitchen but stopped short as a cell phone shrilled. Mine, not Sandy's. I refrained from diving for it but barely. I fished it out of my purse, which hung from the back of a dining room chair. Yes! It was Ben.

I mean, cool. It was Ben.

"Hello?" I said. Totally cool.

"Hi, Jessie. You busy?" Ben asked.

"No. What's going on?" I settled back onto the sofa, his voice sending a charge up my spine.

"So I know I said I would call to set up a date for tomorrow, but I changed my mind."

"You're calling to tell me you're not going to call me?" I teased.

He laughed his warm, delicious laugh. "No, I mean I changed my mind about waiting until tomorrow to see you. I had a great time at lunch yesterday so I thought maybe we could do dinner tonight."

I almost said yes. Almost. But instead I said, "I'm so sorry; I can't go out tonight."

Sandy waved her arms frantically, trying to get my attention. "Liar!" she mouthed. I gestured for her to knock it off.

"Oh." Ben sighed. "I guess it's bad manners to call a girl on a Friday night and assume she's free, isn't it?"

"It's not that. Trust me. I've got nothing exciting going on. Just work."

"You're still there?" He sounded surprised.

"No, but I brought a bunch home with me. I hate making people put in overtime on the weekend, so I'm trying to get some stuff done on my own."

"I see," Ben said. He sounded subdued.

"But hey, does the offer stand for tomorrow?"

"Of course. I'm thinking midafternoon, before it gets dark. Sound okay?"

"Sounds great." I gave him my address and confirmed the time. When I hung up, I turned around to find Sandy staring at me, her arms crossed in irritation.

"How is that fair?" she asked. "I beg the cell phone idols for a call, and nothing."

"False idols?" I guessed. "I hear Motorola is pretty fickle."

"Ha ha." She changed the subject. "That was Ben."

"Yeah."

"Why are you turning him down?"

"I have a lot of work to do. I'll see him tomorrow."

"What's wrong with seeing him today *and* tomorrow?"

"I'll work tonight, go out tomorrow. It's called balance."

"Working at six thirty from home on a Friday night is not balance!"

"Spending too much time with Ben isn't balance either," I answered.

"I'm going to drop this only because you're going out tomorrow. But I know where to find your Häagen-Dazs."

"It's a small freezer. I'm not impressed."

I turned back to my laptop, and Sandy retrieved her cell phone then tapped it against the countertop.

After a minute, I burst out, "Stop."

"What? Oh," she said, looking down at her bouncing cell phone. "I need something to take my mind off of this. I want to talk about your date. Where's he taking you?"

"I don't know."

"Aren't you worried?"

"Why would I be? He's pretty normal."

"I mean, aren't you worried about how to plan? If you don't know where you're going, you can't figure out how to dress. That doesn't concern you?"

I set my laptop aside. "It didn't. It does now."

"A movie matinee and mountain biking require totally different outfits. You should think about that."

I leaned my head back on the sofa and stared at the ceiling forlornly. "Why didn't I ask him? I'm an idiot."

"It's a good excuse to call him back now."

"I don't want him to think I'm obsessing about my outfits."

"Even though you are?"

"Especially because I am."

"Okay, we'll figure it out. For an outdoor activity, he'd have to warn you so you could grab the proper gear, like hiking boots or running shoes, so I think you can rule that out."

"Oh, good. That leaves the theater, a picnic, bowling, or a million other possibilities I don't know how to dress for. Maybe I'll wear about twelve layers and peel off all the ones that don't fit the activity."

"Good plan. But he might think you're doing a weird striptease. Bad on any date, super bad on a Mormon date."

"True. Which means I don't have a plan again."

"Hmm. Middle of the afternoon implies casual, so don't worry about the theater or anything like that. Unless he takes you to a museum or something." She blew a bit of hair out of her eyes. "This is hard. Didn't he give you any kind of hint?"

"At lunch, he said something about a baseball game, but that's about it."

"There's no baseball in January," she protested.

"That's what I said."

"Still, it's the only clue you've got. Come on. Let's hit your closet. I've got an idea."

Chapter 11

Two different jackets lay on the bed, and two pairs of shoes sat by the front door. Watching Sandy stage everything the night before reminded me of what a diabolical genius she could be.

"It's all in the delivery," she explained.

"I thought that was babies and jokes," I replied.

"And mystery dates without a dress code. You open the door, say hi, and figure out if he's dressed for casual or nice."

"He's going to think I'm checking him out!"

"Won't you be?"

"Yes, but I don't want him to know."

"Chicken," she teased. "It'll only take a glance anyway. He'll never catch on. When you know which outfit you need, you tell him to hang on while you get your coat. You come grab the jacket from the bed. Then you slip on the right pair of shoes at the front door, and you're out of here like that's the outfit you planned to wear all along."

"This is why you're my hero," I said.

"It's not world peace, but at least you don't have to stress anymore."

I looked at the time. I had this cool original modular clock from the 1950s that my grandma gave me when she cleaned out her basement. I watched the second hand creeping around the face of it, each tick measuring off what felt like an hour. After a full minute of willing it to move faster, I gave up and headed for my mirror to check my reflection. Again. Ben wasn't due for another ten minutes anyway.

Hair down and loose around my shoulders. Freckles hiding under a dusting of mineral powder. Subtle eye shadow. And, of course, lip gloss. Passable, I guess.

Sandy watched me study my reflection. "You look good."

"Thanks."

She had loaned me her Hudson jeans. When I saw how good they looked, I had to promise not to make fun of her for spending that much on denim in the future so she'd let me wear them. The dark wash complemented my gray sweater. It wasn't expensive or anything, but the slim cut and merino wool made it easy to dress up or down. If it looked like a casual afternoon, I would grab Sandy's trendy puffy vest that fit like a glove and throw on Converse on the way out. If Ben showed up dressed to prowl art galleries and debate foreign policy, I would grab my own black leather blazer and slip on some high heeled ankle boots instead.

Sandy stretched and yawned. "I'm worn out from your outfit intervention. I want to take a nap. When's he getting here?"

"You're not meeting him," I protested.

"Why not? I deserve at least that much after being your personal date stylist."

"I don't want him to feel all ganged up on."

"I'm sure Benny-boy can handle himself. I'll be cool, I swear."

I relented after delivering a threat. "You crack one joke, and I will kill you slowly."

"I'll be good."

When the doorbell rang, I was fastening in some delicate silver drop earrings. My stomach lurched, and I took a deep breath to settle my nerves. *Get it together, girl.* Sandy raced to the sofa and thumbed through a magazine, feigning boredom. I padded out to the front door in my black socks and checked the eye hole. Ben stood there in a blue sweater and jeans. Casual, then. I slipped on my Chucks and opened the door.

"Hi," I said, trying not to sound as dippy as I felt. I stepped aside to let him in.

"Hi back," he answered. He took an interested glance around the room. "I like your place. Have you lived here long?"

"About a year," I answered.

"It's hard to find something in this neighborhood. How'd you luck out?"

"I have a realtor in my ward who gave me the scoop before it came on the market."

"You own it? Nice."

"It seemed better than paying rent."

"Definitely. And you get to pick the colors," he smiled.

Time to make the introductions. "Ben, this is my roommate Sandy. Sandy, this is Ben." I watched his reaction curiously. Even though Sandy had pulled her hair back into a low ponytail and wore jeans and a baggy T-shirt, she still looked gorgeous.

He moved to shake her hand politely, but his face showed nothing more than well-bred courtesy. "So you're the one who's into identity theft," Ben nodded, the teasing note clear in his voice. "Nice to meet you, Sandy."

Sandy looked ready to fire back a snappy retort, but at my warning glare, she said only, "Nice to meet you, and I don't know what you're talking about."

Ben grinned. "Too bad. I thought I owed you a thank you for putting Jessie's info on Lookup."

"I would never do something like that, but whoever did sure must be an awesome and amazing friend to Jessie," Sandy said.

"Must be," he agreed. I rolled my eyes.

"Would you like to sit for a second while I grab my jacket?" I asked. He wandered over to my fireplace mantle instead.

"Do you mind if I sneak a peek at your pictures while I wait?" he asked.

"Not at all. I don't keep the embarrassing ones in the living room anyway."

He laughed, and I went to retrieve Sandy's vest from my bed. It took a talented designer to turn puffy down and nylon into something chic, but leave it to my roommate to find the one who could. I slipped it on and returned to find Ben where I'd left him, standing in front of the fireplace. Sandy leafed through her magazine and studied him from the corner of her eye.

He turned when I walked in and lifted a quizzical eyebrow at me. He held up my graffiti rock in his hand and read aloud, "'This is just a rock.' I'm guessing there's a story here?"

I shrugged. "Not anymore."

"That's all I get?" he asked.

"That's all you get."

"Fair enough. Are you ready to go?"

"Sure."

I locked the door behind us and managed to block his view of Sandy's huge grin and thumbs up gesture before it clicked closed, then I followed him to his car. I half expected a massive lumberjack pickup truck, but instead, he opened the passenger side of an Acura sedan. Sensible and stylish. My, my, my. When he got in and started it, music filled the interior. An old White Stripes song blared out. So he liked his rock and roll loud. That went in the plus column too.

"Sorry," he muttered, fumbling for the volume control. "I should have remembered to do that before I got out."

"Don't worry about it. I like this album," I said.

He put the car in gear and pulled smoothly onto Eleventh Avenue, heading south. "Do you have any idea where we're going yet?" he asked.

"Not a clue."

"Does that make you nervous?"

"No way. I'm one of those totally kickback chicks. I'm going to let it ride."

"Uh-huh. I don't believe you. Kickback chicks don't own condos when they're twenty-five."

"Well, I'm going to be a kickback chick for this afternoon, then."

"So you're not at all curious about where I'm taking you?"

"Of course. But I'm practicing patience."

"How big of you. How about if I let you guess?"

"That works. How many guesses do I get?"

"Three."

"Okay, first guess. We're going door to door to collect canned goods for charity."

"Thoughtful, but wrong."

"Um . . . we're going to try on formals at the mall and crash some high school's winter dance."

He grimaced. "Scary and wrong."

"Then I guess I'd better give you a serious guess." I tapped my chin and pretended to think. "Let's see. We're going to join a group attempting to set a Guinness record for the most people jumping on pogo sticks simultaneously."

He stared at me for a full two seconds before shaking his head and turning his blue eyes back to the road. "Your mind goes to some fascinating places," he said.

"I only wish I could take credit for those, but they're actual dates I've been on," I said with a grin.

"So high school was all about the creative and cheap dates, huh?"

"Oh no. Those were all since I've been in Seattle."

"I'd like to thank those guys for setting a low bar. I'm feeling better and better about our plans."

"I'm looking forward to finding out what they are. Oh, and if there's food involved, I promise to spill first again so you'll feel even better."

"Thanks, but I can't let you do that. It's a guy's job. I'll do it," he said.

"You're a real gentleman."

"My mother taught me well."

This was fun. No awkwardness, no uncomfortable pauses. Now that the stress of what to wear had passed, I found myself trying to guess what Ben had planned. The conversation turned to questions about the pictures Ben had seen on my mantle, and I kept an eye on the scenery. We stayed on Eleventh Avenue, and I watched townhomes pass by on the tree-lined streets. Within a few minutes, the car slowed, and Ben flipped his signal on to make a left turn. Cal Anderson Park, home of the neighborhood baseball diamonds.

"There really is baseball in January?" I asked.

"Only because you requested it," Ben answered. I hadn't exactly, but I wasn't going to spoil the moment by pointing that out.

Instead I said, "I didn't know there were city league games going on this time of year." I was fishing, and he knew it.

"There aren't," he said and clammed up.

Dang.

He pulled into a space next to the closest field, which indeed teemed with baseball players. Short, very cute baseball players. He turned the engine off and grinned at me. "Come on out and meet the team. This is a special exhibition. They agreed to play a game just for you."

As soon as he stepped out of the car, a swarm of boys surged toward him calling, "Ben!" or "Brother Bratton!" in high-pitched, excited voices. When we got closer, I could see most of them were about my nephew Caleb's age, somewhere in the nine-year-old range. What on earth?

He laughed as the boys clamored around him, some trying to give him a high five, a couple of them tugging at the hem of his light blue sweater to get his attention. He held up his hands in mock surrender. "Okay, men. I promise I'll answer everyone's questions in a minute. Yours too," he added with a nod toward me. "Let me make some introductions first." He gestured to the group. "This is the West Seattle Ward Cub Scout pack, along with several of their little brothers." He waved to a small stand of bleachers across the field. "Those are their parents and drivers." About eight adults sat watching with varying degrees of amusement. Lastly, he turned and pointed to me.

"Boys," he said solemnly, "This is Jessie. Sister Taylor."

A chorus of exuberant hellos fluttered up from the herd of Cub Scouts. One little voice came from a cute freckled redhead who looked maybe six years old. "Are you the lady who likes baseball?" he asked excitedly.

My nephews always liked it when I came down to their level, so I crouched and, adopting Ben's gravity, said, "Yes, I am. I love baseball. How about you?"

"Of course," he answered. "That's why I'm here. We're going to play!"

"This is my live baseball game?" I asked Ben.

"It is," he said, grinning. "You are looking at parts of the three finest Little League teams in Seattle, and they're here to show you their mad baseball skills."

A towheaded boy from the back of the bunch piped up. "Actually, my team stinks, but the coach says we have heart."

"That's what matters," I said.

"My big brother says winning all the time is what matters," the redhead said.

"All the time? That sounds boring. I prefer variety," I said. Ben looked at me, pleased—I guess with the way I handled the boys. If he thought they would throw me, he had another thing coming. Six nephews had made me a seasoned pro.

"Game time!" he announced, eliciting a chorus of whoops. "Hit the field, men." They all tore off to their respective dugouts with such enthusiasm I had to laugh again. All except for one, that is. The redhead remained behind, staring at me with a fierce expression.

"Winning *is* important. The most important. My brother Tyler said so."

His intensity surprised me. I opened my mouth to answer him, but Ben intervened. "You're right, Logan," he said gently to the upset boy. "Winning is important. But Sister Taylor is also right that you don't always have to win. It's okay to play for fun."

"Tyler says you should never let someone win on purpose. You have to always fight. I'm going to keep points in my head even though you said we weren't keeping track." He crossed his arms, his knobby elbows jutting.

Ben drew a deep breath and held it for a minute. Then he quietly exhaled and turned to me. "Excuse me for a moment, would you, Jessie?"

"No problem." I took a seat in the bleachers and watched as he placed an arm around Logan's shoulders and slowly walked with him across the field, speaking quietly. Gradually, the tension in the small boy's shoulders relaxed, and he uncrossed his arms and nodded solemnly. He stared at Ben for a long moment before giving him a high five and scampering the last few yards to his team's dugout. Ben turned and headed back toward me.

"Sorry about that," he said when he reached my newly claimed seat. "He's had it a bit rough. His dad took off when Logan was a tiny guy, and his mom's been raising him and his two older brothers. The oldest, Tyler, is overseas in Afghanistan right now. Logan has a case of hero worship."

"Sounds like he should. Is he okay to play?"

"He'll be fine. He's intense, but eventually the kid in him wins out."

"I hope so. He's too young to carry around so much heavy baggage."

"They all relax when they play. It's fun to watch. Some of them are too young for pitches, so they'll be batting off a tee. I know it's not the Mariners, but you don't mind, do you?" he asked.

"Of course not! How did you pull this off?"

"I'm the assistant Cubmaster in the ward. I offered to let the den mothers off the hook for an activity this week so the boys could work on their sports activity badges, and they were happy to go for it."

"That's so funny. Don't you have to have kids to get pulled into Scouts?"

"Usually, yes. But I worked at Scout camp every summer in high school, and the Scoutmaster is the same guy I had back in the day. And my nephew's in the troop."

"So he lured you in."

"He didn't have to try hard. The kids are a blast."

"Which one is your nephew?"

"He couldn't come. He's got the flu. You'd like him. He's a funny kid."

He liked kids. Definitely something for the plus column.

"I better get out there," he said, pointing to the boys happily kicking dirt at each other. "But I brought some supplies for you." He went to the trunk of his car and returned with a blanket and a small cooler. Leading me over to the prime bleacher seats, he padded the bench with the blanket, and when I settled in, he opened the cooler with a flourish.

"What's all this?" I asked.

"You can't go to the ball game without hot dogs and other game staples," he explained. He pulled out a warm, foil-wrapped hot dog and several small packets with assorted mustards, relishes, and mayonnaise. I stared at him in astonishment.

"The 7-Eleven condiment bar has an amazing variety." Next, he pulled out a tray of nachos with slightly congealed cheese. "I wouldn't eat these, but maybe you can sniff them to get the ballpark nacho stand whiff."

Stale nachos and processed cheese were definitely part of the ballpark experience. Ben wasn't overlooking anything, except maybe . . .

Oh, nope. He stuck a plastic bag of premade popcorn in my hand, cheddar flavored, even. He topped everything off with a glass bottle of another exotic root beer. "You comfortable?" he asked.

"Totally. This is awesome."

"Good." His eyes twinkled. "Let me get this game going, and I'll be back." He took off in a jog toward the other side of the field, where the parents sat. Three of the dads came down to meet him and followed him back onto the field. He spent the next several minutes with the boys, reminding them of the rules and giving them direction. He finished with, "Okay, boys. Remember, we're not keeping score today. We're playing for fun and learning. Give it your best!"

The dad on the mound threw the first pitch. By the time Ben had made it back to me, the batter had reached first base, looking very proud of himself. Ben took his seat beside me and fished another foil-wrapped hot dog from the cooler then piled on some mustard and bit into it.

I watched in amusement as he tucked into his food with gusto. "This is great," I told him. "Thanks for giving me baseball in January."

"No problem." He shrugged. "It was nothing."

"I disagree. You thought of everything. Look," I said, scooting closer. His hot dog stopped halfway to his mouth as he watched me lean in slowly. He stared, transfixed, until I reached over and scooped a dollop of mustard off his shirt with my thumb. "You even spilled first. That's so sweet," I said with pretended innocence.

His gaze narrowed as he watched me wipe the mustard off with a 7-Eleven napkin. "I'm not sweet at all," he said. "I'm . . ." he trailed off, searching for the right word.

"Generous? Kind?"

"Don't say that! I'm manly and tough," he said. "By the way, I brought you an extra blanket in case it got too cold today." And he reached into a duffel bag and pulled one out.

"Yeah, you're super tough," I said, accepting the blanket.

"Okay, I'm not. I'm cold. Want to share that blanket?" He waggled his eyebrows at me.

"Not tough," I amended with a laugh. "You're smooth."

"Except for the mustard thing."

"I thought spilling first was part of being a gentleman."

"It is. That's what I meant," he said.

Just then, Logan came to bat. Although the other boys his age and size had hit from the tee and run like crazy, the redhead looked determined to hit a pitch. He squared up his stance and stared at the pitcher, watching for the throw. I stood and gave a piercing whistle then yelled, "Go, Logan!" He didn't turn, focusing instead on the ball. When the pitch came, he swung with every ounce of his energy and hit a pop fly straight to second base. Luckily, the second baseman, distracted by the rock at his feet, didn't notice when the ball landed near him with a thud and rolled to the outfield.

Ben jumped up and hollered, "Run, Logan!"

The little boy looked startled and broke into a mad dash for first base. Ben and I cheered when he beat the throw. Logan turned and waved at me, his arm flapping like a proud flag as he claimed the base as his own. "Look at me, Sister Taylor. I'm a winner!"

"Yes, you are," I called back. I turned to grin at Ben. "I went to a couple of Mariners games last summer. This is so much better," I said.

"Tell me about it," he agreed. "The pros run all their bases in order. Here, half the fun is guessing which base they'll run to next."

Each of the boys took their turn at bat, playing three loosely organized innings. Every time Logan was up, he swung his bat with fierce determination and ran all out, doing progressively sillier things with each base he gained. By third base of his last at bat, Ben and I looked forward to Logan's final performance. As soon as the batter hit his pitch, Logan pelted down the third base line, turning in a respectable, though totally uncontested, slide for the last two feet. He scrambled up out of the dirt and planted his feet firmly on the base then gyrated like a Tickle Me Elmo on too much Mountain Dew.

"Is that the hokey pokey?" Ben asked.

"Nope. I think it's the Macarena."

"Either way," he said climbing to his feet, "I can't let him dance alone." And he loped off toward the bouncing redhead to join his celebration.

How utterly random.

And totally cool.

Chapter 12

"How did it go?" Sandy asked when I walked in around dusk.

I took a moment to lean back against the door and savor the moment.

"That good, huh?" she prompted me when I didn't answer.

I shoved myself up and answered, "I don't owe you ice cream, if that's what you're asking."

She stared at me blankly. "I didn't think you did," she said.

I sometimes forgot Sandy didn't follow the typical LDS girl life arc. "It's a BYU thing," I explained. "The first time you kiss a guy, you're supposed to buy your roommates a carton of ice cream."

"Huh." She digested that for a moment. "Why?"

That stumped me. "I don't know," I said. "I never thought about it before. Maybe to celebrate?"

"Sounds more like an excuse to get free ice cream."

"If I were smarter, I'd have instituted the ice cream rule with you. I'd never buy my own Häagen-Dazs again."

"Funny, Jessie." She crossed her eyes and stuck out her tongue. "You're a real comedian."

"I kinda am," I agreed.

"You're also violating one of our real roommate rules. No withholding juicy details after dates."

"I'm not withholding. I'm digesting."

"That sounds gross."

"I mean that I'm soaking up the moment, that's all."

"I know what you meant. You've soaked for about three minutes now. That's plenty. I want details!"

I plopped myself down on the sofa next to her. Finally cracking a smile, I said, "It was pretty fantastic."

"Because . . ." She prompted.

"Because we had a great time. He set up a baseball game between some kids in his ward and brought me all kinds of ballpark food to eat while we watched. He acted like a total gentleman. He opened doors, made sure I stayed warm. He even spilled first." The look on Sandy's face was priceless. I had probably circumscribed several of her least favorite things into one afternoon.

"Trust me," I told her. "It was perfect."

"Knowing you, it probably was. So when's the next date?" she asked.

"I don't know," I answered.

She stared at me in surprise. "He didn't ask you out again?"

"Well, yeah. For tomorrow."

"A Sunday?"

"His ward's having a fireside."

"That makes sense. Except for the part about why you're not going."

I shrugged. "It's all part of the balance and moderation thing I'm doing," I said.

"Maybe you'd better define those words for me because we clearly don't think they mean the same thing."

"I saw him Thursday, I saw him today, and that's kind of a lot. I think things could use a breather, that's all."

Understanding and a hint of impatience dawned in Sandy's eyes. "You mean *you* could use a breather," she said. "Why? You don't work on Sundays, so it's not like you have that to distract you."

I opened my mouth to defend my decision, but I realized she had a point. I closed it again and thought for a minute. I didn't have to try hard to change my own mind. "You're right," I said.

"You should never sound surprised when you say that. It's a statistical probability any time I speak, accountant girl," she teased me. "So what are you going to do?"

"I guess call him?"

"Ding, ding, ding! Tell her what she's won, Don Pardo. Why, it's a fun-filled evening with a hot guy!"

"Oh, I remember now."

"Remember what now?" Sandy asked.

"I remember why I keep threatening to kick you out."

"You've never threatened to kick me out."

"I haven't? I keep meaning to say it out loud."

"You'll never do it. What would you do with me gone?"

"I don't know, maybe get more work done? I'd never have to hunt for my Pottery Barn catalog. And the pantry would stay organized by alphabetical order." I considered the possibilities and added, "You'd better stay. But you can't have my magazines until I'm done."

"Deal. You should call Ben now."

"I will, but again, I'm only doing this because I want to, not because you told me to."

"Okay. Call Ben now. That's me reaffirming your great idea," she said.

"Uh, what do I say? Inviting myself over for something I already declined is flaky."

"Did you or did you not have a great day today?" she demanded.

I thought about the afternoon again and the hour we had lingered after the game had ended, slowly packing up our picnic and laughing. I thought too about the quickly hidden surprise and disappointment that had flashed across Ben's face when I told him I couldn't make it to the fireside the next day. Our easy rapport stayed intact through the car ride home and his warm hug at the door. But he hadn't promised to call me about setting something else up either. Which meant he had placed the ball in my court.

I weighed everything out in my mind once more. Stay home all Sunday afternoon by myself and take a break from Ben or hang out with a hot, funny guy who I didn't want a break from anyway? When I looked at it that way . . .

I leaned over and rummaged through my purse. When I straightened with my cell phone in hand, Sandy murmured, "Good girl." As I scrolled through my phone book to find Ben's number, she headed for her room. "I'll leave you to do your icky twitterpation thing in private."

When I found his number, I hesitated for a moment. I had never gotten comfortable with calling guys, and my stomach always clenched when I had to do it, but then again, I could only blame myself. If I had accepted Ben's invitation in the first place, I wouldn't be risking possible rejection.

Then again, why did I have to call at all? I selected the "text message" option and typed, *I meant to say instead of a fireside, how about dinner at my place?* Before I could talk myself out of it, I pressed SEND and shoved the phone under the sofa cushion. That way, if Ben didn't text me back, I could pretend the silence stemmed from its location under the sofa cushions.

I ignored the flaws in my logic and sat down with the Pottery Barn catalog I found underneath the cushion currently smothering my phone. A few minutes later, Sandy walked through the living room, dressed to the nines. She paused when a distant chime sounded from my . . . posterior. I could see her debate whether or not to ask me about it, but she said nothing and turned to do her customary once over in the foyer mirror. I sat for another minute, debating whether or not someone would be so fast to text back a heartless, "No, thanks," and then my bum chimed again. Unable to withstand the suspense, I jumped up and tore the cushion off. This definitely had Sandy's attention now.

I took one look at the screen and grabbed my handbag on the way to the door.

"Where are you going?" she demanded.

"To the store. Apparently, I'm cooking dinner tomorrow!"

Chapter 13

I FUSSED WITH THE PLACE settings on the table in the dining nook next to the kitchen. Glass tumblers flanked simple white plates, each place setting framed in a neutral-toned woven placemat. The only touches of color were the green cotton napkins that reflected the accents in the living room. Instead of a centerpiece, I set out a collection of seasonings and sauces for Sandy and Ben to choose from.

Sandy walked in and looked over the table. "It's cute," she said. "But it's a bad idea for me to be here for dinner."

"Why? It'll be fun."

"Like Rob Whitaker fun?" she asked. I flinched at the justified accusation in her tone. I had invited Rob to dinner last year for a second and last date after he spent the meal alternately ogling Sandy and calling her to repentance. Sandy didn't go to church on Sundays, but she lived the same values I did, so his lecture was not only inappropriate as a dinner guest, but it was also completely misplaced.

"Rob is the moron gold standard. Ben's totally different. You have to eat with us. I don't want this to look romantic or anything."

"Yes, it would clearly be wrong to send him any signals that you like him. Since you like him and all," she said.

"I'm trying to keep it light," I said. "Look at this table. It says I put some effort into it, it says I can cook and entertain, and it says there are three places settings, not two, so clearly we're taking it slow."

"It says that loudly," she agreed.

I wasn't going to change my mind. I had to balance seeing Ben three out of the last four days, and I wanted the classic roommate buffer. Besides, I wasn't comfortable with the idea of entertaining any guy alone in my condo. I knew that was the real reason Sandy agreed to stay for dinner. She might find my rules outdated, but she had my back.

I adjusted one of the placemats again. Sandy grinned. "I want it to be perfect," I said.

"Sounds like you're keeping it light, all right."

When I ignored her, she wandered off toward her room while I fluffed a napkin and gave the hot sauce bottle a half turn in the middle of the table. The doorbell rang and sent my nerves twitching. This amounted to one more date than I'd given anyone in almost two years. The two-date rule had been working fine. I had suffered from neither a broken heart nor a psycho stalker in those two years. In fact, since being in Seattle, I'd gone out with over ten different guys and had never been tempted to say yes to a third date. I either lost interest or got too busy or picked up a strange vibe that made saying no to a third date easy. Was it crazy to break the policy for Ben?

My anxiety spiked even higher until the third place setting snagged my attention again.

Oh yeah. This wasn't a date. This was Ben coming over for dinner with me and my roommate. Right, I could do this. This was the same Ben I'd had a great time with yesterday without any nervousness at all.

Armed with this reminder and the knowledge that it would be rude to keep him waiting any longer, I went to let him in. I found him smiling uncertainly, with a six pack of root beer under his arm, and the last bit of my stress evaporated.

"Hi," he said.

"Hi back," I replied. Should I hug him? We weren't at hello hugs yet. I stared at him for a full five seconds while I tried to figure out what to do next then reddened as his smile wavered again. "Come in," I said, and stepped aside so he could enter. I invited him to sit on the sofa while I stuck the soda on the kitchen counter. As I walked back into the living room, Sandy made an appearance in the hallway.

"Are you hungry?" I asked Ben.

"Not until I walked in, but whatever I smell has me about three seconds from starving now," he said.

"Smooth," mouthed Sandy so Ben couldn't see.

"Let's eat, then," I said and led the way to the dining room table. After Ben and Sandy took their seats, I stepped into my kitchen and grabbed a platter of chips and guacamole. When I placed it on the table, Ben scooped up a bite and sighed.

"I love good guacamole. It's been hard to find since I left Arizona," he said.

"Jessie made it," Sandy informed him. "Her cooking doesn't stink."

"I didn't have to cook anything to make it," I said, embarrassed. I rarely cooked for myself, but I knew my way around a kitchen. My mother grew up in Georgia and trained my sisters and me to be old school Southern cooks. Living in California had broadened our food vocabulary to include things like tasty chicken enchiladas, since Mexican food was not a thing when my mom was growing up. Thank goodness times change. She had found a killer enchilada recipe, which I had baked for tonight. Even health-crazed Sandy couldn't resist them.

"Did you know February is the biggest month for avocado sales?" Ben asked.

"Uh, no," Sandy said.

"It's true," Ben said. "It's because of the Super Bowl; people love to make guacamole for their game parties. Surprising, right?"

"Why would you know that?" Sandy asked.

Ben shrugged. "I have a bad habit of getting random facts caught in my head. If I see it or hear it, it's in there. I can list ten useless pieces of trivia on demand that you never needed to know. I think it's a talent to compensate for not being able to play the piano or sing or, you know, something cool."

"Bad trade," she said.

"Definitely. But watch *Jeopardy* with me and you'll think I'm a genius. I own that half hour," he joked.

"You sound like Jessie," Sandy said. "Last time she had the flu, she made me read her Trivial Pursuit cards for an hour. She didn't even want the board out." She shook her head.

"I wanted to take my mind off my misery," I defended myself.

"Is that why you cheated?" Sandy asked.

"I can't cheat if I'm not even playing the real game," I said.

Sandy explained to Ben. "She not only didn't play with the pieces, but she skipped half the categories on the card."

"Only two!" I interrupted her. "I don't like the geography or science and nature questions. They give me a headache."

"I think the flu means you can skip categories if you want," Ben said. "But geography? From someone who loves to travel?"

"I can find a country on a map if I've been there or plan to go there, but none of the questions are about pointing to a map, so I skip them."

"That's fair," he said. "I'm pretty comfortable in those two categories anyway, so we'll play as a team and crush everyone."

I smiled, and Sandy hooted.

"Nerdiness isn't catching, is it?" she asked, waving her hands in front of her face as if dispersing nerd germs.

"Behave, Sandy, or I'll reveal your dirty little secret," I warned her.

"I'm sorry. I think it's great you guys are so smart," she said.

"One, I'm not that smart. I just remember useless stuff more than most people," Ben said. "And two, you don't think I can let a secret pass by like that, do you? Jessie, you can't leave me hanging."

"No, Jessie, what you can't do is throw your roommate under the bus. Don't tell," Sandy ordered.

I wavered for a moment and then made my choice. Carrying a tray of hot enchiladas from the oven, I set them on the table and leaned down to whisper loudly to Ben, "Sandy's not telling you that she can wipe the floor with anyone in arts and literature or history."

"It turns out the brown and yellow questions in Trivial Pursuit are the only real use for my liberal arts degree," she grumbled.

"That is some secret," Ben said. "You feel okay now that it's out there?"

"I'd feel better if we got one of Jessie's secrets out too," she answered. I grimaced while she pretended to think.

"Please don't let it be a fingernail collection," Ben said.

"It's worse," she warned him. "She has all three seasons of *Kung Fu* on DVD. I think she might even have them all memorized."

Ben turned to me. "You do kung fu?"

I shook my head at Sandy. "No, but I might start." She smiled. "I grew up watching that old TV show *Kung Fu* with my dad," I clarified for Ben. "It's got this Buddhist monk guy wandering through the old West and schooling people with kung fu."

"Cowboy karate? How have I missed this? That sounds like the greatest show ever," he said.

I assumed my most Zen-like expression and said, "I have learned the greatest life lessons from Master Po. Mainly, how to squish Craig the Snitch like a bug."

"Bummer," Sandy said. "I thought you were a natural evil genius, but all along your plotting came from some dude who called everyone grasshoppers."

"How about if I serve these piping hot enchiladas right into your lap?" I asked.

"That's my girl," she replied.

Ben grinned. "Dinner and a floor show. Cool."

"So far only a floor show," Sandy complained. "Are you going to let us eat those things or keep waving them at us?" She turned to Ben. "I know I probably sound—"

"Rude?" I interjected.

"*Impatient*," she continued. "But when you eat them, you'll understand."

"I can't wait to try them," he said. "I'm always down for enchiladas."

I took a seat and dished out the food. The enchiladas came out of the pan with strings of cheese trailing off them and clouds of steam puffing in the air. Definitely one of my personal favorites. Ben lifted a forkful to his mouth but paused when Sandy said, "Stop! You forgot the salad."

I jumped up to get it and returned bearing a bowl of romaine lettuce and fresh vegetables in a creamy cilantro vinaigrette. Ben tried to be a good sport and returned his bit of enchilada untasted to his plate while he waited for his salad to be served. Sandy gave him a knowing glance but said nothing, just watched him take his first bite. His eyes widened as he chewed.

"This is awesome!" he said. "What kind of dressing is it?"

"It's the cilantro. It's from Café Rio, one of my favorite restaurants back home," I said.

"They must make a fortune selling this stuff," he said.

Sandy laughed. "They don't sell it. Jessie-All-Or-Nothing Taylor here liked it so much she experimented for a month until she figured out how to make it herself."

Ben's look bordered on . . . respectful? "I used to have a 1955 Chevy I fixed up with my dad. When I couldn't find the upholstery I wanted, we had my mom teach us to use the sewing machine, and then we did it ourselves."

"It's the best way to get what you want," I said.

"Really?" Sandy interjected. "I find asking works pretty well."

"It does when you're the legendary Sandy Burke," I said. "The rest of us mere mortals have to apply more elbow grease to get things done."

Once the salad disappeared, we started in on the enchiladas, which had cooled enough to eat. I waited for Ben's reaction, fighting for a neutral expression so he wouldn't notice how much I wanted him to like the dinner.

He took one bite and chewed slowly, his eyes half closing. Suppressing an impatient fidget, I ate a bite off my own plate. Well, *I* thought it tasted good. A bit of crankiness crept in when Ben took his second bite without saying a word. I chewed my own second bite with more vigor. You'd think a guy who had the manners to spill first would know to compliment the cook.

He set his fork down and stared at his plate for a moment, transfixed. Finally, he looked up at me. "I wish you had one of those 'Kiss the Cook' aprons on. This is the best enchilada ever."

I blushed.

The rest of dinner continued in easy conversation and a few dozen more jokes. After Ben reached sheepishly for his third serving and finished it, he jumped up to help me clear the table. I went to the kitchen for the dessert. Ben's eyes widened when he turned from the sink and saw the large plate heaped with pralines in my hand. Taking it from me and heading for the table again, he called over his shoulder, "These look awesome, but what are you guys going to eat?"

I snapped a kitchen towel in my hand. "Hand over the goods."

"Yeah, Ben. You must not have sisters, or you'd know how dangerous it is to get between a girl and her dessert," Sandy said.

"Actually, I do have a sister, but she's a lot younger, so we didn't grow up together. But I have three brothers, and it's kind of the law of the jungle when we eat. If you don't get it first, you get what's left."

"I'm pretty sure I made enough to share," I said. Sandy snatched up her first praline only a hair less eagerly than Ben did.

"They're good on ice cream," I said. "I'll be right back."

"This is crazy good," Ben said. "I don't know if they need ice cream."

I stopped, and Sandy and I both stared.

He cleared his throat. "I mean, they definitely need ice cream. What was I thinking?"

What a great dinner guest. What a great personality.

I fetched a carton of French vanilla and then sat and took a satisfied bite of my own. Ben licked his spoon and asked, "Can I do the dishes for you?"

What a great guy.

At eleven thirty, Ben noticed me yawn and made polite motions about leaving. Even knowing I needed to sleep, I kept drawing out the conversation until somehow another hour slipped past. Sandy had long since gone to bed. The whole evening had been totally unlike me. I rarely ever invited guys into my home, and I had never schemed to prolong their visits. But with Ben, I reached such an easy comfort level that it felt right to sit curled into the corner of my sofa, listening to him tell stories about his mission and college and work.

The realization of how badly I wanted to know more scared me. I yawned and clapped a hand over my mouth. "Sorry! I think my body figured out it's bed time, but I'm with you right here," I said, tapping my forehead.

He jumped up. "No, I'm sorry. I should have left an hour ago, the first time you yawned."

He helped me off the sofa and held onto my hand while I walked him to the door, suddenly nervous about what would happen when we got there. His hand felt good wrapped around mine, but . . . would he kiss me? I had only known him for a week, but this was technically a third date and . . . I *wanted* that kiss.

He paused with his other hand on the doorknob and faced me. I struggled to keep any anxiety out of my expression. I don't know what he saw in my face, but he slowly pulled me in for a long hug and then leaned back enough to plant a soft kiss on my forehead. After murmuring a thank you, he slipped out the door, and I found myself for the second time leaning against it and smiling.

Chapter 14

MONDAY MORNING DAWNED FAR TOO early. I glared at my clock through a slitted eye, watching it glare 6:33 back at me. I hated setting my alarm for even numbers, like 6:30. My microwave cook times too. It was about the most rebellious thing I ever did. The blinking number changed to 6:34. That meant I'd had about five hours of sleep. I needed more than that to deal with a whole week of Craig and payroll drama. I smacked the snooze button and flopped onto my back, drifting into a daydream about last night.

The grating noise of my alarm's buzzer broke into my reverie as the snooze time expired. I gave the reset button a last, irritated smack and took a moment to stretch in the warm afterglow of my Sunday night memory. I almost had myself talked into emerging from my cozy down comforter when Sandy tapped on the door and poked her head in.

"So, do I get ice cream?" she wanted to know.

I thought about it for a minute and said, "Maybe frozen yogurt."

"You didn't get a real deal kiss? But I wanted ice cream!"

"Sorry for not taking your needs into consideration. Maybe I could call Ben to come over and set it right."

"Great idea. But you can call him later. I don't need ice cream until tonight." And she shut the door behind her before I could muster a comeback. Instead, I shook my head and hauled myself out of bed.

It looked like the only thing that would salvage this Monday was dwelling on Sunday, so I did. My good date buzz lasted until I walked into my office to find Craig already waiting by my door.

He looked like he'd stepped straight out of *GQ* in his perfectly creased pants and hot pink tie. He wasn't a bad looking guy, which annoyed me in the way bleached-toothed, spray-tanned people sometimes do. Why couldn't pasty white be the standard? High-maintenance people like Craig make me feel lazy. And pale.

He smiled as I walked up.

I squelched a flare of irritation and smiled back. I couldn't make him less of a jerk, but I could be less of one.

"Getting an early start?" I asked, proud of myself for sounding like I cared.

"Something like that. I'm glad you're finally here. I have some numbers to go over with you," he said.

He made it sound like I had rolled in late when, in fact, I'd made it five minutes early.

"Great," I said. "It's good your team has decided to be productive." I wasn't picking this fight, but I wasn't running either.

His smile widened. "We're going to do whatever we can."

Lucky us. He laid out spreadsheets on my desktop, papering the whole thing in payroll numbers before I could even put my handbag away. He sat in the extra office chair, drumming his fingers on its arms, his posture reeking of annoyance. Good, then. Time to ratchet it up. Instead of taking my own chair, I walked around to stand alongside him and gain a height advantage with all five feet, eight inches I could muster. He couldn't get back to his feet without conceding that he had made a tactical error by sitting in the first place. Score one for me already.

He plastered another smile on his face and nodded to the paperwork. "I crunched some more numbers," he began. He dove into a technical discourse designed to intimidate me. Ha. I kept up and threw in a few questions where he skimmed too lightly, but uneasiness had settled over me like a sticky blanket by the time I escorted him out of the office with a word of thanks for his work. It might have been a major tactical error to work only Friday night instead of through the whole weekend like usual. Craig had obviously spent hours of his weekend running projections.

Even though it was technically my project, I understood his motivation. Every team got called in to support another one now and then when the scope of a project grew too big for one group to handle. Getting called in to play backup too many times posed a problem. It implied that management lacked faith in that team's ability to take the lead. Craig wanted to make sure he wasn't called in as support again for a long time by attempting to outproduce the lead team. I was sure in Craig's dreams, Dennis Court would call us both in and flip the team assignments.

But that was only in his dreams.

In reality, my own team had been so effective in our support role under my old boss that I had earned my promotion, and I didn't want to rest on it. I'd learned that lesson at my grandfather's knee, puttering in his garden with him during one of my dad's summer school breaks. Grandpa Ray had been carefully tamping the rich Georgia soil of his garden down around a tomato seedling as he explained the steps to ensuring a healthy harvest. He had finished his lesson with a final pat to the soil and the summary, "It has to grow or die, Jessie. Those are a garden's only two choices."

Grow or die. The distillation of the principle of work, something our family embraced. That was Grandpa's real lesson. Grow or die. We were put here to do our own unique job, and if we didn't, we would shrivel, even if only inside. So no one in our family shirked—ever. Especially not me, Jessie "All-Or-Nothing" Taylor.

Time to refocus. If I worked for a couple extra hours every evening this week, I could be four days ahead of the projected deadline. Balance would come from logging all the overtime before Friday so I had no demands on my weekend time and I could see Ben without my work suffering. Two birds, one stone, and good aim could make it happen.

Moderation. Sandy would be proud. I pushed Ben and the associated stomach flip-flops out of my mind and turned back to my work. Time to hunker down.

* * *

I worked like a madwoman for the rest of the day, even skipping lunch. I avoided checking my personal e-mail on the off chance Ben had sent me a message, knowing I wouldn't be able to resist reading and responding if he had. My cell phone stayed off too.

By seven o'clock, I had made the smallest dent in my work, but it was a dent. Taking the first deep breath of the day, I rubbed the knots in my neck and surveyed my computer screen one last time. Every box on my task list showed a neat check in it. Time for a reward. I savored the moment of anticipation before I opened my e-mail, curious about what Ben would have to say after our Sunday evening.

I clicked on the inbox and found out.

Nothing.

He must have had nothing to say because I didn't have anything from him waiting for me. I heard from my Internet provider, a vitamin company, an online bookseller, IKEA, and two of my sisters. But not Ben.

Before I allowed myself to spiral into self-pity, I checked my cell phone, powering it on and trying to mind meld with it so I didn't have to wait through the interminable boot up. A text message chirp greeted me when it connected to the network. Ben!

Hi, Jess. Using my nickname? Good sign. *I had a great time last night.*

The text had come in three hours ago, so I didn't waste time, typing back, *I had a good time too.*

His response came right away. *You're easy to talk to. I had fun.*

Ditto. Okay, that's maybe a cop out, but I didn't want to get all slobbery on him.

Air hockey tonight at FHE. You in?

To be fair, I actually debated with myself before saying no. But in the end, pragmatism won. By a narrow margin, but it won. Instead of the *Yes!!!!* I wanted to send, I texted, *Can't. Am drowning in work. Rain check?*

Definitely, he sent back.

I tucked my phone away with a sigh. Had being responsible always been so boring?

Chapter 15

"You've lost focus," Sandy chastised me an hour later. "I feel like this is the umpteenth time I've had this conversation with you. Why are you so determined to become a lonely workaholic?"

"Is umpteen before a gajillion or closer to a bazillion?" I asked.

"Stop avoiding the question. I can't believe you turned Ben down. He's going to think you didn't have fun last night or that you don't like him or something."

"I doubt guys invest much thought in it," I answered. "And I told him I had fun last night. He knows."

"Couldn't you have at least called to turn him down?"

"No way. I get all distracted and off-task when I talk to him."

"That's fantastic. You should do more of that," she said.

"No! I don't want to get behind at work again. Craig had a field day in our meeting this morning because he almost caught up. If he gets ahead and Dennis hands him the project, I'll never hear the end of it."

"If we had this conversation when I first moved in with you, I would have believed you were supercompetitive or ambitious or something. But now I know better. This isn't about your career or even one-upmanship. This is about you being a mess." She shook her head to illustrate how hopeless she found me.

"I'm not a mess. I know exactly what I want and how to get it," I said.

"Really? And what's that?"

I opened my mouth to answer, but no response came out.

Sandy watched me for a minute and then hammered home her point. "I know this is none of my business, but I'm the only eyewitness to how hard you're pushing yourself, and I guess that makes me the only one who can say anything." She sat down on the sofa next to me and turned to look me in the eye. "You are a cool chick, Jessie. You're doing awesome at work because you've got a lot of natural talent and an insane work ethic, but I don't think you're happy. You're comfortable, and that's different. Maybe it's even bad because you're missing out on stuff."

I dropped my gaze. I hated being transparent.

"I know you've done some dating on and off since you moved here, but you haven't tried to find a relationship. You go out on dates because you think you're supposed to, and you start looking for reasons not to go out again as soon as you get home. That's backwards, don't you think?"

I looked up and sighed. "Yeah. Maybe."

"You're a great friend. You've done some thoughtful things for me. You come back from visits with your nieces and nephews relaxed and happy. And with Ben, you've shown pretty much the first ounces of spontaneity I've seen from you. Work never does any of that for you, so it makes me wonder why you try to make it everything."

"I don't know. It's easier."

"Can we have an Oprah moment?" she asked.

"Are we going to have one anyway if I say no?"

"Yes. So what about this for a theory? You are addicted to forward motion, and you like to be able to measure it."

I nodded in agreement. True.

"Work is an easy place to do that," she continued, "because they give you a pay raise or a new office or whatever when you've shown enough progress."

I nodded again. It was that whole grow-or-die approach to living.

"And you don't even care much about Craig except when he gets in the way of your forward motion, right?"

"He tries to," I muttered.

"You invest more time in worrying about him and your job than you do about the relationship you have growing right under your nose, one you are desperately trying to sabotage."

"I am not!" I protested. "I'm keeping the pace slow and steady. You can't call three dates a relationship."

"You can when your previous record is two dates."

Fair point.

"Why stall here when you charge full steam ahead with everything else? Remember when they called you to be a Primary teacher?"

I had put together flannel board kits and graphic organizers for the next six months of lessons before I taught my first class. I flushed.

Sandy studied me for a moment, trying to marshal her arguments, I'd bet. She fired her final accusation at me.

"The Jason thing messes with your head because you did everything you were supposed to do, and it didn't work. I think you've avoided ever trying again because you don't know what to change to make it work the next time. But I have an answer for you," she said.

"Really? Is this the Oprah moment?"

She ignored that and said, "The only thing that needed to change with Jason was Jason. Not you. Just because that relationship failed doesn't mean you did. I've seen you when stuff goes wrong at work. If something knocks you back, you're up and at it again, finding a different solution. But in your personal life . . . you're treading water, Jessie. You're not getting anywhere. Isn't that the worst thing possible in your type-A mindset?"

"You're acting like I haven't put any effort into my social life at all. You saw all the dates I went on before it got down to scary middle-aged men and other walking social disasters."

"Yeah, but I also saw you shut down a couple of potential candidates for stupid reasons. Like that Dave guy. How come you never went out with him again?"

"Because he was on a break from his girlfriend and still totally hung up on her. That's not my fault."

She shook her head. "Excuses, Jessie. You'll have one for any example I give you."

Her analysis made me cranky. I knew she wanted to help, but it wasn't fun to sit and listen while someone dismantled my entire coping mechanism, as if suddenly doing things differently were a no-brainer. Time to dish back her own medicine.

"Fine. I'm stagnant." I held up a finger to stop her when she opened her mouth. "My turn. I'm stagnant and an overachieving workaholic. I've got problems. But I'm working on them." When she narrowed her eyes, I shrugged. "It's true. Going out with Ben at all was a change of pace for me. Going out with him more than twice is a record. And I plan to go out with him again. But I'm not going to drop everything to build my whole future around him because I have to live in the right now. Right now is where I've got a territory war going on at work and not a lot of time to date."

"How is working all the time a change of pace?" she demanded.

"I'm not going to work all the time. I'll scale it back to fit Ben in where I can. That's more than I've ever done in the past," I challenged her.

"It is, but ask yourself if it's enough. If you were into someone who kept turning down your invitations but who acted like he liked you every fifth time you talked or hung out, how long would it take for you to lose interest? You're going to confuse him."

"No, I'll tell you what's confusing. You are," I said. Here came her medicine. "Let's talk about your love life. You say you believe in the values you learned as a teenager, but you don't go to church. You don't date anyone from church. In fact, the only ones you kiss are the ones you meet at parties or in clubs, the ones who don't share the same values as you. You tell me to get it together for Ben, but you haven't been in a relationship the whole time I've known you. And friends with benefits don't count!" I preempted her.

"Are you done?" she asked without any inflection.

"Yeah, sure," I answered.

"Not everyone who quits going to church does it because they want to become hedonists, Jessie. I can be a good person without stepping foot in a chapel or a bishop's office. And I can have good values without having a testimony. It's narrow-minded not to see that. You're lucky you didn't grow up with a crackpot mother and her religion-of-the-month or a parade of stepfathers. But I did, and it colors things for me. There are a whole lot of shades of gray in this gospel, and I'm not comfortable with that. I can't be there every Sunday pretending I am. I do my best to be a good person without tying up three hours of my weekend beating my brains out over questions that don't have answers. Maybe I do run around kissing cute guys who aren't LDS, but they aren't bad people either. A lot of them are more respectful of my standards than some of the Mormon boys I've put up with. So don't judge what you don't understand."

"I'm just saying I'm not the only one around here who could use some fixing."

Her expression tightened. "Whatever, Jessie. You're right. You've got everything working fine. I'm going to bed."

I watched her storm to her bedroom and slam the door behind her.

And I let her go, smarting over her analysis.

* * *

An hour later, I still sat on the sofa, studying the patch of carpet immediately in front of me. What a royal screwup. I'd hurt Sandy when she only wanted to help, and I didn't know how to make it right. For all our bickering, we'd never been truly upset with each other before. It stunk.

I decided to grovel for forgiveness. Pushing myself up despite the heaviness in my stomach that tried to drag me back down, I squared my shoulders and headed down the hall.

I tapped on her door, not sure she would talk to me, then poked my head into her darkened room. "I'm sorry, Sandy," I said softly. "I never meant to imply that I think you're a bad person. I just think you'd have better luck at church finding someone who understands how you're trying to live." She sat up on her bed and switched her lamp on. I could see a flicker of hurt lurking in her eyes. "I shouldn't have snapped at you," I continued. "It's not fun to look at myself and realize no matter how hard I work, I've got places in my life where I'm standing still, so I lashed out. I swear I'm not judging you. I know you have good values, and it makes me sad that you meet guys who don't know how to appreciate them."

"Even Latter-day Saint guys can forget the *Saint* part of their name," she said.

"I know. I just have a hard time believing you don't have a testimony when you work so hard to keep your standards high. Is it such a leap to go to church?"

"In three years, this is the first time we've ever talked about why I don't go to church," she pointed out. "Why now?"

"I don't know," I admitted. "Maybe I'm paying you back for pointing out some of my unresolved baggage by pointing out a little of your own. I guess that isn't nice."

"It's okay. But your baggage is a carry-on case compared to mine. My baggage is more like a freight car full of screwed-up-edness."

"That's not a real word."

"But I'm fabulous, and fabulous people invent their own vocabulary all the time."

I grinned, knowing she'd forgiven me. "Fine, I'll let screwed-up-edness slide."

She climbed off her bed and turned to look at me. "I know I have to get off the fence at some point about church. But my life works pretty well for me, and I'm good with that right now. I poke my nose into your business because I don't think you have what you want, and I'm not sure you know it. I meant to help, but I'm sorry if I overstepped."

"You didn't. I know you're trying to help. But I can't drop everything to date Ben. I have to figure out how to fit all the pieces in."

"I'm not suggesting you drop everything. But I know most of your work team, and I think they're more ready to help than you give them credit for. Try delegating something every once in a while, and five o'clock might seem like a reasonable time to finish work."

"That's the craziest thing I've ever heard."

"Well, it's true. I read it in a book once. Apparently, the people we hire to work for you are there to help you do your job and not to count the office supplies."

I winced. "Uh . . ." I scrambled to explain this use of human resources to the assistant HR director who was now grinning at me. Oops.

Sandy laughed. "Forget it," she said. "That was genius. Did you know Craig called Susannah Anders to report you for misappropriation of personnel after that stunt?"

I groaned. Susannah was the big boss over HR.

She shook her head. "Don't worry. Susannah had received a half dozen complaints about his supply embargo, so it delighted her to hear that you set him straight."

I leaned over and gave her a hug. "You're the best, Sandy. Now quit bugging me about Ben."

She looked surprised for a moment, given we are not of the hugging-roommate variety, but said only, "I am, and I won't. Now go call him." She clambered off the bed and headed toward the kitchen, probably in search of postconflict chocolate.

I followed her out, plugged in my laptop, dug my cell phone out of my purse, and laid it next to the computer. I eyed them both for a moment. Decision time. Call Ben or work?

Chapter 16

After the fourth ring, relief crept in. I would get the best of both worlds if Ben's voicemail picked up and I could leave a message. No risk of distraction that way. I was mentally composing the witty and flirtatious voicemail I would leave when Ben's "Hello?" interrupted the fifth ring.

Uh . . . "Hi," I said. "It's Jessie."

"I know. The caller ID already sold you out. That's why I picked up," he said.

"Oh, well, good."

A bunch of yells and piercing whistles filtered through the phone.

"I'm at FHE," Ben said, followed by something I couldn't quite catch through all the ruckus.

"What did you say?" I asked.

"Sheesh, it's loud. Can you hold on a sec?"

"Sure," I answered. It sounded muffled for a moment, like maybe he was covering the receiver with his hand. For some reason, I like it better when people do that instead of hitting the mute button. The mute button always makes it seem like someone's got something to hide, like they're going to press it and trash you to whoever they're with. A hand over the phone says, "I'm an open book." Not that I've overthought this or anything.

Ben yelled over the noise to someone about stepping out to take a call. A minute later, he came back on, crystal clear.

"Sorry about that," he said. I heard nothing in the background now. "The air hockey tournament is in the finals, and it somehow became a battle of the sexes, so there's extra loud trash talking."

"No problem," I told him. "So you're at the institute?"

I attended a family ward because I couldn't deal with the later afternoon start time the singles ward had, but I dropped by activities at the institute building every now and then when I wasn't drowning in work. For a moment, I wondered how I had managed to miss Ben there and then realized how many Monday nights I'd spent working over the past several months. Using my superfast CPA mental computation skills, I came up with the precise figure of how many: pretty much every single Monday.

"I *was* at the institute," he said. "Now I'm in my car driving away from it."

"Oh, I'm sorry! I didn't mean for you to leave."

"Don't apologize. I lost big time to a pre-mish freshman in the semi-finals. I think he's a prodigy. You gave me an excuse to leave and save face."

"An air hockey prodigy?"

"Why not? There're already enough violin and piano prodigies running around. Dare to be different, I say."

"Kind of like you and your trivia?" I teased him.

"Exactly like that. What about you? Do you have any savant tendencies? So far, everything I've seen you do seems more like true talent than stupid human tricks, Chef Jessie."

"Thanks," I said, flattered. "It's kind of embarrassing to admit, but almost nothing comes to me naturally. I have to work hard at everything to be even kind of good."

"Wow. So while I know useless trivia because of some freakish wiring in my brain, you have thousands of trivia tidbits filed away in yours that you acquired through actual intelligence and learning?"

"That's not what I meant!" I went from flattered to flustered.

"Too late. You're busted," he said. "You've been found out as smart and hard working." Humor laced his tone.

"Fine. I admit it. I'm amazing," I responded.

This time his laughter spilled out of the phone. "Remember, I said it first," he said. I liked his laugh. A lot.

"I can invent a useless talent if it means you'll quit teasing me," I said.

"This I gotta hear."

I scrambled to think of something absurd. "Uh . . . I can name the patron saint for every country."

"But we don't believe in patron saints."

"I said it was a useless talent."

"Okay, name one."

"All right, Peru. They have St. Judas of the sacred liver."

"Is that true?"

"Kind of," I hedged. "He's the saint of a school near where my dad served his mission."

"Name another one. What's Canada's?"

"St. Francis, patron saint of processed meat products."

He laughed. "And Poland?"

"That's St. Gertrude, defender of itchy long johns."

That really got him going. A pleased grin took custody of the corners of my mouth. I dug that he had a goofy bone. Most people have a funny bone, but very few have a goofy one.

"Whew. I think I bruised my spleen," he said.

"It's okay. That's one of those vestigial organs you don't need." As soon as I said it, I winced. Vestigial? Who says *vestigial*? My true useless talent was probably my massive vocabulary that I'd kept toned down since childhood. When I was a kid, Lane Dorsey accused me of trying to show off how smart I was in Primary when I used the word *pastoral* to describe a picture of Jesus and the lost sheep. Granted, it might have been precocious for a seven-year-old.

"Mmmm, *vestigial*." He paused for a minute. "That's a good word. I like it. Vestigial, vestigial, vestigial."

I laughed. "If only I could use it in Scrabble. I would die happy."

"It doesn't take much to please you."

"No, I guess not. A good book or movie, a cheeseburger, curly fries, and big words. It's kind of sad. I should probably upgrade to filet mignon and rolling around in money for kicks or something."

"Nah. Not unless it's freshly minted cash. Do you have any idea how many hands the average dollar bill passes through?"

"No, but I bet you do. Go ahead, trivia man. Tell me."

"Maybe I will, and maybe I won't. It depends."

"On what?"

"Your answer to my next question," he said.

"Lay it on me," I prompted him.

"Oh, wait. I hate to do this to you, but can I call you back in a second? I saw the time and realized I've got a tiny bit of business to do. I promise it won't take long," he said, his tone apologetic.

Who was the workaholic now? But I had about an hour left of my own work anyway. "No problem," I said. "But you owe me the dollar trivia when you call back."

"I promise, I'll tell you everything you never wanted to know about the lowly single bill. I'll take care of this as fast as I can."

After he hung up, I stared at the phone for a minute, disappointed we didn't talk longer but relieved he had enough self-discipline to take care of business. Goodness knew, I didn't. After all my big talk to Sandy, I had almost abandoned my work just because Ben had made me laugh.

I shook my head at my moment of weakness, found my backbone, and dug out a new audit report. When Ben called fifteen minutes later, I was immersed in a payroll discrepancy from the marketing department. I surfaced long enough to murmur a distracted, "Hello?"

"Hi, Jess. Sorry that took longer than I thought. But I'm armed with dollar trivia."

"Oh. Uh . . ." Even as I stared at the stupid payroll report, temptation urged me back toward a conversation with Ben and away from work. Again. Dang. I needed to focus on my project, but I didn't want to blow him off.

Ben rescued me as I stumbled around, trying to find a polite way to extricate myself. "Uh-oh. Sounds like my window of opportunity closed."

"I'm sorry. I kind of hit my groove on the work stuff I have to do."

"No problem. Don't work too hard though. You might get a hunched back and a squint," he teased.

"That only happens to people in Dickens novels. I'm more in danger of carpal tunnel or a Craig allergy," I answered.

"Yeah, well. Remember to take breaks sometimes. I usually solve my toughest problems after I step away for a while because I can look at them with fresh eyes."

"I know. I just have to get this done."

"I can respect that." He was quiet for a moment, and I didn't know what to say. "I guess I better let you go," he said.

"Thanks for the invitation tonight," I offered lamely. "I'm sorry I couldn't go."

"There will be other air hockey tournaments, I'm sure. Good night, Jessie."

"Good night," I parroted back.

"Oh, one more thing," he said.

"Yeah?"

"You should take a look on your doorstep when we hang up."

I was already heading for the front door when he ended the call. When I opened it, I found a bag with a cheeseburger and fries and a rental copy of *Saturday Night Live*, best of Will Ferrell. Ben had tucked a napkin under the corner of the DVD box and scrawled, "A dollar goes through hundreds of hands in its life span. Gross. I'd rather spend it than roll in it!"

I ran for my living room window and strained to see down into the parking lot. A car pulled into the main road, and as it passed beneath a street light, I could see the deep blue shape of Ben's Acura slipping away.

I grabbed my phone and called him, but it went straight to voicemail. Instead of leaving a message, I hung up and typed out a text. *I refuse to watch Will without you.* I sent it and retrieved my burger. I was wiping up the last of my ketchup with an exceptionally tasty curly fry when I got a text back.

Ben had replied simply, *I rented him for a few days. Call me if work lets up.*

The ball landed back in my court. Again.

Chapter 17

In three years at Macrosystems, I've never had a week drag so much. Each day crawled by, sloth-like and agonizing.

Working late didn't help speed things up any, and I was sick of eating three meals a day at my desk. Craig worked just as late every night, which did nothing to validate Sandy's opinion that I only imagined the competition between us.

Now staring blankly out the office window, half my brain tried to puzzle through an audit problem, and the other half brooded over how much I didn't want to work the long hours stretching before me. This time last week I had been counting down the minutes until lunch with Ben, and everything looked brighter and shinier. Quite a contrast to my current mood, which mirrored the gray Seattle sky.

When I'm stuck idling, sometimes the best thing to do is switch gears. I picked up the phone and called Sandy.

"I'm bored," I snapped when she answered. "Quick, tell me a joke."

"Knock, knock," she said without missing a beat.

"Who's there?"

"Pathetic."

"Pathetic who?"

"Pathetic girl who calls me as a poor substitute for the hot guy she should be calling because she has her priorities all screwed up."

I snorted. "That's stupid."

"I should have made it rhyme. You would have liked it better."

"I don't think it was the rhyming. I think it's the part where you called me pathetic. That wasn't my favorite part."

"Give me five minutes, and I'll make it up to you."

"It'd better involve your emergency sugar stash," I grumbled.

"This will be way better than candy."

"Cheesecake? Don't tease me."

"No. I forgot to shove a cheesecake in my purse this morning. Check your e-mail in five minutes." And she hung up.

I spent the next five minutes in the ladies' room, fixing a strand of my hair engaged in angry rebellion, then made a brisk return to my desk for my coworkers' benefit. Inwardly, I slouched and cringed in resistance. I wasn't only sick of eating at my desk. I was sick of my desk, period.

I clicked open the e-mail from Sandy.

To: Jessie Taylor
From: Sandy Burke, Assistant HR Director
There once was a girl in Seattle
Who fought Craig the Snitch in a battle
She worked hard and won
But never had fun
So go call Ben or you're lame

I snatched up the phone again. "Worst limerick ever," I said when she answered the phone.

"Limerick writing wasn't in my liberal arts program. If you give me a week, I could render the spirit of the limerick in an abstract sculpture."

"Please don't. Your poetry makes me scared of your art."

"It's abstract. You won't be able to tell if it's good or bad. For all you know, I might reshape a couple of wire hangers and call it an interpretation of a girl who works too much."

"Cool. Will you sell it?"

"For hundreds and hundreds of dollars, none of which I'll share because you mocked my creative process."

"I have to go now," I said.

"Are you mad I'm not sharing my hanger art money with you?"

"No. I'm calling Ben."

"Yes! The limerick changed your mind, right?"

"More like the fear of more coming if I don't call him."

"Interesting." I heard papers rustling. "I'm entering 'pathological fear of limericks' in your permanent employee file as we speak."

"If it helps me to avoid them from now on, go right ahead."

"Oh," she breathed. "Uh-oh, I feel another one coming on. There once was a plaid covered lumberjack—"

I hung up.

I tapped my forehead, right between my eyes, like it could focus my thoughts or something. I hadn't heard from Ben either way in the last three days, not since Monday, but that was kind of my fault. I debated between a phone call and an e-mail. Ultimately, I chose neither and went with option C, as in *cop out*, and sent Ben a text again. *Knock, knock.*

It's not like every comedian out there hasn't helped himself or herself to someone else's jokes at least once. It was a tribute to Sandy.

A minute later, Ben's reply came back. *Who's there?*

Hooray! He used the proper form of *who's*! Be still, my word-nerd loving heart. *Will*, I typed.

Will who? he responded.

Will Ferrell. Some girl's had me trapped for three days, and I can't get out. Save me!

After a long pause, he texted back. *Okay, but only b/c the video store expects you by tmrw. Tell the crazy lady to call me.*

I punched his number in.

"Hello," he said.

"Hi. I don't know if you remember me or not, but my name is Jessie. We've hung out a few times?"

"Jessie . . . Jessie. Sounds familiar. Are you tall-ish, with brown-ish hair and green-ish eyes?"

"Sounds me-ish. Keep going," I encouraged him.

"Let's see. If I have the right person, you have a cool condo, you're pretty, and you're funny."

"Almost. I'm just pretty funny."

Ben laughed. "No, I definitely had it right the first time. You're pretty, and there's no ish about it."

"Well, thanks." I had developed the ability to accept compliments through years of my mom's coaching. She insisted to all of her girls that accepting compliments with good grace was a way to let other people practice kindness, whether we were comfortable with praise or not. But I didn't mind one bit being complimented by Ben.

"So, Jessie, long time, no talk."

"Yeah. Sorry. Work again."

"Man, that place sounds brutal. How did you ever get away for lunch with me last week? Did you have to sneak past the guards?"

"Oh, them," I said. "We get an hour every day in the yard, like real prison. I used it to grab lunch."

"And when do prison hours end today?"

I eyed the pile of work sitting in my in-box and turned my back on it. "The guards leave at 5:30, and I'll be right behind them."

"Good. That means you can eat dinner with me. I think it's my turn to cook. I open up a mean box of takeout," he offered.

"But you already bought me a burger," I protested.

"That was a cheap bribe in a bag. Let me bring you something from an actual carton to prove I know how to treat a lady right."

"How can I refuse?"

"You can't. Say yes."

"Fine. But I expect phenomenal cartons."

"I'll meet you at your place at seven?"

I agreed and disconnected the call.

I switched back to the desk phone and dialed Sandy again. When she picked up, I announced, "I called him."

"And?"

"And he's coming over and bringing dinner. Are you going to be around?" I knew she would want us to hang out without her even if she didn't have plans already, but I also knew she would play chaperone if I wanted her to.

"Jessie, it's not BYU anymore. There's no 'chastity line' in the condo," she pointed out.

When I had explained about the BYU rule of no boys ever leaving the common areas of a girl's house or apartment, she had fallen off the sofa laughing. She loved my tales of BYU housing rules and honor code guidelines, especially the beard card for guys. She still didn't believe it existed.

"Sandy . . ."

"No, I don't have anything major going on, and I can sit and measure the distance between you all evening. Can I borrow your Book of Mormon?"

"Are you getting religion again?"

"Nope. It's one of the few details I remember from logging time at the stake dances. Book of Mormon width is the standard distance to help protect your morality, right?

"Uh, are we talking the width of the cover or width of the spine?"

"This ain't BYU any more. I'm only counting the spine."

"You're definitely the right girl for the job."

"Yeah, yeah," she grumbled. "Do you really think he's the type to bust a move on you on your sofa?"

I stayed silent for a long moment. "Is it bad to say I hope so?"

I could still hear her laughing when I hung up.

Chapter 18

I THREW OPEN THE FRONT door when Ben knocked at exactly seven.

He smiled and stepped in to hug me.

"You're prompt," I complimented him. "I like that."

"I'm also clean, loyal, honest, friendly, cheerful, brave, reverent, and I can sew on my own buttons."

"Were you born a Boy Scout, or did you have that beaten into you when you were twelve?" Sandy called from the sofa.

"Remember I mentioned having brothers?"

"Ah. Beaten into you, then."

"Don't get me wrong, I was almost an Eagle Scout."

I raised an eyebrow. Almost? Ben noticed the question inherent in the brow arch and explained, "I had a difference of opinion with the Scoutmaster about my Eagle project." His mischievous grin suggested he wasn't at all sorry about it.

"Goody. A story. Sit down and tell us," I said.

"Wait!" Sandy interjected. Her nose twitched, and her eyes zeroed in on the large brown paper shopping bag in his hand. "Is that food?"

"Yep. And three separate desserts. I learn." He smiled.

"Okay. Then we'll listen to your story," she said.

"Hold up, hungry girl." I took the bag from Ben and pulled one of his hands in mine, leading him to the kitchen. I plunked the food down on the counter, opened up the cabinet housing my dishes, and stepped out of his way. "Show me how the magic happens."

"I'm not great in the kitchen. What's the scooper thingy called?" He mimed using a spoon.

I laughed and pushed myself up from the counter then slapped a spoon in his outstretched hand. "I don't know what you brought, but it smells awesome."

"I brought the best noodles in the city," he said.

When he pulled the first box out of the bag, I couldn't hold back a cheer. "Yes! Boom Noodle! I love their food!"

His face fell. "You've been there already?"

"Ha!" Sandy hollered from the living room. "She's turned me down three times when I've invited her to go there."

I rolled my eyes. "No, I haven't been to the actual restaurant," I said. "But coworkers have brought takeout when we're putting in overtime, and once, Sandy even let me have some of her leftovers."

"Well, the only thing better than Boom Noodle takeout is eating there in person. It's a cool place. We should go there sometime."

"I'd like that," I said, smiling.

He pulled off lids and opened more boxes, releasing incredible aromas as the steaming food poured into plates and bowls. *Lots* of plates and bowls. The bag disgorged an alarming number of containers.

"Whoa," I protested. "I know we went back for seconds when you ate with us on Sunday, but seriously, we've never been this hungry for one meal. Ever."

He pulled yet another dish down from the cabinet. "I didn't know what you would like, so I got a bunch of different things to make sure you guys get what you want." He spooned a spongy looking brown curd soup into a bowl. "I even got tofu," he called to Sandy.

She wandered in, following her nose. "You're all right, Bratton," she pronounced.

"It's so bizarre to me that anyone would thank another human being for putting them in proximity of tofu," I said.

"Sheesh, Jessie. Tofu isn't a punishment. It's kind of good if you cook it right, and Boom Noodle most definitely does it right." She leaned past me to pluck out the piece of tofu I was trying to protect her from, popping it into her mouth and smiling. "Yum."

I shrugged. "If you say so."

"So, Ben, do you have any riveting tofu trivia?" Sandy asked.

"You have no idea." He shook his head. "There could be a whole *Jeopardy* just on soybeans. Soy farming, soy based products, soy poetry." He slid her a look. "Should I go on?"

"I'm going to take your word for it," she said.

"Too bad. What I know about soy sauce would blow your minds."

"Now I have to know," I said. "What about soy sauce?"

"Remember a couple of years ago when a thing went around about putting Mentos in a Diet Coke and making a crazy soda explosion?" he asked.

"Yeah. I saw it on Letterman or something."

"That's nothing compared to what happens when you stick a potato in soy sauce. Talk about explosive." He shook his head.

We stared at him.

"You don't know anything about soy, do you?" Sandy accused him.

"Nope."

"You're such a dork," she said, but she laughed.

"Since he's my guest, I have to defend his honor or something if you insult him," I warned her. "I *will* fling noodles at you, if necessary."

"How is that different from when you test your pasta?" she wanted to know. "I distinctly remember picking spaghetti out of my hair."

"That's only because you walked right in front of the cupboard when I threw it to see if it would stick," I said.

"Isn't that an old wives' tale kind of thing? How do I know you weren't waiting to ambush me with a whole fistful of Barilla and Ragu?"

"First, because I make my sauce from scratch. Second, because I do it the way my mom taught me, and if she says to throw it against the door to check it, I do it. I don't ask why. I quit arguing in the kitchen when I was nine and she told me the secret ingredient to beef stew is stirring it with your finger to make it taste better."

"Seriously?" Ben asked.

"Very seriously. My mom is a Southern cook and a God-fearing woman, but I swear there's a pinch of voodoo in every recipe below the Mason-Dixon line."

Ben folded the paper bag and announced, "No voodoo here, but dinner is served anyway, buffet style. Grab what you want."

Sandy needed no further invitation and scooped a bit of everything into her bowl and plate.

I took a more scientific approach. "What do you recommend?" I asked him. "Do you have any favorites?"

"Yeah, I do." He dug into a bowl of flat noodles flecked with peppers that smelled like heaven. "This is spicy but awesome."

"You like spicy food?" Sandy asked. I knew she was thinking of her spicy-food-means-good-kisser theory.

"Love it," he answered.

She shot me a naughty grin, but luckily she said only, "You chose well, Jess."

Ben looked confused, so I hurried to explain before Sandy did. "She's talking about the food," I said.

"Yep, that's it. Talking about the food," she agreed.

Well, it was true on some level.

After we all made our third (or fourth) trip back to the makeshift buffet, I folded my arms across my chest and narrowed my eyes at Ben. "Deep, dark secret time again," I said.

"Isn't it enough to know about my secret alter ego, Nerdy Trivia Man?" he asked.

"Not nearly enough. I think we have an episode with your Scoutmaster to discuss."

"Jessie's right," Sandy said. "You're the floor show this evening."

"Meaning, I'm supposed to do a dramatic reenactment while I tell you the story of my misbegotten youth?"

"Yes," I said. "Don't leave anything out."

"Okay, but I warn you. The truth is ugly. This is a tale of malice, revenge, and ultimate redemption."

I turned to Sandy. "And you thought you might want to go to bed early tonight."

"Shhh . . . I want to hear about the revenge and stuff."

"Long, long ago in Brother Atkins's Scout troop, I was on track to get my Eagle by fifteen. My final project was simple: organize a work party to fix up a rundown park near my house. Slap paint over the graffiti, upgrade a couple of benches, and pick up the trash."

"That doesn't sound too controversial," Sandy said.

"It wasn't. Brother Atkins liked the idea. We got the whole thing done in a Saturday."

"So where did it all go wrong?" I asked, propping my chin in my hands.

"On Sunday. After church, my dad suggested a walk over to admire my handiwork. That's when we discovered that someone had trashed the place, probably during the night."

"That stinks," Sandy said.

"Yep. Tagging everywhere, trash cans emptied out all over the park. They'd tied all the swings into big knots so the little kids couldn't untangle them."

"That's so mean," I blurted.

"Yeah, it bummed me out at first. But then I noticed my sister Lindsay crying. She was only five at the time, and I got mad."

"So what did you do?" Sandy asked, caught up in the story.

"Nothing. At least not at that moment. I let my parents try to make me feel better, and we left. But when we got home, I pulled Dean and Logan, my older brothers in for a powwow."

"Uh-oh."

"Exactly. We grew up on too many A-Team reruns. We figured the vandals were probably a crew of troublemakers who hung out in the park after sunset, but they weren't exactly a criminal brain trust. It wasn't the kind of area that had issues with real, hard-core gangs or anything."

"Yeah, we had a group of kids like that at my high school. They always graffitied the desks and bathrooms and stuff," I said.

"Well, we decided to do something about it. I don't want to spoil your image of me as a guy who is all that is good and holy—"

Sandy snorted.

"—but let's just say the plan involved an ambush with our quads and paintball guns, a potato shooter, water balloon launcher, camo and greasepaint, and about eight other Scouts out way past curfew."

"Your Scoutmaster caught on to what happened?"

"He overheard another Scout talking about it at our campout the next weekend. He confronted me, I told the truth, and it turned into kind of a thing."

"What thing?" I wanted to know.

"He thought I had exhibited the wrong kind of leadership, and I thought I had done exactly what I needed to. Those kids never messed with the park again. He wanted me to plan another project, and I refused as a matter of principle. He wouldn't sign off on the park project, which my parents agreed with, and I wouldn't change my mind. And that was that."

"But this is the guy who called you in as a Cubmaster."

"As the assistant, yeah. He's a great guy who felt at the time like I should have been setting an example of turning the other cheek and not seeking revenge. I saw it more as teaching a lesson than seeking revenge. We agreed to disagree, but I never held a grudge about it. It was my choice not to do another project." He shrugged, his tone unconcerned.

"Boy, you're full of all kinds of juicy secrets," I said. "You got any more you can spill?"

"A few dozen, but I'm limiting them to one per hang out so you'll keep coming back for more," he joked.

"Feeding her old *SNL* skits will do the trick," Sandy reassured him.

"Speaking of . . ." I gestured to the sofa across from the TV. "Sorry about the television," I said. "It's a girl TV."

"I don't know what a girl TV is. Does it only show *Bachelor* marathons?"

I raised an eyebrow. "You know about *The Bachelor* because . . ."

"That sister I keep mentioning? Loves it," he said.

"Got it. And no, no *Bachelor*." I flushed. I had the whole current season on the DVR. "The TV's old school. Under fifty something inches and no plasma screen."

"Yeah, Ben. What's your TV look like?" Sandy asked.

"It might be a fifty-something inch plasma," he mumbled.

"Because you're a guy and truly believe you must have a giant TV to be complete as a man," she said.

"Oh, I thought they bought them because they like shiny buttons and blinking lights," I said.

"No, Sandy's right," Ben said. "It's encoded in American male DNA."

I shook my head and grabbed the DVD box. "Time to let Will out." I stuck the disc in the player and went to settle into the sofa. Sandy sat curled up in her usual corner, and Ben hadn't taken a seat yet. It was going to be mighty cozy with all three of us on the couch. I guess I hadn't thought through the movie seating when I insisted on Sandy joining us. I stood there, wavering for a moment about what to do when Ben said, "Don't worry about it. I'll find a spot. Go ahead and sit."

So I did, stretching my legs to the side and feeling like a bad hostess. No sooner had I sat, though, than Ben settled onto the floor in front of me, his back leaning comfortably against my legs. Twisting around for a quick glance at me he asked, "Is this going to bother you?"

I smiled and placed my hand on his head, gently shaking it from side to side. "Not at all," I answered.

"Good." He took my hand off his head and tucked it comfortably under his own on his shoulder.

"This DVD was the best idea ever," he pronounced. "I hope it's really, really long." And he gave my hand a slight squeeze.

Since I had temporarily lost the power of speech, I squeezed back. And discovered a new favorite way to watch TV.

* * *

We were laughing like punch drunk hyenas over Will Ferrell as a Spartan cheerleader when Sandy broke into a huge yawn, which she tried to smother behind her hand.

"Sorry, guys," she apologized. "I'm so sleepy. I think I'm going to crash for the night."

The clock showed it was barely after ten, but she looked thrashed. "Night, kids," she called over her shoulder as she headed for her room.

"My cue to exit?" Ben asked, his head tilted back to look at me.

I gnawed on my lower lip, torn about what to do. I wanted him to stay, but I didn't want to risk staying up so late that it made me useless for work the next day.

Ben watched me for a moment, and then pushing up from the floor, he took the middle cushion on the sofa next to me. "I probably need to go. I think if I overstay my welcome tonight, you'll find some reason not to hang out with me this weekend, and I have every intention of tying your weekend up."

I started to explain that only my weekdays were occupied when he stopped me with a knee-weakening grin. "I'm onto you, Jessie. And I think I might like you as more than a Saturday and Sunday friend, so think about that, okay?"

I watched, mesmerized, as he reached up to cradle his hands around either side of my face and leaned in. He smiled, but his eyes gleamed with intent. My hand crept to his chest. I meant to steady myself but instead gave his shirt a tug. His grin widened in the split second before his lips touched mine. My eyes drifted closed, and I quit thinking, quit worrying, quit overanalyzing. I fell into the moment and that first, amazing kiss.

Chapter 19

My oldest sister, Callie, likes to brag that she can count on one hand the number of guys she kissed before she married her husband, Gary. Now, I'm not exactly a kissing bandit, but I've been going on dates for almost ten years, and I'd have to at least take my socks off to count and get the number right.

But it didn't matter because Ben's kiss jumped to the top of the list. I'd been kissed under a full moon, in a rowboat on a lake, at the peak of a mountain, and next to a waterfall, but nothing compared to that kiss on my living room sofa. Ben's kiss made my previous best kiss, a sunset-by-the-ocean smooch, seem like a clumsy peck.

Ben's kiss . . . it was in a league of its own. My toes curled, I think. A zing of electricity snapped through me the second he touched me, and when he drew back an eternity later, he stared at me for a few seconds, like he couldn't figure out what had happened. He reached up and brushed my hair off my forehead, tucking it behind my ear with a feather-light touch that sizzled anyway.

He leaned forward, so close our lips nearly touched again. "I want your weekend, Jessie. All of it," he whispered and brushed his mouth over mine.

I don't do well with orders—usually. It's probably from being bossed to death by my sisters as a kid. But from Ben, it sounded like a challenge, and I don't back down from those, ever. Especially not when it means getting exactly what I want. So I kissed him back, hard, and then I leaned away and quirked an eyebrow at him. "Make it worth my time."

"Name your bribe."

I kissed him again, drawing back enough to say, "Those, whenever I want them."

"Done."

"And chocolate."

He laughed. "And chocolate."

"Then you've got my weekend."

"Good. What time are you done at work tomorrow?"

I tensed. "Friday's not the weekend, Ben. I won't be free until Saturday."

He sat back. "You're working tomorrow night?"

"Yeah. I should have been working tonight too, so tomorrow I'm going to have to play catch up if I'm taking the whole weekend off."

"Taking it off? Macrosystems has accounting shifts on the weekend?" he asked.

"Not exactly. I just don't seem to finish stuff during regular office hours."

"Stuff you have to do, or stuff you think you have to do?"

"Same thing," I said.

"Is it?" His expression shifted to watchful. "They're asking an awful lot from you."

I shrugged. "I choose to give it." Tension grew between us, creeping into my neck and shoulders.

Another moment slipped past, and he smiled and tapped the back of my hand. "It's your prerogative, right? I love what I do. I respect that you love what you do."

I sighed. "It's not even that. My boss has learned to expect miracles from me, and I feel like I have to keep delivering. So I work a lot." It sounded pretty lame when I said it out loud.

He picked up my hand and clasped it then raised it until our elbows touched. "I'll arm wrestle you for your Friday."

I laughed. "I can't. I'd let you win so I could get out of work."

"You'd *let* me win? I've got six inches and fifty pounds on you. How are you going to do that?"

"Remember Master Po?"

"Oh yeah. You're a kung fu expert." He put my hand down, and I was bummed.

"I've watched hours of the stuff. Osmosis has to count for something."

"I surrender. No arm wrestling. Maybe we should do sumo wrestling. That involves lots of hugging," he mused.

"And you would get to wear that cool loincloth," I reminded him.

"Right, no sumo wrestling. So you're working tomorrow."

"I am," I agreed with some regret.

"Then I call Saturday, twelve to twelve."

"Deal. And I call Sunday evening again." I felt bold, playing his game.

"All right, you get Sunday." He stretched and climbed to his feet. "You better come walk me out before I think of another reason to stay."

When we reached the door, he turned and pulled me into a hug. "One of my Young Men leaders once told us that hugging a girl longer than ten seconds is inappropriate, and I try to live by that." He squeezed tighter, and I listened to his chest rumble as he counted, "One Mississippi, one-and-a-half Mississippi, one-and-three-quarters Mississippi, two Mississippi . . ."

I pushed gently at his chest and smiled up at him. "Accountants are experts at reinterpreting the numbers, but I think I could learn a few things from you."

He pressed one last kiss to my lips and left, closing the door behind him.

Sandy came in a moment later, toothbrush in hand.

"Ben left? How'd it go?" she asked.

"I thought you were tired," I said.

"I am. I was getting ready for bed when I heard the door close." She waved her toothbrush at me.

"You better hold off," I said. "We're having ice cream."

"Hallelujah!" She tossed the toothbrush over her shoulder. "Now dish, and I'm not talking about the Häagen-Dazs."

"There's not much to say." Sandy's face fell. "Except it was kind of awesome."

She perked up again. "That's what I'm talking about! Are you getting married?"

Since I knew she was kidding, I rolled my eyes at her and muttered a drawn out, "*Anyway . . .*"

"I won't interrupt again," she promised. "Give me details. I need them now that my love life has dried up."

I obliged her with a retelling of the action after she'd left, hitting the high points and skipping the parts about how my insides went all mushy.

"I have to say, Jess, you totally lucked out. I should hate you for stealing the only guy like that left in North America."

"That's not true. I think there's a handful of them in Canada."

"Yuck."

"What's wrong with Canadians? Do you have some latent anti-Canuck sentiments I don't know about?"

"No. They're just so . . ." she groped for the right word. "Kind," she finished.

"Yeah. Kindness. That's a problem, all right."

"Never mind. Congratulations on finding such a cool guy."

"Thanks. And what do you mean your love life is all dried up, by the way?" I'd never known anyone who dated as much as Sandy, including one college roommate who was built like Barbie and had the personality of a turnip, making her a hit with the guys.

"Blah. Everything's blah. I'm so bored with the same old faces when I go out that I don't even feel like going anymore. And even when it's a new face, it's the same old thing."

I stared at her. How unlike Sandy.

She gave a tiny shrug. "I blame Jacob," she said. "Ever since he ripped my heart out and stomped on it, nothing's been the same."

I missed a heart stomping? "Who's Jacob?" I dared to ask.

She dropped her chin into her hand and grumbled, "Hot guy from the club who never called back."

"Jacob is a hot guy name. Much better than that Phil guy you were so into last month."

"I could use some moral support here. Besides, it's not like they name themselves. You can't hold people responsible for their parents' bad taste."

"I can hold Phil responsible for not calling himself Phillip. Tell me that's not better than Phil," I argued.

Instead of responding, she dropped her head into her arms and moaned pitifully.

"Okay, okay, I'm kidding," I said. "Look, maybe this Jacob guy lost your number. It happens."

She picked her head up enough to eye me for a moment. "Good try, except remember, I told you I programmed my number directly into his cell?"

"Oh yeah." I tried again. "Then he probably lost his phone."

She didn't even raise her head this time, just shook it against her arms, causing her hair in front to bunch into a bright red blossom of tangled curls. No response.

"Seriously, Sandy. I bet he did lose it. He's from out of town, right?"

"Boston, I think," she mumbled from inside her arm cave.

"So I bet they confiscated it when he went through security on the grounds that it looked suspicious."

She picked her head up all the way. "How is a cell phone suspicious?"

"I don't know. Was it bedazzled in the national colors of any terrorist states?"

"You're weird."

"No, you are. Plenty of other guys haven't called. Why is this Jacob character getting under your skin?"

"They don't call because I don't give them the right number. I wanted him to call though. He was different."

"Different how? You only talked to him once. Maybe he's as clueless as the rest of them."

"I don't think so," she said, shaking her head. "We talked most of the night. Lots of stuff was different about him."

"So name them," I said.

"First of all, he's not into clubs, but he was in town on business and he met his clients there at their request. So he didn't do all the usual club stuff."

"Define usual."

"I don't know. He didn't stand around ogling all the girls in skimpy clothes. He didn't drink anything harder than a Coke or bug me about why I didn't either. He wore a business suit but not because he was trying to seem like a high roller. It's how he came from work. And he had interesting opinions about something besides the football playoffs."

"That does sound pretty cool. But if he's not calling you, there's definitely something wrong with him." I grinned. "Maybe he doesn't like girls."

"That's not it," she said. "I can tell when a guy is into me. We were for sure connecting. I don't get it."

This was a strange state of mind for Sandy. I'd never known anyone as confident as her or as social. I'd watched guys flock to her in droves in the three years I'd known her. Her wild red hair and gorgeous face hooked them, and her personality reeled them in. But she left a wake of bewildered Romeos behind her, scratching their heads, unable to figure her out. It never surprised me when she cut them loose; it happened the second a guy asked more than she was willing to give of herself physically or emotionally, which was not much at all. But I was as clueless as anyone as to why she prowled the clubs and bars. She discarded guy after guy she found there, always frustrated when they turned out to be exactly like the guy before.

If she hadn't quit dating LDS guys a long time ago, living vicariously through my misfires in the Seattle area would have put her off of them for good. I decided a year ago, after listening to her complain about another jerk, that she clearly knew what she didn't want, but she had no idea what she *did* want.

I tried to come up with some reassuring girl power slogan to share with her but failed. She popped her head off her arms and pushed away from the table.

"I'm done," she said. "I'm done with the stupid guys and the stupid clubs and obsessing over stupid Jacob."

"Good."

"In fact, it's time for a makeover."

"Right this second?" I asked.

"There's no time like the right now."

"True, but I don't think anything's open, so where . . ."

She broke into my question. "I don't need anything from a store. This is going to be a life makeover. You've started yours, and now I'm going to do mine."

"I'm not doing anything as drastic as a makeover."

"Maybe not a total one, but rearranging things and spending time with Ben is kind of like getting new highlights or something. If you start leaving work on time every day, that's practically like going blonde."

"I'd look terrible as a blonde."

"Fine. Red, green, blue, whatever. The point is, there are degrees of change. You stick a toe out there to test the water, but I'm diving in."

All the metaphors confused me. "Okay. I don't follow anymore. Are you diving into a vat of hair color that's an analogy for your life?"

"What?"

"Yeah. What?"

"I'm doing a one-eighty. I'm quitting the club and party scene, refusing all dates, and finding inner peace." She whipped around and strode down the hall.

"Inner peace is in your bedroom? It's all the feng shui, right?"

"Ha ha. No. I'm going to sleep so I can wake up a new woman."

"Someone you know or a total stranger?"

"Keep it coming, Jess. I'm finding my bliss, and even you can't stop me."

"I wouldn't dare. I remember when I got between you and your curl enhancer that one time. I'll never stand in your way again."

"You couldn't if you tried. I'm evolving. That makes me a force of nature."

"Sandy?" I called before she shut her door.

She poked her head out. "Yeah?"

"You're already pretty great."

She smiled. "Wait 'til you see what's coming."

Chapter 20

FRIDAY NIGHT I STAGGERED INTO the condo after eight. Normally when I got home so late, I found only traces of Sandy, who liked to start her weekends as early as possible. This time, instead of a slight mist of the hairspray and expensive perfume she trailed behind when she took off for the night, the aroma of . . . something . . . cooking smacked me as soon as I opened the door.

Following my nose, I peeked into the kitchen and found my roommate standing over the stove. Flour dusted her arms to her elbows, and the steam from the pot she stirred had caused the topmost tendrils of her curls to escape her pony tail. It didn't smell bad exactly, but I wasn't going to beg for a taste.

I watched for another moment as she stirred, her attention completely focused on the pot. "What are you making?" I asked.

Without looking up she answered, "Broccoli soup."

"Oh, like with cheddar or something? Sounds good."

"No. Just broccoli. It's not coming out right." She tasted a spoonful and wrinkled her nose. "Maybe it needs salt. Will you check and see what you think?"

I hate broccoli, but I didn't want to get sucked into a lecture about antioxidants and vitamins, so I stepped into the kitchen and grabbed a spoon. Scooping up a bit of the brew, I took a small taste and schooled my face into a thoughtful expression instead of choking like I wanted to.

"Is it the salt? Should I add some?" she asked.

"Yeah, I pretty much taste broccoli. What seasonings did the recipe call for?"

"Oh, I didn't use a recipe. I wanted a healthy soup, and I figured soup is mostly cream and pureed stuff, so I blended up broccoli and skim milk and cooked it, but it's not coming out right."

My gag reflex nearly undid me. I cleared my throat. "Is this part of the life makeover?"

"Uh-huh. I'm going to develop new talents instead of going out all the time. I'm starting with healthy cooking."

I had a feeling cooking wasn't going to be her most special talent.

"So what do you think I should add to the soup?" she asked.

I couldn't exactly say, "The garbage disposal," so I reached for the spice rack in the cupboard. I handed her the lemon pepper, garlic, and cayenne.

"Try these," I told her. "Use a lot of cayenne." Maybe it would be so hot it would temporarily disable her ability to taste the concoction. It was the least I could do.

I rummaged through the fridge while she shook stuff haphazardly into the soup. When I sat down to eat a turkey sandwich, the oven buzzer went off. Sandy leaned in and pulled out a loaf pan. I couldn't see the contents, but I watched with interest as she stabbed it repeatedly with a fork.

"Whatever it did to you, I'm sure it's sorry," I said after a particularly vicious poke.

"It's bread, but it doesn't look like the recipe picture. How come it didn't puff up?"

"Maybe you didn't let it rise long enough before you put it in," I suggested.

She looked at me blankly.

"You know how you're supposed to cover it and let it sit for a while after you add the yeast?"

This time I got a brow furrow.

"Did you follow the recipe exactly?" I asked.

"Mostly. But I didn't have any of the yeast packets it asked for, so I did baking soda. That's a rising agent, right?"

Oh boy. "It is for cookies and stuff but not so much for bread."

"Oh." She plopped into a chair across from me, looking disgruntled. "Cooking is hard."

"Only at first." I smiled. "It's like everything else. It takes practice."

"How long did it take you to get good at it?" she asked.

"I don't know. My mom's been teaching me since I was a kid. I learned a little at a time, and now I can handle myself in the kitchen. It took me a long time, I guess."

Disgruntlement morphed into discouragement on Sandy's face, so I hurried to reassure her. "I wasn't trying to learn to cook when my mom taught me. I just did what she said, and eventually it stuck. I bet it'll go faster since you're really trying."

"Maybe." She got up and peered into the soup again. "I think I'm rocking a salad tonight though."

I didn't need another whiff to tell me to encourage plan B.

"Sounds like a good idea. What's next on the life makeover list?" I asked.

"I'm getting to know the great outdoors," she announced.

"You mean, like, nature walks and stuff?"

"Nope. I'm going to do hiking and camping and rock climbing. All that stuff. It's stupid to live in Seattle and not take advantage of it."

I refrained from pointing out that she had ignored those activities for the last three years with perfect contentment. Sandy was the girliest girl I knew. She worked hard to keep herself in fantastic shape and could probably handle the exertion easily, but her muscles came courtesy of an expensive Pilates studio and her devotion to yoga. Those two things didn't usually lead to encounters with stuff like bugs and rain. And dirt. Struggling between wanting to encourage her and wanting to warn her, I asked, "You're aware that outside isn't climate controlled, right?"

She rolled her eyes. "Yes, Jessie. I'm aware of that. I know it might rain and stuff—"

"It's Seattle."

"Okay, I know it *will* rain and not always be perfect, but I think it's important for me to change my perspective and explore something new."

"I think it's great. But it's more challenging out there than you probably think," I said.

"Quit worrying. I can run three miles in under twenty minutes. I'm in pretty good shape, Jess."

"Those are treadmill miles."

"I'm not a delicate flower," she said, sounding impatient.

"I know, I know," I said. "I'm sure you'll love it. What are you starting with?"

"Rock climbing. It looks cool. It'll be a metaphor for overcoming personal difficulties."

It was hard to believe one unreturned phone call had turned her inside out. I mean, her life seemed pretty sweet. She had a good job with a great salary. I knew for a fact she had an awesome roommate. But she wanted to trade her active social life for a daunting list of activities and projects I couldn't fathom. I watched her shred the lettuce for her salad with more force than necessary.

Considering she had all those things going for her, I wondered if the void she needed to fill was a spiritual one. But she clearly wasn't quite ready to tackle her faith, and it was none of my business. She was a smart girl, and she'd eventually get there.

I stifled a sigh at the thought of change. It wouldn't be easy for her. It's human nature to hold on to what's familiar because that's what I had been doing: I was clinging to work instead of opening up to Ben because he wasn't a known quantity. I watched the stress etched in every line of Sandy's tense figure as she hovered over her salad bowl, and I resolved to be more open to change too. At least I knew what changes I needed to make.

I looked at my gorgeous, unhappy roommate and considered the upheaval she would face when she finally figured out what she had to do. Spending more time with a hot guy I liked was a downright fantastic alternative.

Chapter 21

The doorbell rang at exactly twelve the next day. This time, I approached the door without any wardrobe drama; an e-mail from Ben that morning had suggested dressing for the outdoors.

When I threw the door open and reached up for a hug, I took note of his hiking shoes, jeans, and down jacket. A perfect match for my own almost identical outfit. Except he had on flannel, and I wore a comfy green cotton Henley. I knew I'd better get him out of the house before Sandy saw him. She'd be thrilled for an opportunity to renew her lumberjack jokes.

I grabbed a coat and stepped outside into the chilly Seattle afternoon.

"Are we in a hurry?" Ben asked with a grin.

"I'm trying to save you from Sandy," I explained.

"Why? Did I do something to make her mad?"

"It's your shirt. I don't want to send her over the edge," I answered.

"Is it bad?"

"No! It looks nice," I said. The blue and white pattern shirt sported a trendy Western cut with snaps instead of buttons.

"Well, back at you," he said. "That shirt goes great with your eyes. They're extra green today."

I smiled, happy about the compliment. At some point, I would run out of green shirts to wear and I'd have to figure out what color accented my hair or something, but it pleased me for now that he noticed.

On the way to the car, I trailed behind him in order to better appreciate the view. Yep, it was official. All of him was good looking.

When he started the engine, I tensed, but his radio didn't blare. Seeing me relax, he laughed and said, "I remembered this time." He handed me his iPod, which synched to his stereo. "Want to play three-song deejay?" he asked.

"Sure, if you explain it to me."

"It's a game my parents used to play with us on road trips. Every kid got to pick three songs in a row so no one would fight over the radio. I like to do it now when I have passengers because it's good for personality analysis," he teased.

"How so? It's all your music. Maybe my iPod is loaded with the smooth sounds of the seventies and some elevator jazz."

"I doubt it. But to answer your question, I have multiple music personality disorder so there's a ton of stuff on there. You'll probably be able to find something you know and like. What do you say?"

I twirled the iPod dial. "I say, game on."

He grinned and waited while I scrolled through the selections. Eclectic didn't come close to describing the range. I zoomed from Beach Boys to Sufjan Stevens in about twenty seconds. I made a selection and settled back to watch Ben's reaction as Jack Johnson's "Bubble Toes" filled the interior.

"'Jack Johnson when it's not,'" he said.

"Excuse me?"

"I'm quoting your e-mail. You like Jack Johnson when it's not raining," he reminded me.

"I do. Who do you like?"

"You, Jessie. I like you," he answered.

I blushed, thankful he had to watch the road and couldn't see me. "I meant music."

"I know what you meant."

I floundered, unsure of how to respond. I could see the corner of his mouth twitching and realized he meant to unsettle me. Poking him in the side, I growled, "You're not funny, and you will pay."

He grabbed the finger that poked him and drew my whole hand into his grasp then rested it in his on the console between us. "You'll have to wait on my deejay turn to find out my favorites."

"Fine. How about telling me where we're going? Is it a surprise this time?" I asked.

"Nope. No surprise at all. I thought we'd grab lunch at my place, since it's closer to the park, and then we'd do a light hike. I'm leaving the day open so we can do anything or nothing at all."

"How do you do nothing?"

"What do you mean?"

"I mean, don't you read or watch TV or sleep if you're not working?"

He shot me a glance to see if I was kidding. "Sure, but that's all doing something. We can just do nothing."

"Um, you're going to have to explain that to me," I said.

"I'll show you instead. We'll find a point in the afternoon where we want to do nothing at all, and then we'll do it."

I shrugged. "Okay. I'm curious to see how it works."

My next selection came on: "Birdhouse in Your Soul" from They Might Be Giants. Ben quirked an eyebrow at me but commented only on the weather. Nodding at the gray but dry sky he said, "I hope the clouds keep the rain to themselves. I wouldn't miss it today."

"No kidding. I'm not used to all this rain yet, and it's been three years already."

"It doesn't rain in California?" he asked.

"Well, yeah, but a normal amount. It's not an everyday thing like it is here." I sighed. "What about you? You lived in Arizona for a while. Didn't it spoil you for this kind of weather?"

"A little," he admitted. We spent the next couple minutes comparing notes on our favorite kinds of weather (drizzly: boo; thunderstorms: yay). Small talk usually drives me crazy because I fluctuate between feeling like I'm babbling and being bored out of my mind, but with Ben, it interested me. Who knew I could be so into the weather?

My third choice came on. Bob Marley crooned about three little birds.

"Wow," Ben said. "I thought *I* had a multiple music personality."

"Do you have enough information to conduct your analysis?"

"Oh yeah. You're totally busted," he said.

"How so?"

"My extensive practice in the field of music profiling leads me to believe you're excessively happy. I dare you to deny it," he said.

"That's a sucker's dare. I *am* happy," I said.

"Good. Is it the company or your natural state?"

"Maybe both. And those are all songs my sisters used to blare on the way to seminary. They were part of our wake-up sound track," I explained.

"You were a good kid. I made my brothers drive and slept the whole way there."

"What about when they graduated?"

"Then I drove myself there, half awake, listening to whatever came on the radio." He reached for the iPod and fiddled with the dial. "My turn." He grinned. "Now you have to figure out what kind of sound track these three songs would be on."

We swapped stories of terrorizing seminary teachers and playing practical jokes on other youth leaders. It embarrassed me that I had a story or two to contribute. One part of my brain listened as each of his three song choices came on, turning them over and looking for a connection. He played selections from Death Cab for Cutie, the Avett Brothers, and Amos Lee. The third song finished. "Well?" he asked.

"Is that the combo that suggests you have good taste in music?" I guessed, hedging until I came up with the answer.

"That's a secondary function. Guess again," he said.

After a couple of more fruitless guesses, he took pity on me. "That's my perfect moment playlist." He smiled. "I only play those when I'm in the middle of a moment where I wouldn't change a thing."

A strong urge to reenact our Thursday night kiss seized me. To resist the impulse, I looked out the window, watching a green blur of trees whip past outside.

"Jess?" he asked. "Did I overstep? I'm sorry. I don't want you to be uncomfortable."

I turned to face him again, noting the concern in his blue eyes. He had let go of my hand when he queued up his song selections. I reached over and tucked my hand back into his and ignored the nervous churning in my stomach.

"I haven't been uncomfortable with you yet," I said, and it was true. The nerves I quashed grew from my own overly analytical tendencies. But if I refused to overthink, to worry about an outcome . . . I sat back and felt the moment. It was a pretty great moment.

Chapter 22

A COUPLE MORE SONGS PASSED before he surprised me by pulling up to a cute bungalow on a quiet street. I thought he would have an apartment; instead, we sat in front of an older home, but fresh paint and a well-trimmed yard made it inviting.

"This is where you live?"

"Yeah, home sweet home. Come see," he said, and I waited while he jumped out of the car to open my door.

"You don't have to open my door every time," I said after thanking him.

"Yes, I do. I believe in modern, liberated women, but my mom believes in old-fashioned manners, so when in doubt—"

"Listen to your mama," I finished.

"Exactly."

"What other cool tricks did she teach you to do?" I asked.

"Laundry, ironing, yard work," he listed as he unlocked the front door. When it opened, a delicious smell rolled out. "And a couple of fall-back recipes."

"You open doors *and* cook too? Do you have *any* bad habits?" I demanded.

"Sure, but you'd have to ask my brothers for a list of those. And don't be too impressed because five of the six things I know how to make are on the grill, and I only learned because I liked playing with the fire."

"So what do I smell?"

"The sixth thing in my weak playbook, and the only thing that doesn't involve a barbeque," he confessed. "Why don't you have a seat, and I'll go check on it."

He showed me to a comfy sofa and headed into the kitchen. I looked around, trying to gather clues from his living room. It didn't say much. A couple of landscape paintings hung on the walls, the furniture was slightly worn but clean and all in a matching tan corduroy, and no knick-knacks cluttered the end tables. I wandered over to investigate his bookshelf. When he came back from the kitchen, trailing a spicy scent behind him, I was leafing through a crime thriller.

"You like mysteries?" he asked.

"Yeah, I do," I said. "But only if they're not too scary."

"You'd probably like that one," he said, indicating the book I held. "It's about a conservation officer who's tracking down some poachers."

He laughed at my doubtful expression. "I know it sounds weird, but the guys at the office are into this series, and they gave me a couple. It's not bad stuff."

"I believe you," I said, not trying to sound convincing. I picked up another book, a collection of short stories from J. D. Salinger. "'Great Day for Banana Fish?'" I asked, quoting one of the titles inside it without looking.

"You know your *Nine Stories*," he complimented me. "I'm impressed."

"No, I am. Mystery poachers aside, you have some pretty cool books in here," I said. I recognized two or three poetry volumes and some computer programming books, but his collection also included a couple of Russian classics and some literary fiction I'd read about in newspaper reviews.

"There's not much to look through," he apologized. "Most of my books are in Arizona."

"There's enough here for me to do my own personality analysis," I responded.

"Take your best shot," he said. "What do my shelves tell you?"

I pretended to think hard, crossing my arms and tapping a foot while I developed my theory. He waited patiently until I delivered the verdict. "Turns out you still have a split personality," I said.

"That's okay. All my personalities are nice, and we get along with each other pretty well."

"That makes me feel tons better," I said. "Can you introduce me to the personality who cooks? Because I have to know what I'm smelling."

"Sorry! I meant to feed you right away. Let's go to the kitchen before I lose awesome host status."

The kitchen, like the living room, didn't say much about his tastes. White walls and cabinets with beige paint and older model appliances told me nothing more than that Ben kept things pretty clean. Even the refrigerator door boasted only ad magnets from a couple of local pizza chains. The kitchen opened to a breakfast nook, occupied by a small table set with plain white dishes.

"Go ahead and have a seat over there," Ben said. "I've got beef stew coming up."

I took the seat he indicated. "Beef stew, huh? It smells awesome."

"It's not fancy, but I think it's pretty good. My mom figured my attention span in the kitchen was so short that she'd better focus only on stuff I'd like eating, and beef stew is an old favorite."

"Good thinking," I commented. "Your mom sounds like a wise woman."

"She's very Zen," he agreed. "I think she learned it from raising four boys. Not much gets to her anymore."

"So you're saying you put her through that much as a kid?"

"Anything you can imagine and more. My brother Dave had a knack for troublemaking, and we were always on board. Each brother after him sort of inherited the job."

He grabbed the bowls and dished out soup from the giant pot on the stove. Every time the cover came off, more insanely good smells wafted through the kitchen. My mouth watered. It felt weird. Ben set my full bowl in front of me then made one more trip, returning with a loaf of bakery bread. Impressive. I hated to stereotype, but I'd expect a guy to think of Wonder bread at best. This nutty whole grain had a delicious, yeasty, fresh-baked scent.

One bite confirmed it tasted as good as it smelled. "This is so good," I murmured.

"There's a cool bakery a few blocks away. I like the good stuff for dunking in my soup," he said and promptly plopped a healthy-sized hunk into his stew.

It looked like such a good idea that I copied it. The flavor of the stew equaled the rich aroma. This time I couldn't even form words, just a happy "Mmmm."

"You like it?" he asked, looking pleased.

"Oh yeah," I answered and set about making sure my spoon traveled a quick route from the bowl to my mouth, with a few bread dunks in between. When my stomach finally signaled to my brain to slow down, I asked questions.

"Do you have roommates?"

"Nope. I'm renting this for a few months from my aunt. She was nice enough to let me do it month to month since I didn't want to get stuck with a closed lease."

"It's a nice place," I said.

"Yeah, it's not bad. It came furnished, which was the other nice thing, but it doesn't feel like home yet."

That explained the lack of clues. "What would you do if you could trick it out your way?"

He thought about it for a minute. "Tear out the carpeting and put in wood, switch the old sofas out there for a cool leather sectional, add more bookshelves, and repaint the outside to something more modern."

"And the kitchen?"

"Something Asian style. Clean, interesting shapes, minimal clutter." He gestured at the durable Corelle bowls holding our stew. "Definitely some cooler dishes. Square bowls. That kind of thing."

"Wow. That was off the top of your head?"

"I might have thought about it a time or two."

"So if this doesn't feel like home, where does? Arizona?"

A fleeting frown slipped over his face, and he shrugged. "It used to."

I thought I heard tension in his voice, but he looked relaxed. Deciding I imagined it, I asked, "Do you still have friends down there?"

"Some, but most of them have married in the last couple years. They're busy with new babies and stuff, so it's not like we hang out much anymore."

"It's kind of strange when your friends cross over to the married side," I agreed. "Being married seems like this big mystery. Like there's some kind of secret to finding who you want to marry and then existing in this altered newly married state. They're automatic grown-ups or something."

He looked amused. "You don't feel grown up at twenty-five?" he asked. "You seem so mature and adult-like."

Despite his teasing tone, I answered him seriously. "Sometimes I feel like I'm still seventeen and impatient for the rest of my life to happen."

"I guess in the Mormon world, marriage does come next," he said. "It's strange when one of my friends ties the knot, but they all seem pretty happy. It must not be that bad."

"So you haven't found who you want to marry?" I asked. "I guess that's a pretty good reason to wait."

He put down his spoon and gave me a long look I couldn't read. When he spoke, his voice sounded much softer. "I thought I did find the right person once," he said. "But I was the only one who did, and I hear it takes two."

I couldn't imagine someone passing on Ben if he was that into her. "Was she nuts to let you go?" I asked.

He shook his head and smiled. "Look how hard it is to get you to come out."

"Only during the week and only because of work," I reminded him.

He grew serious again. "Actually, I was engaged before. For a long time, and that was the problem. I met my ex-fiancée when she joined the Church in Phoenix. She was a college senior, and she made it into law school right before we started dating. She studied long, crazy hours, which worked out fine because I was only in the second year of having my business, and I worked just as much."

He broke off and sopped up his remaining stew with his bread. He took a bite but tossed the rest into his bowl, uneaten. "Things moved slowly, but they moved, and I thought we had reached the next level. I proposed; she accepted. But she wanted to wait until she finished law school, so I said fine, and another year went by. When she graduated, I thought we would set a wedding date, but she wanted to get through her first year at a big Phoenix law firm.

"It was a great opportunity for her, and she was brilliant and talented and incredibly committed to her job." He smiled distractedly. "She just wasn't committed to me."

"Did she cheat on you?" I asked, horrified.

"No, nothing like that. She kept postponing the wedding talk until I gave her an ultimatum. Pick a date, or walk away. She had a thousand excuses, so I walked."

"That's rough," I said. "How long ago did this happen?"

He fidgeted and cleared his throat. "We broke up right before I moved here. It's part of why I changed my scenery."

This wasn't good. Not good at all. Did this make me the rebound girl? A consolation prize to pass the time while he figured out what to do next? I looked down at my soup, trying to process what it meant.

"Hey," he said. He reached over and touched my hand. "I know it sounds like a big dramatic ending, but giving Carie an ultimatum forced an ending I could see coming anyway."

I wanted to believe that so much it unnerved me, but I'd been burned once before by a guy with his heart in two places.

"Believe me, Jess. That relationship was over months before it ended. I tried to be a stand-up guy by sticking it out, but I didn't do either one of us any favors."

"And does Carie agree with you?"

He smiled. "Yes. She's nothing if not practical."

I took a deep breath and nodded. "Okay," I said. "I hope you're right."

"I am," he promised. "Just because we weren't right for each other doesn't mean I don't understand her pretty well."

"It's more a question of whether she understands herself. What if she takes a look around and decides you're the one for her, after all? That's a long time with someone to throw away," I said.

"It wasn't wasted time," he said. "I learned a lot about myself and what I want. But to answer your question, she won't. She and I are so fundamentally different that now that we've broken the habit of being in a relationship with each other, neither of us could consider getting back together. Yes, she feels the same. And no," he forestalled my next concern, "I'm not on the rebound."

"Nobody ever thinks they're on the rebound," I muttered.

"True," he said and laughed. "But if I were, I would have run out as soon as we broke up and dated like crazy. I didn't though."

He lifted my hand and rubbed his thumb over my knuckles. "I took a few months to get my head straight, and then you came and found me."

I tugged my hand away in embarrassment. "I didn't find you," I protested. "Sandy was behind the whole thing."

He sat back, grinning. "So I'm dating the wrong roommate?"

"No!" I burst out and blushed when he laughed. "It sounds all needy and desperate to say I went looking for you, that's all."

"Jess, you're about the most self-sufficient, independent woman I know," he said. "I don't think you have an ounce of neediness in you."

"That's not true at all," I said, finding my composure.

"No? Then what do you need?"

I leaned forward ever so slightly. "I think a kiss would totally reassure me."

What an understatement.

Chapter 23

I FELT STUPID. I LAY on Ben's living room floor with the top of my head touching his as he stretched out in the opposite direction, both of us staring at the ceiling.

"I—"

"Shh," he hushed me.

"But—"

He shushed me even louder.

"You—"

He groaned and rolled over to his elbows to glare at me, but our positions put his gaze upside down.

"Are you giving my chin the evil eye?" I asked.

"You are hopeless at doing nothing," he announced.

"I don't get the point. What are we supposed to be doing?"

He growled. "Nothing. We are lying here, staring at the ceiling, doing nothing."

I sat up and turned around. "I didn't think you actually meant nothing at all. Why would we do that?"

"To see if we can. The answer is, you can't."

"It's hard," I said.

"Only if you're Jessie Wiggle Bum Taylor," he said.

"Wiggle bum?" I asked.

"It sounded marginally better than 'ants in your pants' in my head. I was wrong," he conceded.

"So, so wrong," I agreed.

"We're going to have to go to plan B," he decided.

"Oh good. What's that?"

"Plan B is doing something."

"I like it already," I said. "Tell me more."

"How about that hike I mentioned?" he asked. "There are two good ones within a ten minute drive."

"Sounds good. Race you to the car," I said and jumped up to run for it. I made it as far as the front door when he grabbed me around the waist and swung me away from the handle.

"That's cheating!" I complained.

"No, this is called honoring my father and mother."

"How do you figure?"

"I only manhandled you so I could get to the door first and open it for you," he explained.

"I don't believe you."

"How sad. And here I thought we were building a relationship of trust," he said. A mischievous undertone laced his words, but I followed him out onto the front porch anyway. As soon as he locked the door, he bounded over the three concrete steps leading to the lawn and sprinted for the car, not looking back until he was leaning against it. He had covered half the lawn before I figured out what he was up to, and when I reached him a moment later, he made a big production of stretching and saying, "I won."

"Cheaters never prosper," I retorted.

"Don't be mad. I had to win so I could pick my prize," he explained.

"Let me guess. A kiss?"

"Good guess, but no."

Really? Bummer. "Then what?" I asked.

"I get a weeknight next week."

I eyed him. "How do you mean?"

"I mean, instead of waiting until next weekend to see you, I get to see you one night during the week."

He held up his hand when he could see me forming a protest. "Pick any night you want, a two hour window that coincides with dinner, and I'll come eat with you and then get out of your hair."

Instant quandary. Yearning and panic wrestled inside me; he was breaching my boundaries! Yearning pinned panic down and held a pillow over its face, allowing me to say calmly, "Okay. Wednesday. And I'll call you to tell you when and where." I felt better for yanking back control and setting the terms. But the tiny voice of panic taunted, *Yes, but he still carved out more of your time.*

I ignored it, glad when he grinned and said, "Good."

He walked around to open my side of the car. I liked that. I felt dumb waiting for him to help me out of the car, but I liked the chivalry of him helping me into the car. Modern women are studies in contradiction, I guess.

Within ten minutes, we stood at the foot of a hike at the High Point Trailhead. Despite an overcast sky and a January chill permeating the air, it didn't look like it would actually rain, and the midafternoon sun shone weakly enough to make it tolerable. I knew if Ben set the pace, I'd work up a sweat soon anyway.

He headed down the trail at a brisk pace. I liked a good hike, but the last one I took had been the previous summer, and all my exercise since had come from the gym. When I could fit it in. Hustling behind him reminded me that selecting the hill course on the elliptical machine was nothing like being on an actual hill. Within minutes, my calves burned in protest, and I fought to keep my breathing even. Ben had picked the easy trail, and I could barely keep up. How embarrassing! Pride prevented me from begging him to stop after five minutes, but when he turned around to point out something in a nearby tree, he took one look at my face and dug into his backpack for bottled water.

"Drink this," he urged me, concern drawing his eyebrows together over worried eyes.

"I'm fine," I gasped.

"Sounds like it. Drink it anyway," he insisted, wrapping my gloved fingers around the bottle.

"Well, if it'll make you feel better . . ." I said.

"Tons better."

I took a few deep swallows and tried to regulate my breaths, hoping he wouldn't notice, but they betrayed me, emerging in uneven puffs of steam. He had the good sense not to comment. Instead, he pointed again at the tree he had stopped for in the first place, angling his gaze away and wandering off a few feet so I could suck down more air without worrying that I looked like a wide-mouth bass out of water.

"I think there's a flamingo up there," he said, pointing to the top of an evergreen.

That distracted me from gulping down my next mouthful of precious, delicious air.

"Yeah right. Where?"

"Okay, it might be a cardinal." He grinned.

"I am cursed with funny friends," I muttered.

He took a couple steps back toward me. Cocking his head to the side, he asked, "Are we friends?"

"Sure," I said, too out of breath to say more without wheezing.

He narrowed his eyes and nodded. I didn't know what that meant. Maybe narrowed eyes meant, "I don't want to be friends," or the nod said, "Cool, we're friends." But since he didn't use any words, I couldn't tell for sure. I didn't have the energy to follow up on it, but I filed his reaction to "friends" away for further study. I'd get to it when I could breathe.

He didn't say anything else, only crossed his arms and slowly rotated in a circle, taking in the surrounding forest. We stood at its edges, and the faint winter sunlight still penetrated the leaf canopy. Not much moved or rustled. Even the usual sounds of skittering squirrels didn't disturb the peace. I guess the little guys were hibernating with their acorns, it being winter and all. Wait a minute . . .

"Cardinals don't hang out in the Northwest during January," I accused.

"Your point?" he asked politely.

"So why did we stop? You think I can't keep up?" The assumption irritated me. Even though it was true.

"Nope. I mean, yes, I think you can keep up, so no, that's not why we stopped."

"Well, for sure, it wasn't for flamingo watching," I said.

"It's that tree," he said, pointing to the evergreen tree.

"The one where the imaginary flamingos and cardinals live?" I asked.

"That one," he confirmed. "Do you see the vine-looking thing growing all over it?" When I squinted and nodded, he asked, "Do you recognize it?"

"Uh, no. What is it?"

"Mistletoe." He grinned.

My jaw dropped slightly as I stared at him. "That's a pretty roundabout way to ask for a kiss," I said. "Is that why you picked this hike?"

"No. This is dumb luck," he admitted.

"Hmm. Not that dumb," I said.

He grinned again and pressed a light kiss on my lips then settled back on his heels. "Today I love forests, hikes, and mistletoe," he announced.

After he urged me to take another swig of water, we took off up the trail again, this time side by side. It meandered through the copse of trees that grew thicker the farther in we hiked. Neither of us said much. I couldn't talk, and I could tell Ben enjoyed the quiet.

I'm not a chatterer. I listen a bit more than I talk. Dates are different though. Awkward pauses make me feel bad, like I am guilty of breaching good etiquette or something, so I often grope for ways to fill in the silences. Being with Ben felt easy though, like when Sandy and I hung out.

After several minutes on the winding path, he stopped again and pointed to another tree.

I smiled. "More mistletoe?"

"I wish," he said. "There's a woodpecker. It's the first one I've seen since I moved back."

Sure enough, I could see a large black and white bird with a red crested head clinging to the bark about midway up the tree. He dug into the trunk with a cheerful rat-a-tat-tat, looking for grubs to eat.

"That's the good life," I said.

"Eating worms?"

"Yep."

"Do I hear jealousy of the woodpecker?" Ben asked.

"It's easy out here, you know? You pick a nice tree and build a nest with your sticks and raise your baby chicks, and no one ever bugs you. Not a bad life," I said.

I expected Ben to crack a joke, but when he didn't, I glanced over to see if he'd heard me. I found him studying me with a curious expression.

"What?" I asked, feeling self-conscious. "Did that sound too cheesy?"

"Not at all. I'm just surprised," he said.

"Because I want to be a woodpecker?"

"No, that you want a quiet life with babies."

Oh no. Did he think I was sending out marriage hints? Embarrassed, I backtracked. "I'm probably more of a bee than a bird," I said. "Busy in my honeycomb of office cubicles, working like crazy to make the hive run. That's more my thing."

Ben didn't smile. Puzzlement flickered over his face, but he turned and gestured down the trail. "We've got about a half mile to go before the trail turns and winds back. You up for it?" he asked.

"Sure, of course," I answered with forced cheerfulness, and I hoped Ben didn't sense it. I couldn't pinpoint what had changed, but in a few short moments, the vibe between us had morphed from easy to awkward. I pushed the feeling to the side for the moment. Obsessing now would only make me feel more uptight when I wanted to relax back into the comfortable rapport we'd had moments before.

I took a deep breath, both because I needed the oxygen and to help me let go of the slight tension settling in my shoulders. Ben cruised nearly even with me on the path, a few scant inches away. Deciding to treat those inches as an opportunity instead of a gulf between us, I edged close enough to bump him gently with my hip. He glanced down, startled, then bumped back. He slung his arm around my shoulders and pulled me to his side. "Get over here, Queen Bee."

I liked the solid, reassuring weight of his arm across the back of my neck. The awkwardness evaporated, and the next hour passed in companionable silence with occasional pauses to "identify" increasingly outrageous wildlife in the forest. When we rounded one curve and Ben claimed to have seen the back end of a baby Yeti disappear into the brush, I threw up my hands in surrender.

"I give up," I said. "You are the King of the Forest. I don't know why I tried to compete. My albino fox is nothing compared to a baby Yeti. You're in the wrong field, by the way. You should quit computers and get an Animal Planet show where you wrestle bears on the slopes of Mt. Rainier."

He looked disturbed. "I think I've falsely misled you into believing I have, you know . . . muscles." He flexed and stared at his biceps in mock frustration. "I'll have to outrun the bear because I'm pretty sure I can't wrestle it."

I laughed. Ben definitely tended toward the lean side, but I knew from his hugs that he wasn't at all scrawny. "Okay, so you're no wrestler. Your neck is visible so that rules out football. Let me guess," I said, poking his bicep. "I'm betting on swim team in high school." He had the perfect frame for it. Not that I was looking. Much.

He smiled. "Good guess."

We walked again, comparing notes on high school activities. Me: volleyball, school paper, honor society, and orchestra for two years. I play a mediocre violin. Ben: swim team, water polo, chess club, and cheer squad.

Wait, what?

"*Cheer* squad?" I choked out.

"Yep," he said, his grin growing wider. "On swim team, all the girls are in bathing suits, and cheer squad—"

"—they're all in short skirts," I finished for him. "Genius."

"It's a Bratton thing," he said. "Two of my older brothers did it too."

"What about the one who didn't?" I asked.

"Dean? He didn't need an inside edge. He's the good-looking one, so he joined the football team and got girls anyway."

"Somehow, I doubt you needed extracurricular activities to get girls."

"You'd be surprised. When you have good-looking older brothers, the girls don't tend to look at you. I had to think of creative ways to compensate. Didn't you have the same problem with older sisters?" he asked.

"They always dated guys older than them, so the ones my age never really tried to get their attention. Besides—"

But I stopped, weirded out by the idea of bringing up Jason. I'd never needed to explain him to anyone before.

Ben looked at me. "Besides, what?"

I swallowed. "I always had a boyfriend."

This didn't seem to alarm him. "No surprise. I can see guys lining up to date you the second you were available."

"It was the same boyfriend the whole time, actually. In high school, I mean. And also in college."

Now he looked interested. The concerned kind of interested. "How long were you together?"

"Four years."

His eyebrows shot up. "What happened?"

"He met someone else. And married her."

"Idiot."

I smiled. "Maybe. Unfortunately, I hear they're happy so it turns out I just wasn't the right girl for the job."

"Unfortunately? No way. Super lucky break for me," he said. He pulled me in for a hug, and I soaked up his warmth. After several long moments, he leaned his head back and studied the tree canopy. More light streamed through, meaning the trees had thinned and we were near the end of the trail. "Excuse me for being nosy, but I gotta ask, are you done with that? Like, over it done?"

I pictured the Jason box disappearing in the flames of my fireplace. I was trying my hardest to be done. I hated the idea that Jason still had any kind of hold on me, but it scared the heck out of me to feel so strongly for someone again. So I told the truth I wanted to believe. "I'm so done," I said.

Without saying anything else, Ben took my hand once more, and we strolled out of the forest.

Chapter 24

By the time we neared Ben's place, dusk had already fallen at barely past five o'clock. What came next? A tinge of anxiety shadowed the last mile to his house as I wondered if the awkwardness from the trail had put the kibosh on the rest of our day. Did I want it to?

We'd already spent a pretty great afternoon together. Maybe I should get while the getting was good and cut out for the evening. No danger of more uncomfortable sharing that way. *You didn't share much*, a voice whispered in my head. *And Ben didn't push you to tell more than you wanted to. Stay.*

Even as I hustled to shore up my defenses, they crumbled under the realization that I wanted to spend time with Ben more than I wanted to run away. He had breached my first line of defense.

I didn't care.

How interesting.

He pulled into his driveway and turned to look at me.

"What do you say, Miss J?" he asked softly.

"Why are we almost whispering?" I asked him in a near whisper of my own.

"Because you look like you want to bolt; I'm trying not to startle you."

I blew out an exasperated sigh. "I'm that obvious?"

"No," he said. "But you seem to have a limit to how much of me you can take, and I thought we might be reaching it."

I could sense he was only half joking. Instead of reaching for the rope he threw me, I pushed it aside and kicked the rest of my outer wall down myself.

"Today, the sky's the limit, I think. I have nowhere to be," I said.

"How flattering. It's good to know that here's at least better than nowhere," he teased me.

I took a deep breath and said, "No, I meant to say there's nowhere I'd rather be." I couldn't meet his eyes, so I stared more in the vicinity of my fidgety fingers as I said it.

"Hey," he said, his tone soft again. He waited until I looked up. "I'm glad," he said. He leaned over and kissed me.

My eyelids fluttered open a moment later to find him watching me again, his expression thoughtful. "I've made an executive decision to change our plans for the evening," he said. "Would it be rude if I stepped out of the car to make a short phone call?"

"No, that's fine."

I watched him through the windshield as he walked toward the house, thankful for the chance to collect myself. He pressed his phone to his ear while he fiddled with the door lock, and I wondered what he was up to. Wondered what *I* was up to, really. This was no way to play it safe. But I didn't bother lecturing myself on staying focused and keeping my priorities straight. For this one Saturday evening, I decided I didn't care. I had spent the last nine years being driven by priorities that kept me safe and comfortable. And bored. Time to take Sandy's advice and live a little. No more stressing about what every glance or gesture meant, the million things I should be doing instead of spending a whole evening with Ben, or the countless ways this could go wrong.

For tonight, I cared only about the moment, not anything that came after. A small weight lifted off my shoulders, and I smiled at Ben when he ducked his head through the driver's side door, done with his phone call.

He raised an eyebrow. "You mean, all I have to do to get a smile out of you is leave?'

"No, you have to come back."

"Jessie?"

"Ben?"

"Are you hitting on me?"

"Is it working?"

"Like a charm." He hung a garment bag in the back and slid into the driver's seat.

"Where are we going?"

"I'm taking you back home."

What?

"If it's okay with you," he continued, "I booked us a table at a nice restaurant, and I thought you might want to change. Is that okay?"

I looked down at my comfy shirt and picked off a twig stuck to its hem. "Yeah, a change would be good. Uh . . ." and I said nothing but gave his worn flannel a quick once over.

He grinned. "That's what the bag is for. I was a Boy Scout, remember? Always prepared."

"Well, you didn't make Eagle, so I thought I'd better double check."

"Ouch," he said, but he smiled again and merged onto the highway.

"So where are we going?" I asked.

"It's another surprise."

"Can I get a hint?" I wheedled.

"Sure. It's your idea."

"Okay, so what's the hint?"

"That was the hint. Where we're going tonight is your idea."

"Now I'm confused."

"Good."

I gave him a mock scowl and settled back, enjoying the smooth ride to my house. I drive a newish Honda Accord, and it's a good car, but Ben's Acura was a luxurious step up. I'm not into cars beyond making sure mine's reliable, but it didn't mean I couldn't appreciate a nice car when I saw it.

At my place, Ben walked me to my front door. "I'll be back in twenty minutes. Does that give you enough time?"

"Er . . ."

"Thirty?"

Yeah, I thought. *That should give me enough time for a wardrobe freakout and still get my hair brushed.* "Thirty works."

"Are you sure? I can make up some errands to do."

"Thirty will be fine," I said. "Do you need to borrow a bathroom to change and stuff?"

"Nope. Don't worry about me. I'll be ready when I come back to pick you up. See you in half an hour," he said on his way out the door.

"See you," I answered back, already preoccupied with my new wardrobe challenge. "Sandy?" I called into the house, but when I wandered down the hallway, I could see her empty bedroom.

I would have to make do with my closet. At least I knew to dress for a fancy restaurant. I scanned my hanging racks without much hope. I could always stick with classic black slacks and a button down. Except Ben hadn't invited me to a business dinner. This was a *date*, for pity's sake. Surely I had fancy date clothes in here somewhere.

I resorted to pulling out anything that had a prayer of being dressy and threw it on the bed, quickly amassing a pile of clothes rivaling Sandy's unfolded laundry mounds. I sorted through my choices, discarding one pair of pants after another and shoving aside my tailored blouses in disgust. Even the few skirts I owned for church would look boring and conservative with those tops. I had to have at least one girly thing that would work for a night out with a good-looking guy. Didn't I? I mean, I couldn't own only gym clothes, jeans, and business suits.

After ten minutes of sorting and rearranging, desperation overwhelmed me. My closet had become Sandy's best argument against my work-driven lifestyle. In three years, I hadn't bought one party dress I could now draft into service for a romantic evening out. I kicked an innocent suit jacket lying on the floor. Stupid suits.

In a last-ditch effort, I yanked open my dresser drawers and plundered them. Finally, in the bottom drawer under an old intramural softball jersey, I found a solution. A sweater set.

Normally, that wouldn't sound like an improvement on a suit jacket, but this wasn't any old sweater set. Two years ago, my sister Evie had drawn my name for Christmas. She'd seized the opportunity to inject some glamour in my life and enclosed a card with the sweater set that read, "Live a little." I had smiled and thanked her at the time, knowing I would never wear it, but now I knew I'd owe her the hugest hug and cheek-smacking kiss of her life. The set, spun out of a sparkly silver thread, draped beautifully without clinging. A thin tie accented my waist.

I scrounged up a black skirt I'd bought on a whim. It fit snugly through the hips and ended in a slight flare at my knees. It made me feel self-conscious, so I rarely wore it. Sandy said it was because it gave away the fact that I had hips, but when I checked out the effect with the cardigan in the mirror, it looked trendy and festive, not suggestive. I let out a relieved breath. This would work, especially with the pair of black stilettos I fished from Sandy's closet.

I lifted out my favorite silver chain with matching hoops from my jewelry box. It came from Tiffany's, a gift from my dad on my sixteenth birthday. I ran a quick brush through my hair, touched up my makeup, and finished it off with one of Sandy's sheer lip glosses in a plum shade. She would be proud.

I studied my handiwork with a critical eye and smiled. It had been years since my sisters had henpecked me into learning how to do a full face of makeup, and although they might have gone heavier with the eyeliner and mascara, even they would admit I had done all right. I'd forgotten how fun getting all done up could be.

A knock sounded at the door, and I hurried to let Ben in.

He stared.

"Holy smokes," he managed. "You look hot."

"Thanks," I said, trying not to laugh.

He reddened, embarrassed for the first time since the vase incident during our first lunch. "Sorry, that didn't come out very smooth. I meant to say you look amazing."

Ben cleaned up nicely too. I'd seen him in his work clothes on that first lunch date, but the slacks and button down shirt hadn't even hinted at the good things he could do to a suit. A faint pinstripe ran through the charcoal gray, and a light blue shirt and silvery gray tie accented the whole thing. "You're not half bad either," I said. "Great suit."

"No one's going to notice with you next to me," he said.

"You're making me blush," I teased, trying to lighten the moment. "But I think you're wrong. Your suit owes you a big thank you for making it look good."

"We're incredibly attractive. Let's go make everybody jealous." He offered me his arm, and we headed out to his car once more. When Ben revved the engine, my stomach gurgled in an excited chorus. I didn't know where we were going, but I already couldn't wait to get there.

Chapter 25

Ten minutes later, we drove right into the heart of Seattle Center, a combination of high-rise corporate buildings and tourist traps selling Space Needle key chains. I had no idea what we were doing in this part of town, unless . . .

Sure enough, Ben pulled into the parking lot for the Space Needle.

"Let me guess," he said. "You've never been here."

"How'd you know?"

"It's one of Seattle's great ironies. Its most famous tourist attraction is one most locals have only seen at a distance."

"I always meant to come check it out."

"Now's your chance. You're the one who said the sky's the limit."

"So *that's* how we ended up at the Space Needle."

He smiled and climbed out of the car, hurrying around to open my door. "You're not afraid of heights, are you?" he asked as he helped me out of the car.

"Spiders, yes. Heights, no."

"You're scared of spiders?"

"They're creepy," I said, my tone defensive.

"Okay, I'll be the designated spider squisher for the evening, but I suspect Sky City will be spider free."

Sky City, a world famous restaurant, rotates slowly at the top of the Needle, giving an incredible panoramic view of the entire Puget Sound down below. How had Ben managed last-minute reservations for us on a Saturday night?

He anticipated my question, placing a hand at the small of my back and guiding us toward the elevator that would take us to the top. "I know someone," he said before I could even ask.

"How have you barely moved to Seattle and yet you have hookups that I don't?" I wondered.

"The manager, Nate Greely, is in my ward. I gave him a call, and he said he'd hold a spot for us."

"Nicely done, Ben. Nicely done."

He accepted the compliment with a pleased smile and punched the button to take us to the restaurant. The glass elevator arrived, and we stepped in and watched the city spread out before us as we rose. Lights twinkled below us, shining out from homes and cars and stores, all humming with energy and intent. To be up above it felt peaceful, like we were curious observers somehow detached from the bustle.

When we reached the restaurant, a guy in a button-down shirt and tie hurried over to Ben, who introduced him as Nate, the manager. Nate led us to a prime table on the outer ring of the room, directly overlooking the city. After he settled us in with menus and a basket of piping hot sourdough bread, he left, and Ben leaned back in his chair to fix me with a concerned gaze.

"Is this all okay with you?" he asked. "Are you comfortable? Is the spinning going to bother you?"

"Yes, yes, and no," I answered. The spinning was almost imperceptible as the restaurant revolved around the tip of the Needle. "This is better than okay with me, I'm completely comfortable, and I love that we get to see the city. Great idea."

"I'm glad. I haven't been here in years, but tonight seemed like a good time to check it out again."

I soaked up the details. The Sky City restaurant wasn't the fanciest in Seattle, but it had the best views by far. The dining room was filled only halfway because we had beaten the dinner rush. Modern leather, crisp white table linens, and simple white brasserie place settings created a clean, contemporary look. Crystal stemware and heavy silver utensils with spare lines finished off each table. The interior didn't need fussy details that could never compete with the amazing skyline. The other customers in our section wore everything from jeans and sweaters to suits and dresses, like Ben and me. It reflected the city's aesthetic. I loved that about Seattle, the diversity on display at every turn.

I hated to tear my eyes away from the window, but my stomach reminded me we were there for dinner. I picked up the menu and tried not to flinch when I glanced over the prices. I sure hoped Nate hooked Ben up with a discount and not just a reservation. When the waiter approached to take our order, I followed another one of my mother's etiquette rules; I waited for Ben to order first and then made sure what I ordered cost less. My mom always said nothing showed less class than eating lobster while your date picked through a salad. However, since Ben ordered an expensive filet steak, I suspected he wasn't too worried about the price. I ordered roasted vegetables and lamb cooked in puff pastry.

"That sounds good," Ben said. "Will I sound stupid if I ask what a puff pastry is?"

"Not to me. I don't know what it is either. But it's been my experience that nothing in a pastry ever ends badly."

"Good reasoning. Have I complimented you on your incredible brain lately?"

"Thanks." It genuinely pleased me. I'd received compliments on my looks in the past, and I got plenty of praise about my job performance at work, but not a lot of guys took the time to compliment my intelligence. Maybe they thought girls wanted to hear more about their outfits or hairstyles, but Ben looked past that. It was thoughtful, and I appreciated it.

I glanced back out at the blanket of winking lights far below us, wondering which of them represented my house, my chapel, and my job. I appreciated being away from it all for a while. The massive hulk of Macrosystems's corporate offices barely made a speck as I hovered this far above it, a reminder of how small it was in the grand scheme of things.

Ben quietly interrupted my reverie to ask, "What are you thinking about?"

"Work," I answered. His face tightened, but before I could explain my small epiphany, the waiter arrived bearing steaming platters. The moment got lost in the shuffle of accommodating the large plates on our table. For the first time in my life, I cursed the food for being so prompt. Ben cut into his steak as soon as the waiter walked away. With all his energy directed at his dinner, bringing up work again felt awkward, even though it would only be to clear up a misunderstanding.

Besides, what would I say? "I meant to say that sitting with you and enjoying this moment makes my work seem stale and antiseptic"? While totally true, it would come out sounding needy and lame, so I dropped it. Our hike had shown me that awkward moments evaporated between us if I let them go and didn't stress about it.

I bit into my puff pastry, releasing a cloud of fragrant spices. I savored it in silence. Finally, Ben asked, "How's yours?"

"Even better than I'd hoped," I answered.

"Good." He smiled. But he didn't say anything else.

Despite my resolve to let the awkwardness dissipate on its own, it crept back in. I hated not knowing whether my imagination had manufactured the unease or if it was really there. Another minute slid by, punctuated by the clinks of our forks and plates.

I swallowed, but my food felt like it wanted to stick in my dry throat. "How's your steak? Any good?"

"It is, yeah."

Not exactly an invitation for further discussion. I focused again on my puff pastry. Anxiety replaced the hunger in my stomach. This wasn't my imagination; Ben wasn't being cold, exactly, but an unfamiliar distance stretched between us. I wished we were back on our hike so I could wander over and clear it all up with a friendly hip bump. This didn't feel like it would be so easy to fix.

The tension deepened with each bite I forced down, until my nerves stretched to the point of snapping. Taking a breath as deep as I could without being obvious, I tried again. Gesturing outside, I asked, "It's beautiful, isn't it?"

"Definitely."

My reporting days on the San Luis Obispo High School paper should have taught me better than to lead with a yes or no question. "What's wrong?" I asked.

"I don't know." He took another bite of his steak and chewed it purposefully, like it was the most important thing he could be doing right at that minute.

I paused, on the brink of vulnerability, knowing I stood at a crossroads. Did I wave away the awkward moment with an easy joke, or did I tell the truth like a grown-up? I teetered between safety and risk for the space of a heartbeat and then tipped.

"I'm sorry, Ben. I guess I wasn't clear before." I pointed out the window. "Somewhere out there is the Macrosystems building. Do you see it?"

He peered through the glass intently and shrugged. "No."

"Me neither. That's what made me think. That place dominates my life, but up here, looking down, it's nothing."

His face relaxed slightly, so I continued. "I think you're mistaking my commitment to my job for passion. I'm good at what I do, and I'm determined to give it my best because that's me. But I don't love it. My parents taught me to work hard, so I do. But I'd work this hard if I were a mail lady or a rock star."

"A rock star? Can you sing?"

"Is that really a prerequisite?"

"Good point."

The tension between us ratcheted down several notches, and I paused, unsure how much more I wanted to say. "I didn't grow up wanting to be an accountant. It's what I do now, so I do it the best I can. But it feels good to sit here for a while and remember that my office isn't where the world starts and ends. I'm sorry it came out wrong the first time," I said.

Relief softened the lines bracketing his mouth. "Don't apologize. I shouldn't have jumped to conclusions." He pushed a piece of asparagus around his plate, dragging it around the perimeter twice before looking up. "I feel bad."

I shrugged. "Don't. You had a good reason to be frustrated."

"Let me make it up to you. What can I do?"

I eyed his poor, bedraggled piece of asparagus. "How about you quit abusing your vegetables and let me try a piece of your steak?"

He looked up, his eyes bright. "I want to make nice, but this is a good piece of steak," he protested.

"I named my price, Bratton. It's steak or nothing."

He cut off a large piece and held it out to me. I bit it from the end of his fork, and he smiled. "I'll order another filet and feed it to you if it will help make peace," he said.

I swallowed the bite and answered, "Not necessary. That was so good; we're even now."

His expression turned serious again. "I really am sorry, Jessie. I'm sensitive about the work thing because of my ex-fiancée, but I know how much time it takes if you want to be the best in your field. I've been building my own business up for four years, working crazy hours, and now that I have free time every now and then, it's not fair to expect someone else to drop everything too."

"It's okay. I probably don't need to work seventy hours a week. I forget to come up for air and fun."

He looked at me curiously. "How did Sandy talk you into Lookup after she confessed to setting up your profile?"

I fidgeted, not wanting to answer. "Uh . . ."

"Come on, you can tell me. We've been spilling our guts for the last ten minutes anyway."

"Wellll," I fudged. "I might have seen your profile and thought you might be worth dating." Heat climbed up my neck.

He grinned. "So we're dating?"

"I meant—"

"No take backs," he said. "I heard it."

I sat back, nonplussed. By anyone's definition, we were dating, but it sounded so different when he said it out loud. What did that mean? Did "dating" imply "relationship"? Was I ready for that? Did dating mean we were suddenly exclusive? Ben was the first guy I had gone out with since I lifted the dating embargo. Was it smart to stick with my first try? And did that mean he was dating only me now? Maybe—

"Whoa." Ben's voice broke in. "I don't know what you're thinking, but I can tell by your eyes you're in the middle of a freak out." He poured some ice water from the carafe into my half empty goblet and pushed it toward me. "Maybe you should drink this before you hyperventilate."

I did, feeling better and stupid simultaneously.

After I swallowed a few sips, he reached over for my hand. "I didn't drag you up here for a define-the-relationship talk. Breathe," he said, smiling.

I followed orders, for once.

"I do want to tell you this," he said. Determination laced the humor in his tone. "I'm twenty-seven, and I spent three years in a relationship taking it slow because of someone who had other priorities. I respected her and her priorities, but if she had truly loved me, she wouldn't have found it so hard to make time for me."

I shifted in my seat, uncomfortable with the discussion of his past engagement.

He squeezed my hand lightly to get my attention again and smiled when I looked up. "By the same token, if I really loved her, I would have fought harder to reorder her priorities. But I didn't. I let it drop and eventually picked up this contract with the Forest Service and went wading in the dating pool."

I smiled. "I'm glad."

"Good," Ben said. "Let's celebrate with dessert."

"What specifically are we celebrating?" I asked.

"That we each found the only other normal person on LDS Lookup."

"I could raise a forkful to that."

Ben waved the waiter over. We settled on splitting the most famous Sky City dish: a crazy ice cream concoction served on a bed of dry ice and topped with a raspberry coulis. It arrived at our table trailing long ribbons of swirling vapor. When the last bit of ice cream had been scraped from the dish, I thought I would burst. Ben pushed back from the table with a satisfied sigh.

"Yum," I said.

"Yum," he agreed.

We sat for a few minutes on the verge of a food coma but content. Ben lazily swept his thumb back and forth over my knuckles, and I leaned my chin on my other hand and gazed out of the window, thinking of nothing at all.

Ben stirred. "How'd you like it?"

"How'd I like what?"

"Doing nothing. By my watch, we did nothing for about five minutes."

"It was awesome," I admitted.

"Way to be open to new experiences," he teased. "Stick with me and I'll have you totally unproductive and lacking direction in a couple of weeks."

"Nah," I said. "I have it on good authority that you've got a pretty mean work ethic too."

"I'm going to have to stop spreading that rumor," he said.

"Relax. I find hard workers kind of attractive."

"Hard workers like construction guys or hard workers like someone who bangs on a keyboard all day? Because I bet it's not too late for me to get into construction."

"No, don't go have a quarter-life crisis on me," I teased him. "I know sometimes it's the hardest thing in the world for me to stay glued to my computer for eight hours at a time, so I'll give you credit for that."

"Good because I think my last construction effort was my Scout project. But I would have learned for you," he said bravely.

I rolled my eyes in amusement. "Don't worry about it, Ben. I don't require my dates to have hammer skills."

He laughed. "Lucky me."

He turned my hand over to gently uncurl my fingers then massaged my palm, his touch light. "You're hard to read, you know," he said after a while.

"What do you mean?"

"I don't know. I mean, we hang out and have a great time, but it's hard to get you to commit to another date or meal without bribery or coercion. And then when I think you're totally closed off, fun and open and relaxed Jessie shows up. And I so dig her, but which one is you?"

His observation stung, even though he made it with no malice, only curiosity. Picking up words to say and throwing them away again, I wasn't sure I had an answer. I didn't know what I wanted to say because I didn't know what I wanted, period.

I sighed. That wasn't true. I did know what I wanted. Buried under the brain files of countless spreadsheets and accounting formulas lay my dream of being a wife and mother with a house full of kids and laughter. Between me and that image stretched a deep, scary gulf of doubt and uncertainty. Jason's desertion had sent me sailing over the edge of the chasm once, and it had taken sheer grit to climb back out on the other side. I didn't want to go there again.

Ben said nothing, only watched and waited, his face showing no impatience.

I opened my mouth, attempting to explain that I wanted balance, a tidy explanation that didn't say much at all. Instead, my lips croaked out a barely audible, "I don't want to fail."

Ben leaned forward, head cocked to the side, and nodded that he'd heard me, like he was waiting for more.

There wasn't any more. I didn't know what else to say.

After a pregnant pause, he gave me some gentle encouragement. "You don't want to fail at . . . what? Skydiving? Or knitting? Handball? Origami?"

I laughed in spite of myself. "I guess that wasn't a helpful statement," I murmured.

"Helpful? No. But fraught with tension and mystery, if that's what you were going for," he said.

His lightheartedness eased my confusion.

"Here's the thing," I began again. "That high school and college boyfriend? I'm not hung up on him at all, but thinking about that situation makes me wonder if it's smart to put the energy into a project where I can't control the outcome."

"Ah, business lingo. Tell me if I've got this right. You don't want to commit your emotional resources when you're not sure about the return on your investment?"

"That's it in a nutshell."

"Do you know why most businesses fail?" he asked.

"Um, they're selling something crappy?"

"No. Their growth outpaces their capital." He sat back, pleased.

True. Most start-up companies fall apart because they don't plan for growth, and they can't keep up with the demand for whatever they're selling. But I didn't understand the relationship metaphor.

"My job is to make sure a business spends wisely and within limits so they don't go broke," I hedged.

"That's an established business. I'm on the entrepreneur side, and I can tell you that if you start a business without risking some of your assets, you'll never be able to grow it fast enough to succeed. You've got to invest the time and money for it to get off the ground, or it's doomed to fail from the start."

The metaphor cleared up. "So you're saying I should drop everything and spend all my time with you so I can see where this goes? My inner accountant is whimpering in a corner somewhere."

Ben laughed. "No. I'm suggesting you take a small risk and see if it pays a dividend."

"What kind of risk?" I asked.

"How about instead of me visiting you for a dinner break on Wednesday, we turn it into a date, one where we spend the whole evening together."

"A whole Wednesday night? You're asking me for a pretty sizable investment," I said.

"I'm convinced there's a huge payoff," he said, shrugging.

"You're going to see me most of the evening tomorrow after church. Aren't you worried about burnout?"

He mimicked my posture, resting his chin on his hand and leaning forward until his nose nearly touched mine over the table.

"No," he said. "Not even a little." And he stole a quick kiss. "What do you say, Jessie?" he asked. "Are we in business?"

Chapter 26

Monday came too early again. I went through the morning ritual of slapping the alarm clock silly before I rolled out of bed on the third snooze. I swung my legs over the side of the bed and cringed when my stomach muscles protested. Evidently, laughing for three hours straight with Ben last night would replace my ab workout today.

I stumbled to the bathroom and groped for a toothbrush, eyeballing it through puffy lids to make sure I held my own trusty Oral-B and not Sandy's pink-handled glitter monstrosity. She insisted that kids' toothbrushes offered a much better selection.

The fresh tang of minty toothpaste, followed by a splash of cool water on my face, dispelled any lingering grogginess, and by the time I rubbed in my moisturizer, I felt ready to face the day. I knew it would be a long one, but I intended to make it as productive as possible.

I fished a charcoal gray wool suit out of the closet and then, feeling like I was imitating Ben's outfit from our Saturday night date, discarded it in favor of a navy one. I pulled on a pink button down to soften the severity, wondering why I cared. It's not like my suit would be the main event at our morning staff meeting anyway. I recalled the lyrics to an old Smiths song. "I wear black on the outside 'cause black is how I feel on the inside." My borderline frumpy suit reflected my attitude toward work pretty accurately today.

Sandy popped her head in. "Do you still have my boots?" When she saw my outfit, she stepped farther in. "A *navy* suit, Jess? Really? You must not be seeing Ben today."

I picked up her boots and handed them to her. "Out."

She hugged the boots to her chest. "I'm just saying, you've been doing so well with your outfits lately. That suit is a regression."

I sighed. She'd been using lots of therapy-ish, self-improvement terms since starting her life makeover. "This suit means business. That's why it's called a business suit."

"That suit means sad. Seriously, we need to take you shopping. Your closet needs to *suit* you better." I groaned at the pun, but she shot me a mischievous grin and continued. "You are growing out of the navy suit phase of your life. Think about it," she called over her shoulder as she headed back to her room.

Sandy always dressed to her mood. The better her day, the brighter her outfit. Lately, she'd been favoring muted olive greens and subdued browns. They were still terminally chic outfits, but they must have come out of the introspective part of her closet. I imagined a closet with the clothes organized by mood, and I smiled. Mine would have three sides of boring work colors, all very proper. But I'd have to keep a space free for a new section, one with vibrant colors and whimsical styles, or else what would I wear when I saw Ben?

Last night I'd worn a caramel colored corduroy skirt with a sage green merino wool turtleneck and Sandy's BCBG boots, which I had tugged off as soon as Ben and I returned from the fireside I'd dragged him to. Well, I guess I didn't drag him. He went as my willing guest for the CES broadcast at the stake center. The talk was titled "When Weak Things Become Strong" and focused on Ether 12:27. My dad had quoted that to me all the time during my school days when I overextended myself and collapsed in a stress puddle. I could still hear his patient voice saying, "If they humble themselves before me, and have faith in me, then will I make weak things become strong unto them." I liked sitting in the darkened chapel, listening, my hand in Ben's.

Since our ward showed the broadcast live, it ended at six, and I maneuvered us away from the mingling singles and back to my place for dinner. I had stuck a pot roast in the slow-cooker after lunch, the perfect dinner for a cold Sunday evening. It's so hard to screw up a slow-cooker meal, it almost felt like cheating. Of course, I wouldn't mention that to Sandy any time soon. She'd managed to scorch a turkey breast earlier in the week when she forgot to add water and left it on high for eight hours. The aroma of Sunday roast had enticed her from her room, and she'd joined us for dinner.

I could blame her for my aching side muscles this morning after her epic story about her first foray into indoor rock climbing. Ben had to beg her to stop so he could breathe. Then he'd set us off again with a tale about a camping trip with his brothers gone horribly wrong, and it got worse from there.

Standing in my unglamorous round-toe beige pumps and smiling at the memory, I concluded that the "Time with Ben" section of my closet should be filled with spangled neon if my outfits reflected my mood every time I was with him. With a sigh, I shut the door and gathered up my work stuff before trudging off toward the Macrosystems battle with Craig.

* * *

Thunk, thunk, thunk.

After the last whack of my forehead against my desk, I rested it there and gave into my exhaustion for a moment.

"If you get a concussion, you can't file for workman's comp because I'm a witness it was self-inflicted," Sandy said from the doorway.

"Wrong. This is one hundred percent Craig-related," I retorted.

"Ah, good old Craig. The rash that never stops itching." Her lips twitched in amusement as she wandered into my office.

"It's dark," I said. "Why are you here?"

"It's January. It gets dark at four o'clock."

"Right. That's my point. Why are you here? Don't you have a fake rock wall to climb?"

"Nope. Tonight's hot yoga. It doesn't start until seven."

I almost demanded an explanation of hot yoga then shut my mouth and thought better of it. She dropped a paper bag on my desk with a thunk slightly less noisy than the one my head had made.

I eyed it suspiciously. "What's this? Because I'm telling you now if it involves sprouts, I'm not touching it."

"Relax. It's only marginally healthy. I found a new deli, so I grabbed you a sandwich. Sprout free."

I poked it. It didn't move.

She rolled her eyes. "It's a turkey club, but I swapped the regular bacon for the turkey kind and had them use low-fat mayo."

It sounded retch-worthy, but I decided to choke down a couple bites so I didn't hurt her feelings. I reached in and grabbed the wax-wrapped sandwich inside, along with a fistful of napkins. Nothing else fell out. I turned it upside down and shook to make sure. "Chips?" I asked, hopefully.

"Of course." Sandy reached into her own bag and tossed me something.

I picked up the package distressingly free of Frito-Lay colors and examined it. "Veggie crisps?" It emerged as more of a whimper.

"I'm not enabling your fried potato addiction. Just be glad I'm not force feeding you goji berries."

"You were a lot less scary when you only ate *mostly* healthy. I think a lack of real food is making you cranky," I said.

"I'm not cranky. I'm centered. And I eat real food."

Eyeing her dinner, I had my doubts. She had unwrapped a sandwich that appeared to be filled entirely with vegetables. No meat. Bizarre.

"Seriously, why are you still here? You're always gone by five," I said, returning to my original question.

"It's part of the life makeover. I'm rededicating myself to work."

"Yeah, but you're in *human* resources, and we're some of the only humans left in the building. What is there for you to do?"

She shrugged. "I have no idea. You find stuff to do when you stay late, so I thought I'd give it a shot. Is accounting so much harder that it legitimately keeps you busy a billion hours a week?"

"Not a billion. Maybe a hundred million."

That garnered another eye roll.

I laughed. "It's not hard to keep up. It's getting ahead that's the trick."

"You mean, get ahead like 'welcome to the rat race and may I slit your throat' get ahead?"

"No, I mean, 'Craig is one of many breathing down my neck, so I like a little distance because hot breath on my neck feels weird' get ahead."

She snorted. "Believe it or not, there are plenty of women who would enjoy closer proximity to Craig."

"If there are women who want men with bigger salon bills than them, I believe it."

"It's true. Remember, HR is an acronym for Hilarious Rumors. He is a wanted man."

"Ew."

"It takes all kinds," she mumbled around a mouthful of bread. "What did he do this time?"

"He's being extra helpful," I complained.

"The problem is . . ."

"I just don't buy it," I said. "Craig does only what gets him a step ahead. Helping me scores him minor points in the team player ratings, but it's not the kind of glory move he normally makes. If he's going out of his way to help, it's because he has something else up his sleeve. It's bugging me," I concluded.

"But I thought Dennis specifically assigned Craig's team to help you."

"Yeah. I'm telling you, I don't like it. He sends Brad over at least twice a day with something for my team."

"How dare he do something thoughtful? You want to file an official complaint? I can draft it for you right now: *Jessie Taylor alleges Craig the Snitch is going out of his way to be helpful and a team player.* We have to nip this kind of behavior in the bud. What if he starts being genuine? No, ma'am. I'll fast track your complaint in my office tomorrow morning."

"Should I throw my veggie crisps or my sandwich at you?" I asked.

"Neither. The sandwich will fall apart, and the veggie crisps are too light. But I can duck faster than you can throw, so don't bother looking for anything else either," she said.

"Come to think of it though, I do want to file a complaint," I said. "Against you. For creating a hostile work environment."

"You're the one threatening to throw stuff," she pointed out.

"Oh yeah. Can I accuse you of anything that will stick?" I asked.

"Nope. I know how to hide my trail," she answered.

"All right. I tried my best, but if you aren't going to write up Craig or yourself, I don't have any ideas for what you should work on this evening," I said. "I'm going to sit here for another five minutes and think about what Craig is up to while I digest my sandwich, and then I'm wading through more time sheets. Want to join me?"

"About as much as I want a poke in the eye from a sharp stick." She grimaced. She pushed out of her chair and gathered her wrappers from my desk. When she got to the door, she turned and said, "I'm calling it a night. It's too spooky in here after hours." She studied me for a second. "Look, I'm going to tell you something off the record. One of our HR admins, Lisa, has been spending time with Craig. She let it slip to him that he's been ruffling more than your feathers around here with his attitude lately and he might want to think about how he comes across. I guess he took it to heart because he's been playing nice with everyone since. It might not be sincere, but I think he's smart enough to kiss up, so maybe you shouldn't look a gift horse in the mouth. Take it for what it is and be glad he's off your back, you know?"

"Sure." I smiled. "He hasn't attempted any sabotage in almost a week. It's a new record, so maybe you're right."

"I'm definitely right. You say that like it never happens."

"I guess there was that *one* time . . ."

She snorted and headed down the hall.

I took a bite of my sandwich, chewing carefully. The turkey bacon had a strange plastic taste. Or maybe that was the low-fat mayo. Wrinkling my nose, I set the turkey club aside and decided to fire up another Lean Cuisine in the microwave later.

I considered Sandy's tip. It would be a novel feeling to let Craig do his team player routine without having to worry about his ulterior motives. If he only wanted to improve his likeability quotient, there probably wasn't anything to worry about.

Probably.

When it came right down to it, I'd much rather do my job, minus the Craig distraction. If he was trying to improve his image, I could definitely count on him to become the Happy Little Office Elf to resolve his interoffice PR problem. Choosing to trust Sandy's information, I gave my full attention to the time sheets looming in my "in" basket, even tapping the part of my brain I reserved for keeping an eye on Craig.

Heaven knew I needed some priority changes myself. I shrugged it off and reached for my keyboard. Might as well tackle the problems I could do something about. I sank into the numbers blinking from my monitor.

Chapter 27

I'd had at least three dozen Primary lessons in my childhood about speaking kind words to and about others, and now karma had shown up to have its way with me. It was all my fault for branding Craig a snitch. I should have just kept my mouth shut and said only nice things. Then maybe karma would have passed me by to go mess with some other name-calling dummy.

"What are you going to do?" Katie asked, standing as still as possible in the doorway.

I breathed in and breathed out, searching for a cool and professional reaction to this emerging disaster. "I'm going to fix it, that's what," I said.

"Oh." She shrank farther back through the doorway and glanced over her shoulder to the pod, where Mike sat with his head out of sight. Smart guy. At least he'd gotten that part right. His mistake had cost me big. But I knew part of this was my fault—I'd missed the data obfuscation because I'd been so distracted lately.

Data obfuscation referred to the practice of deriving test data from real data, only with everything slightly tweaked. It showed salaries as several percentages higher than the reality and changed people's birth years, for example. That allowed the database guys to give data to employees who weren't cleared to access sensitive salary or personnel information so they could test new accounting modules. Mike had acted as a guinea pig six months ago for a software redesign and had a good relationship with the database administrators, so he volunteered to use his connections to help us avoid the normal three-day waiting period on data requests. But he forgot to explain to them that he needed real data instead of test numbers. We'd been angling for an edge over Craig, but getting the tweaked data had wiped out our advantage completely.

"What can I do to help you fix it?" Katie asked. I detected a faint tremor when she squeaked out the word *fix*.

"Calm down, Katie. I'm not the Dragon Queen. No one's getting hurt," I said. The Dragon Queen had reigned over Craig's team before his promotion. During the last tax season, she'd suffered some sort of psychotic break. According to Sandy's sources, the rumor circulated for a while that Craig had provoked the episode, but no one knew exactly what had happened. In any case, that's when Craig made manager.

Struggling to regain control, I flipped my chair away from Katie and stared out at the parking lot. I counted and divided the cars by color, using the task to keep a cap on my temper. After establishing there were thirteen silver cars, nine white ones, eight beige, eight black, three red, and seven total of the rest combined, I turned to face Katie again.

"Bring me Mike," I directed her.

"He didn't know, Jessie. I—"

"That's painfully clear. Send him in," I said.

She didn't dare argue. I watched her hustle to the cubicle divider hiding him and whisper something over the edge. Mike's head rose a few inches above the divider, and his big, sorrowful eyes met mine. I crooked a finger and beckoned him to come.

He shuffled into my office, gaze now on the floor.

"Sorry," he said.

"I'm sure you are," I responded. "But that won't make this go away."

Even as I watched him flinch, amusement bubbled up. He looked genuinely worried, and I'm sure he expected to be fired. Lucky for him, I liked him. Besides, Sandy would probably kill me if I made extra paperwork for her. I had a different plan for my shaking associate.

"Do you have any idea what a headache you've caused here?" I demanded.

"Yes?" At the sight of my raised eyebrow, he choked out a more convincing, "I mean, yes."

"Are you sure? Because it's Wednesday, and that changes everything."

He looked confused.

I stood up and wandered back to the window, waving him to the vacant seat opposite my desk. Psychological height advantage again.

"This is an important Wednesday. I've put in over twelve hours of overtime already this week so I could leave on time today. And now I can't. Why is that, Mike?"

"Because I screwed up."

"That's it exactly. You probably think you're here to get fired," I continued and ignored the hope in his eyes at the word *probably*. I turned to face him. "I'm not going to do that because part of this is my fault too."

He started to object, but I forestalled him with an upheld hand. "I should have noticed your error before now."

He looked nervous now instead of scared. With firing off the table, I could see him scrambling to figure out his consequence.

"First of all, we're going to have to work a lot of unpaid overtime through the weekend to get this straightened out," I informed him. "Since you're the only one I can legally compel to stay, you're going to have to find a way to persuade the rest of the team to stay with us by using bribery. Start with Katie. She hates making copies, and I'm sure she won't mind handing that job off to you for a couple weeks."

He swallowed. "I can definitely make copies."

"Lauren likes chocolate."

"I'll take care of it."

"Peter would love to get into a Seahawks game. Or three. You have season tickets, right?"

"But—" his protest died on his lips. "Yes."

"Go start making this right. We're going to need everyone if we want to straighten this out by next week."

"I'm on it." He jumped up to leave, ready to grovel, then paused and walked back to my desk.

"I screwed up big. I'm sorry. I should have been looking more closely at the report. I assumed I got the right data."

"You got exactly the data you asked for, Mike. The problem isn't with the database administrator. You asked for the wrong thing."

He hung his head. "I'm sorry," he said again. "I'll buy all the stay-late dinners?"

"At least," I said. But I let a teasing note creep in so he knew he was making his way back to solid ground. When he looked up with a tentative smile, I smiled back.

"I promise I'll triple check everything from now on," he said.

"You do that," I said. "In the meantime, you'd better go smooth talk your team. This will take a couple of days to untangle."

"I'll get right on it."

I waved him out and watched as he hurried over to Katie's desk, knowing she would be the easiest to convince to kick in some free overtime.

I took my seat again with a sigh and picked up the telltale requisition sheet. Although Mike's mistake had been innocent, it had cost us big time. One stupid sentence had undone almost a week of work and put us dangerously behind on our timeline. And I hadn't caught the problem until Katie's salary showed up much higher than it should have. With our report due to Dennis in barely more than a week, this was a nightmare.

I could go to Dennis and get an extension, but that posed two problems: First, Craig would be ready on time, making me look like a slacker. And second, my pathological refusal to fail wouldn't let me. I fought the urge to thump my head against the desk again, instead unwrapping a consolation piece of chocolate. Mike reappeared in my door, excitement chasing away the sad puppy look he'd worn all morning.

"This might not be so bad," he said. "Or at least it's equally bad for everyone, which is sort of the same thing if you think about it the right way. Kind of."

I put my chocolate down and stared at him. "What are you talking about?"

"Well, I did something last week that I thought you might not like, but now I think it's going to be fantastic for us!" he said.

"Keep going."

"I mentioned to Brad that I had a connection on the data, and he mentioned it to Craig, who called me and asked me if I wouldn't mind requesting his data too. And since I didn't want to get on his bad side, I did. Which means he's as far behind as we are, only he doesn't know it yet. And if we don't tell him, he's going to blow it big time next week when he presents." He broke off his explanation and finally took a breath, looking pleased.

Popping the unwrapped chocolate into my mouth, my inner Evil Jessie leaned back for a moment to savor both the candy and the image of Craig's total humiliation if we neglected to warn him.

Way too soon though, I found myself choosing the right. Grrr. I just couldn't dig a pit for my neighbor. With regret, I said good-bye to the mental picture of a red-faced and furious Craig and shoved back to go face the man in person.

"Where are you going?" Mike asked.

"I have to tell Craig what's going on," I said. "In the end, it only hurts the company's bottom line if we let him spend any more time chasing the wrong data. It's only fair."

"But—"

"Two wrongs don't make a right, blah blah blah." I sighed and stood.

"I'll do it," he said. "It was my mistake."

"No, you keep working on your bribes. We're going to need all the help we can get to fix this. I'll handle Craig."

He nodded and scurried back to the pod. I headed for Craig's office, irritated with my conscience but unable to stifle it. When I knocked and poked my head around his door, he looked surprised and then annoyed. Conjuring his plastic smile, he said, "Jessie. Nice to see you."

Yeah right.

"Sorry it's not a social visit, but I need to give you a heads up."

"Really?" he drawled. A calculating gleam flashed in his eye. "Have a seat."

"No, that's fine. I'll only be a minute," I said, but I stepped all the way into the office and closed the door behind me. His expression grew even more curious.

"What's up?" he asked.

"Mike tells me you went through him for a data request last week," I said.

"Is that a problem? I assumed you wouldn't mind pooling resources."

"Of course not." Then again, with Craig, that meant a pool of my resources he could dip into anytime he wanted without returning the favor. But that was beside the point. "But I think our pool might have been tainted," I confessed.

"That sounds bad."

"It is. Mike's connection sent you obfuscated data instead of listing actual salary." I waited for the slow climb of red to his forehead that usually indicated his anger. Instead, I watched a satisfied smile creep over his face.

"I know," he said.

"Excuse me?"

He shrugged. "I noticed last Thursday that my own salary was way off, so I checked around and realized I had a test report. So I got the real one." His smug smile set my teeth on edge. His next words dripped with insincerity. "I hope you guys haven't spent the last week working with the wrong numbers. That would be such a waste."

My temper flared with frightening intensity, but I kept it on a leash. I couldn't believe he had let us charge ahead on misinformation while he sat back and cackled. But I came to Craig's office to do the right thing, and I wouldn't let him bait me with his blatant mean-spiritedness.

"I'm glad you caught the error," I said. I'm sure he was waiting for me to accuse him of costing our end of the project precious time, but I didn't feel like giving him the satisfaction. At the door I turned to say, "I look forward to seeing your report next week. If you guys have found the same kind of savings we have, Dennis is going to be ecstatic."

I shut the door behind me, noting his confusion with grim pleasure. I had neither confirmed nor denied that we had wasted a week with the wrong information. Now he'd be left to wonder until my presentation what his silence had cost us.

I hoofed it back to my office for more chocolate. Deciding I needed the big guns, I dug into the back of my pencil drawer and pulled out my king-size Hershey bar with almonds. The first half served as a great movie refreshment while I played a single loop of film in my mind: me beating Craig about the head with a sheaf of the wrong data while throngs of wronged coworkers cheered. The second half of the Hershey bar was for courage: I had to call Ben up to cancel for that night and several nights after.

Man, did I not want to make that call.

Chapter 28

My toes curled when Ben's warm, "Hi, Jess," came over the line.

"Hey, yourself," I answered back. "Having a good day so far?" For once, I desperately searched for small talk to procrastinate coming to the point.

"Not bad," he answered. "Looking forward to tonight is making it go faster though."

Darn it. No reprieve.

"Right. Tonight . . ."

"Uh-oh," he said. "I don't like how that sounds."

"I don't either. I'm sorry, Ben, but I have to cancel. Something came up here, and I need to handle it."

Silence.

I wondered if the call had dropped. "Ben?"

"Yeah. I'm here."

"Oh."

More silence.

Finally, at about thirty seconds way past awkward, Ben cleared his throat. "I guess this must be a pretty big something," he said.

"It is. We had a huge glitch in our project, and I'm going to have to pull everyone in for major overtime to get this straightened out by next week." I injected my explanation with the most apologetic tone I could.

"So how long is this going to take to fix?"

I couldn't read anything in his voice.

"It's hard to say. It depends on how much overtime my team is willing to give me. It will be at least through the weekend," I said.

"I see." He fell silent again, but I didn't hurry to fill in the gap. I didn't know what to say.

"Okay. You gotta do what you gotta do, right?"

"Right," I said. "Was that a real okay?"

"No." He sighed. "This totally stinks, and I don't understand, but I'm trying not to whine."

"I know. I'm so, so sorry. It's Craig and a stupid clerical error . . . and now it's getting ugly."

"Craig again? Maybe I could beat him up for you," he offered.

"You shouldn't tempt me like that," I said.

"All right, but I would even put on my shining armor and find a horse."

"I appreciate the offer, but Craig is more of a fly who needs swatting than a monster."

"Are you sure about that? Because if he's behind this crisis, I kind of think slaying him wouldn't be that bad."

I laughed. "Unfortunately, he's only a contributing factor. This is a multilayered mess."

"I'll let the offer stand," he said.

"I appreciate it. Maybe I could call you when I need a brain break from the craziness around here."

"You mean squeeze me in when you're not too busy?"

I wrinkled my nose. "I guess that didn't come out right."

"Maybe not, but it's what you meant. And as much as I don't want to be just a convenience in your life, I'll take what I can get." He hesitated. "You should take care of business, Jessie. I know it's important to you. But maybe . . . don't take too long, all right? I'm trying hard to be patient, but it bums me out not to spend time with you again."

I settled on, "I understand." And then I felt stupid as the words hung out there, an unfinished thought. "I'm sorry again for canceling tonight. I was looking forward to it. I'll blow through this project as fast as I can, but it's gnarly, and it's going to take time."

"I get it. I've been there, done that," he said.

"I'll call, Ben. As soon as I'm done."

"I'll answer."

We said our good-byes and hung up, but I kept the phone in my hand and sat staring at it for a while. Ben deserved more than my leftover time and energy, but I had no idea how to fix this current mess without giving it my all.

I found myself tapping out a text message. *I really am sorry.*

It's okay. I'm patient. Kind of.

I guess that's all I can ask, I sent back.

Wrong guess. But it'll do for now.

Huh? I saved the message, not quite sure what it meant, and then reread it several times, puzzling through his cryptic remark. Wrong guess? What did that mean? That I *should* ask him for more?

* * *

I dragged through Thursday and Friday with the energy and enthusiasm of a summer school student repeating algebra for the third time. I showed up, I did my work, but I didn't have to like it. Even the friendly bickering between my workmates during our pizza-fueled late night sessions lacked entertainment value. I doubted anyone noticed since I laughed along with the others, but I felt like my laughs were the equivalent of verbal golf claps.

Since most of the people on my team were working their first post-college jobs, Mike convinced all but two to commit the extra time. The two who didn't stay after both had small kids at home, and no one blamed them for clocking out at the end of their eight-hour workday. But the three other employees besides Katie and Mike were content to put in the time for free as long as Mike picked up the bill at the bar afterward. I had overlooked a couple of morning "headaches" bearing a striking resemblance to hangovers in light of their hard work. As long as their job performance stayed sharp, I wasn't going to stir up trouble. Sandy had once told me a hangover versus a headache was hard to prove anyway as far as personnel issues went.

Saturday morning dawned with anemic sunlight filtering through my window, but it was more than I'd seen in a week. I wanted so badly to get out in it and bike around the nearby lake or wander through an outdoor market. Stupid work. Even bribery couldn't induce most of the team to give up their Friday night *and* Saturday, so today it would only be Katie, Mike, and me.

I schlepped into my office right before nine, but neither of them had arrived yet. I busied myself getting the proper spreadsheets sorted for the next fifteen minutes until Mike showed up. I greeted him and asked about Katie.

"She's not coming. She said it's either take the weekend off or she'll quit in defense of her mental health. Should we get started?" he asked, a notable lack of enthusiasm in his voice.

I felt his pain. "Yeah. We'll make shred and copy piles for Katie and hope she doesn't kill us on Monday," I said.

"Do you find it at all ironic that we're spending massive amounts of overtime trying to figure out how to get departments to trim their payroll budgets?"

"No, because we're not getting paid for this overtime, thanks to someone in this room who isn't me." I gave him the stink eye.

"Right. So like I was saying, I'm glad we have such a great work rapport that we can devote every last spare second of our free time to fun projects like this," he said.

"That's what I thought I heard."

For the next three hours, we worked with minimal conversation beyond occasional requests for documents from the other person. The silence grew too loud after the first hour, so I hooked my iPod into my computer speakers and let The Aggrolites fill in the blanks. When the minute hand dragged itself past noon, I called for a break.

Even working efficiently and producing a massive stack of audited documents for Katie to shred, we had barely made a dent in the work we had left. I dipped into my energy reserves and found them empty. The deserted Macrosystems office spread outward, a sea of gray cubicles.

"I don't want to be here anymore."

Mike turned down the speakers. "What?"

I looked at him. "I don't want to be here anymore. I don't think I'm going to be good for much more today, even after lunch."

He nodded. "I hate to say it, but me neither."

"So should we bag it and get out of here?"

He grinned. "Try to keep up!" And he hustled to sort the last of our work into the shred or copy files.

When we had everything separated, he grabbed his water bottle and waved it jauntily at me on his way out of the door. I eyed the phone. Suddenly, I had half a day of nothing to do. If I was a very, very lucky girl, I would find Ben equally available.

I punched in his number.

Chapter 29

WE'D TEXTED BACK AND FORTH since Wednesday and exchanged e-mails too, but I wouldn't let myself pick up the phone to call him until now, afraid of lacking the willpower to keep the conversation to a few minutes when I so badly wanted to talk to him for hours. I listened to the ringing, hoping he'd pick up, hoping I wouldn't giggle like an idiot at hearing his actual voice.

He answered after the third ring. "Hi, this is Ben. You've reached my live voicemail. If this is Jessie calling to tell me your major project is done ahead of schedule, press one. If this is Jessie calling for any other reason, press two."

Amused, I asked, "Isn't it going to hurt your ear if I press a button?"

"This is Ben's live voicemail," he replied. "You have to follow directions."

I pressed two.

"Ow."

"I did warn you," I said.

"Yeah, but it's all going to be worth it if you pressed one. Turns out, I have no idea what the beeping sound means."

I laughed.

"So what is it? Did you press one?" he demanded.

"Not exactly," I hedged.

"What do you mean, 'not exactly'? One is one, not kind of one."

"Well, two is made up of one plus another one, so it's kind of the same thing."

"You accountants and your funny math. You can't run a business like that," he said.

"Thank goodness I'm not running a business, then. Just trying not to run this one into the ground."

"So you're still in emergency mode?"

"I will be on Monday. I called it quits for today though."

"Good for you. How many hours does that make for this week?"

"Seventy-five, maybe."

"Ouch," he said. "It's that bad, huh?"

"Unfortunately. We have a huge report due to my boss by this coming Friday, and we're working like crazy people to get it done."

"Wow. That does not sound fun."

"Uh, hold on . . . Nope, I can't think of anything less fun."

"So is this a brain break for you?"

"No. Like I said, I'm done until Monday. I thought maybe if you had some free time before then, we could hang out or something."

"Hang out or something, huh?"

I held my breath while he paused, hoping he'd take the offer. But when he spoke again, my heart sank.

"I'm sorry, Jess." He sighed. "I would love to, but I think I'd feel like you were squeezing me into your schedule, and I don't want to go there again. I want to be with you and not wonder if your mind is on all the work stuff you've got to deal with or could be dealing with if you weren't with me. I'll wait out your deadline and see if things calm down for you."

All I could come up with was a lame, "Oh. I see."

"Do you?"

"Yes, but even in my best weeks, I put in more than forty hours. I don't know what to do about that," I said.

"You're generous with your time, considering you don't get paid for the extra," he said.

"I guess. It's just that I'm a new manager, and I don't want them to regret promoting me, so . . ."

"That translates to a lot of hours?"

"Basically."

"Has anyone suggested that you shouldn't have been promoted?"

"Yeah. It's kind of stressful."

"Who said that? Your boss?"

"Well, no, not Dennis," I conceded. "Actually, it was—"

"Craig?" he finished for me.

"Craig." I sighed.

"So you're working yourself into a stroke because Craig said 'Nanny nanny boo boo?'" Ben sounded frustrated. And condescending. It irritated me, and I didn't say anything.

Ben didn't say anything either for a moment and then mumbled, "I'm sorry. That was lame."

"Apology accepted."

He sighed. "Do you ever feel like Craig's pushing your buttons just to see if he can?"

"It's not like that. Craig is obsessed with climbing the corporate ladder, which is fine, but Dennis Court watches our teams pretty closely, and I need to make sure I'm staying on top of things so I don't look bad by comparison. And I need to set a good example for the people I manage too. It's not just Craig," I said, hating the defensive note in my voice.

"Does Dennis require anyone else to work so many hours?"

"No."

"Does anyone else work so many hours on their own?"

"Sure, sometimes," I said, feeling like I was standing on more solid ground.

"But not all the time? Not as often as you?"

I didn't answer.

"Jessie?" he coaxed. "Does anyone work as much overtime as you?"

I wasn't in the mood to hand him my psyche and have it returned sliced and diced. "What's your point, Ben?" I bit out, despite the fact that his questions were both patient and reasonable. "That I work too much? You'd have to stand in line behind my mother, all of my sisters, and Sandy to take your shot at beating me over the head with that news flash."

"Whoa. I'm not trying to pick a fight here. I'm trying to understand why you push so hard," he said.

"I told you, I like to be the best," I said.

"The best overworked and underpaid accountant at Macrosystems?" he asked.

"Why is this such a big deal to you?" I asked him. "Didn't you say you had to put this kind of time in when you first started out?"

"I did. But it was totally different. I was working for myself, building a big enough client base so I would never have to work eighty-hour weeks again. And I don't. I work a regular week now, and all the money goes straight to *my* company, not someone else's. I set my hours and my terms, and that's exactly how I want it. But I paid a price to get here because I'm looking around at friends who are married and having kids and trying to figure out how I let that pass me by. Don't you worry about that?" he asked softly.

"No. This isn't going to go on forever."

"Let me ask you this. When is the last time you worked only forty hours in a week?"

I didn't answer. I couldn't remember.

"How about a vacation?" he pressed. "Have you taken off a week or more in the last year?"

"Sure. I visit my parents a few times a year."

"For how long? Over holiday weekends?" he challenged me.

Yes. I never missed more than a day or two of work if I planned it that way. But I didn't want to admit it.

"Why is this a big deal?" I asked again. "We barely know each other. There'll be plenty of time to get this figured out if we're still hanging out later."

"You keep using that phrase, 'hanging out.' Or calling us friends. Or talking about later like it's the distant future." He sounded frustrated, and I heard him draw a deep breath and sigh. "I didn't want to do this, but I'm going to lay out my reality for you. I've been in Seattle for almost five months, and I have a six month contract. All my stuff and most of my clients are back in Arizona. I came up here to get a job done and clear my head, and I have. I'm as clear as I've ever been on one thing: I don't want to be your friend or your hangout buddy or your side project or your part-time boyfriend."

"What do you want?" I almost whispered. Ben was leaving?

"You," he said. "Not your leftover time and energy. I thought you felt the same crazy click I did from the first time we talked on the phone. I hoped that meant you would want to spend as much time with me as I do with you. I feel like an idiot even having to tell you I've only got a month left here so that maybe you'll want to hang out with me more instead of giving this thing between us time to do whatever it's going to do on its own. I just—"

He paused for a breath, but the revelation of his contract expiration had stolen my breath, and I didn't say anything.

"You say we barely know each other, but I disagree, Jessie. Big time." He sighed, and it sounded so frustrated. "I know you make me laugh, and you make me think. You have an amazing mind, and you're incredibly disciplined. But when you relax, something different happens, and I see something inside of you that drives me to know more. I could spend months learning new things about the way you work and look at the world. But I don't have months. I have one month."

"Ben . . ."

"I'm a risk taker with good instincts, and every one of them is telling me that time with you is the best investment I'll ever make. Tell me how I convince a risk-averse accounting genius to see it the same way."

"Ben . . ." I trailed off again. I had no idea what to say. Funny, laid-back Ben had disappeared, replaced with this intense Ben who unnerved me and fascinated me at the same time.

"I know you want time to think this over. And as much as I want to hoard every free hour you have, I do respect that you have a deadline next week and a job to do. So how about this? Don't answer. Think about what I said. And if you're feeling even half the impulse that I am to explore whatever is going on between us, come to dinner at my place next Saturday, after your deadline is done. You don't even have to call and let me down easy if you decide this isn't what you want. If you don't show up, I promise to leave you alone, and if you do, we can talk this out and see if there's even any reason to worry about where I'm going to be at the end of the month. Okay?"

"Okay." Bewilderment swirled in my brain, like when my sisters used to twirl me too fast on the death trap of a merry-go-round at the playground near our house. Even as I begged them to stop, I reveled in the giddy, dizzy thrill of whirling out of control. As a kid, as soon as they let me off and I caught my breath, I'd screw up my courage and hop right back on, spinning around like mad again. It was tricky though. They never slowed down, so I had to pick my moment to leap.

This time, though, Ben had stopped the ride to give me a breather. And I already missed the thrill, but I didn't know if I had the guts to make the leap again.

Chapter 30

I DON'T USUALLY PAY ATTENTION to the passage of time. I work until the job is done, or I fall asleep, whichever comes first. Then I start again the next day. Watching time drag by on a clock was a Ben-related phenomenon. The last twenty minutes before I knew I'd see him were always the worst. Imagine, then, how painfully slowly the weekend passed. The seconds stretched like pulled taffy, time morphing beyond recognition. I couldn't even imagine enduring the rest of the week.

Saturday after I got off the phone with Ben, I went home and collapsed, sleeping the afternoon away and then hitting a movie with Sandy, an independent film she had picked to "expand our cultural horizons." It was mostly independent of a plot or good acting, but chock full of people sitting around and staring at each other meaningfully. Oh, and the director had included at least two dozen artistic shots of rain. Rain on a child's face, rain on a car window, rain on a beach, rain on a dog.

I live in Seattle. I was over it.

I tolerated Sunday only because I threw myself into my Primary lesson and taught it with so much energy and enthusiasm that one of my kids offered to share his ADD meds with me. At home, I tried to do the thing where you lose yourself in service so you can forget your problems, but when I baked cookies for my visiting teaching sisters, I burned the first batch while I mooned over Ben. The second batch looked fine, but a nibble revealed I had oversalted the dough, so I pitched the batter and spent the rest of the day trying to work through *Jane Eyre* for the fourth time. Not my fourth time finishing it, my fourth time trying to get past the halfway point.

By midevening, my nerves reached the snapping point. I pounced every time my phone rang, but each time, it was friends or family calling to catch up. When the phone shrilled for the fifth time with someone other than Ben on the caller ID, I gave it up as a lost cause and turned the phone off.

Sandy wandered in from her room with a book in her hand, her finger marking her spot in *Healing the Inner You.* "You should read this," she said. "I'm learning a lot. For example, did you know that whatever our predominant emotion is, it's almost always just a masking emotion for something else?"

"I didn't know that," I said. "So what your book is saying is that whatever I'm feeling is not what I'm really feeling? That makes total sense."

"You keep joking, but you're as messed up as me in a whole different way, girl-who-haunts-her-phone. You'd be having a more satisfying life experience if you did a little soul-searching." She floated toward the kitchen with a serene New Agey expression on her face.

"You know, there's a book I could suggest that would probably do more to help you figure out your life than anything you've picked up so far," I said with a grin.

She poked her head back around and scowled. "No church talk. It's on my list of stuff to work through, but I'm not there yet."

I held up my hands in surrender and tried out an innocent expression.

She rolled her eyes. "Seriously, you need to think through your emotions. Avoiding them isn't helping you."

She reached for a cookie, and I decided not to warn her about the measurement mishap. It served her right for snitching. And pointing out uncomfortable truths. She took one bite and spit it out. "Mean," she said.

"No one told you to take it."

"Point goes to Jessie," she grumbled and then fished a yogurt from the fridge and retreated to her room.

I dumped the rest of the salty cookies into the trash and considered her advice. I had nothing else to do. Maybe I should muck around in my muddle of feelings to see what I could find. In my room, I stretched out across my bed, feet propped against my wall in my favorite thinking pose. Trying not to think about Ben certainly hadn't gotten me anywhere, so I gave in and brooded over him instead.

I peeled back the lid I kept on my feelings and stirred them up a bit, examining each one that rose to the surface. Anxiety and curiosity mingled with longing and insecurity and anger.

What?

I separated anger out to study more closely. Why was I mad?

It was a subtle feeling, much less obvious than when my temper flared over Craig's antics. But anger definitely underlined some of the other anxiety and insecurity. I explored the possibility of being mad at Ben, but I didn't turn up much. While I didn't love his Saturday ultimatum, I understood why he'd given it. Kind of. He didn't exactly demand that we do things on his terms, but he controlled the pace right now. I found that uncomfortable. But not maddening.

Something else was at work here. Frustration, confusion . . . about what? Ben had been direct in his intentions. I was the problem.

Wait. *I was the problem.*

My confusion frustrated me. I felt like every dumb girl in every dumb chick flick I'd ever seen who gets in her own way with the guy she likes. She has commitment issues or workaholic tendencies, and it makes the audience want to whack her in the head with their overpriced theater sodas and say, "Go for it, already! We want the big kiss!"

Maybe I needed my own head whacked, but for the first time ever, I found myself in sympathy with the Dumb Girl in the chick flick. If I were living a movie, I'd take a long walk in the rain, leave a voicemail at work that I wouldn't be back, and then I'd drive over to Ben's house in soaking wet clothes but perfect makeup and pound on his door. It would fly open, and I would profess my idiocy and my love, and we'd have our own big kiss. So exciting.

In my real life though, I felt something more like a boring responsibility to my job and absolute confusion about Ben. Was Ben even the right guy for me? He respected my commitment to my job but not enough to tolerate the long hours it sometimes demanded. Driven women attracted him, but it hadn't worked out for him before, so maybe that wasn't what he really wanted. Did I want to risk another relationship implosion if he changed his mind? I thought about the year after my breakup with Jason, the days where it was hard to even get out of bed and face the day because the hurt made it hard to breathe after losing someone who had been woven into my life's fabric. I wasn't sure

I had the emotional currency to invest in a compromise that would let Ben in further but that also might fall apart. Who knew how different our priorities would be if we sat down and hashed it all out. The more entangled we were with each other, the worse it would feel if I wasn't what he really wanted after all.

Tension squeezed the back of my neck, sending a headache creeping behind my eyes. It matched the twisting in my gut as I examined each fear, looking for a resolution. Ben embodied the guy every girl wanted; he had success, good looks, a sense of humor, and a testimony. He treated me like gold, and if I were a braver girl, I'd go tearing down the freeway in search of my movie ending on his doorstep.

Instead, indecision paralyzed me and made me furious with myself.

Rolling off the bed, I landed on my knees and took some of my dad's advice. God probably wondered what had taken me so long. Offering a simple thank you for my many blessings, I then asked for clarity and courage to find the right course. Then I collapsed back into bed, exhausted, and listened until I fell asleep.

* * *

When Monday dawned, for the first time in a month, I welcomed my alarm clock's announcement of a new work week. At least with work, I could concentrate on something other than Ben.

Ha.

I sat in our Monday management meeting and watched Craig do his thing. He wore a lavender shirt with shiny gray trousers, a skinny man belt and pointy-toe shoes. His hair didn't move with the roar of air from our overtaxed office heating vent, and his voice maintained a pleasantly calculated cadence. Surveying the faces of the other managers, I saw one woman listening with a dopey smile on her face. The other women were all married and indifferent to his show. The men mostly watched with polite interest, one of them contributing a head nod here and there. A couple of people jotted notes, but I suspected it was only to convince Dennis that they were paying attention.

Craig concluded his update about three minutes after he should have and sat down with a self-satisfied smile. The group moved on to the next report without any discussion, leading me to wonder how Craig could dominate so much of my work energy when he barely registered as a blip on anyone else's radar. Did I rate any higher than he did with my peers? Surely hours and hours of extra work deserved some type of recognition.

Three more managers presented their productivity recaps and outlined their tasks for the current week, and then it was my turn. Normally, I said my piece and hurried to reclaim my seat as someone who didn't enjoy public speaking. Today, I paid closer attention to people's expressions while I delivered my weekly report. The captain of Craig's fan club had lost her grin and now looked moderately bored. Other than that, I faced the same range of disinterest to polite attention that Craig had faced.

For some reason, this floored me. How could I have pulled in my team and invested twice as much time as Craig had last week and garnered exactly the same level of inattention and, in a couple of cases, borderline disrespect? I made my report succinct and sat down to consider this.

Somewhere between my promotion and this latest project, my focus had switched from doing the best job I could to beating Craig. I told Ben I liked to be the best, but I realized that wasn't strictly true; I liked to give everything my best, but I disliked competition. It didn't matter whether I beat someone else as long as I met the standard I set for myself. Often I ended up "winning" anyway, but it was a fringe benefit, not a goal. So why this fixation on Craig? True team spirit would be congratulating him if he improved the company's profitability, not pushing to keep a foot on his neck in a mad scramble upward.

I thought back to the view from the Space Needle, the moment of clarity I had when I realized how small Macrosystems measured in the big picture. Craig's significance measured even smaller compared to the important people in my life. It bothered me that it was so hard to maintain that perspective in the middle of things. When the morning briefing ended, I walked back to my office in deep thought, oblivious to the swarm of cubicle dwellers rushing around me. Katie had to shift out of my office door so I wouldn't collide with her on my way in. Only her amused, "Jessie?" dispelled my daze.

"Are you okay?" she asked.

"Yeah. What's up?"

"Are you trying to drive me to quit or to the nuthouse?" she asked.

"What?" I felt cotton-headed.

"The raging shred and copy piles? Really?"

"Sorry about that," I said, finally picking up the thread of the conversation. "Mike and I audited a couple more months on Saturday."

"Are you sure it wasn't a couple of years? Those are huge piles," she said.

"No, I promise. We didn't have the stamina for more."

"I guess the piles you made reproduced and spawned more evil paper files. This is going to take all morning."

"Don't worry about it. Do what you can, and I'll make Mike work through his lunch to finish whatever you don't."

"You're the best boss ever." She grinned, satisfied. She whirled around and hurried to share her good news and his bad news.

I shook my head and opened up my e-mail, hoping maybe something from Ben might be waiting for me. Nothing more than the usual clutter of spam and family messages filled the screen. I guess he really meant that he would wait to talk to me until Saturday. If I showed up. I mean, he had practically *threatened* me with a define-the-relationship talk. No one with good sense would walk into one of those if they saw it coming.

But . . . I wanted to see him, no question there. And the crazy hours were paying off; the report would be ready on Friday. I could easily meet that condition, but more than that held me back. I was caught on my own mental merry-go-round, spinning the same questions around like mad. If I showed up, what was I agreeing to? That I would hang out with Ben for a month and then wave bye-bye, like he hadn't gotten under my skin? That if we totally clicked for a month, I'd accept a long-distance relationship when he went back to Arizona? Would my showing up to Ben's house signal my readiness for some kind of leap? Of faith? Of hope?

I closed my e-mail in frustration and clicked open the next report in the massive string of remaining files to audit. Thinking about Ben accomplished nothing. I got off task and confused, and I found no answers. At this rate, not only would I not "beat" Craig, but I'd also fall far short of my own expectations. I had no answers and no time to find them while we hit the home stretch of prepping our presentation for Dennis. I told myself to get through five more long, fatiguing days in the office, and then I would think about Saturday and what to do.

I had that conversation with myself on Monday, Tuesday, and Wednesday. I had that conversation with Sandy when she asked why Ben hadn't been over in a while. Her side of the conversation involved a whole lot more answering back and sassiness than when I talked to myself, but the gist was the same. I would think about Saturday when I finished this stupid report. I mean, this incredibly important report.

The conversation would not go away.

I suppressed it, repressed it, oppressed it, and ignored it. It lingered there, asking, "What are you going to do about Saturday?"

I desperately wanted to see Ben. But I didn't feel ready to sign up for a new complication. For the fiftieth time since hearing the news, I cursed his contract expiration. The curse sounded something like, "Dadgum-shoe-licking-ditch-dwelling-puppy-kicker-of-a-contract." Which almost covered my utter contempt for its existence. Almost. It would take real curse words to encapsulate my full loathing. I needed more time with him. Way more.

Grrr. Thursday offered me my only break from the stupid internal argument. In the insane crunch of last-minute preparations for the presentation, the question of what to do drowned in a sea of spreadsheets and PowerPoint slides as I worked with my team to polish our projections for Dennis. Once, late Thursday as I drifted out of an argument between Mike and Doug the New Hire about whether blue or red looked better in the slide background, the dilemma intruded again. In barely over twelve hours, this whole project would be over, and I'd have all day Friday to think about anything besides our audit findings. I'd *have* to spend it figuring out the best thing to do. I wanted to show up at Ben's on Saturday, but that didn't make it a smart move. I distracted myself with a meditation on why Doug the New Hire held that title when he'd been with us for almost three months.

Near midnight, I dragged myself into bed, exhausted but ready for my meeting with Dennis and Craig. I stared at the ceiling, willing sleep to come and running through the facts and figures I would unveil the next morning. Satisfied I had every last statistic at my fingertips, I rolled over to crash for the night, but my cell phone caught my eye. A red light pulsed, indicating a message. I flipped it open, and my stomach fluttered when the screen said, "1 new text msg." It was from Ben.

I pulled it up. *I know it's a big day for you tomorrow. Good luck, although you're so good you won't need it. I'll be thinking of you.*

Well.

Who was I kidding? I knew exactly what I'd do on Saturday.

Chapter 31

Craig met me in front of Dennis's door. He smiled and exuded smugness like a cheap cologne.

I smiled back. "Ready to go?" I asked him.

"I was born ready."

I refrained from blowing a raspberry of disgust and was saved when Dennis opened the door and herded us in.

"I know you both worked hard over the last two weeks, so how about if we dive in?" he suggested.

"Absolutely," Craig said. Kiss up. "Do you mind if I go first?" he asked.

I waved for him to continue.

He powered up his presentation, opened with his first slide, and announced, "Audit Findings and the Profitability Implications for Payroll Adjustments."

Oh goody. A real barn burner.

Next came a forty-five-minute analysis of the last three years of Macrosystems payroll records, suggestions for curtailing payroll costs, including layoffs in nonpriority departments like shipping and data entry, and an impressive bottom line savings bigger than the number my team had produced. But Craig had reduced payroll costs to mathematics and had overlooked the "resources" part of human resources again, leading to a flawed analysis.

Dennis studied the report for several minutes after Craig had wrapped up, flipping through pages of the hardcopy overview and asking questions, which Craig answered readily. Dennis turned to me. "Do you agree with his findings?"

"Some of them, yes."

"But not all of them?"

"No, sir. We interpreted the data differently," I explained.

"Let's take a look."

I pulled out my jump drive. "We're going to bounce through a couple of different programs to examine the data." Working through a quick overview in PowerPoint, reviewing a few condensed spreadsheets in Excel, and returning to PowerPoint for a summary, I completed my presentation in fewer than fifteen minutes. My report was much shorter and offered less payroll savings, but I knew it had addressed some weaknesses in Craig's analysis. Since a smile played around his lips, I could tell he didn't know he'd been beaten.

Dennis said nothing for a few minutes as he clicked back through the documents.

"Thank you both for investing time into this. Craig, good work. Why don't you take a long lunch and revisit your supply audit to investigate whether or not we're experiencing any savings yet?"

"Sure, Dennis," he said. "Can I bring back some lunch for you?"

Gag.

"No, that's fine. I'll send Leslie out for something later," Dennis demurred.

"Okay. I'll probably eat at my desk, so feel free to call me if you have any questions about my report," Craig said.

Dennis fingered Craig's bound report. "It looks pretty comprehensive. I'm sure it'll be fine. I do have some questions for Miss Taylor here, so if you could get the door . . ."

"Of course." Craig left, pulling the door closed behind him and then practically strutting back toward his office.

Dennis gave the door a small head shake and turned to me.

"You gave me a lot less information than Mr. Jaynes," he said.

"Yes. I gave you bullet points. We have all the hardcopy details if you want something more in-depth."

"I really, really don't."

I smothered a smile.

"How did you come up with a smaller savings than Craig?" He sounded curious rather than disappointed.

"Like I said, we interpreted some of the data differently. I don't think he took into consideration how eliminating some positions would negatively impact worker productivity when those tasks are transferred back to individual departments," I said.

"I see. So you feel in the broader scheme of things, there's a more efficient solution?"

"Yes. I think if you can get supervisors to quit forcing overtime out of their employees and monitor departments with high absenteeism more closely, you're going to reduce payroll expenditures significantly."

"Cut back on overtime, huh?" He eyed me. "Seems like I've heard your team has made a significant overtime investment of its own over the last week."

"Not exactly." I flushed. "Several of us stayed to correct a data error that threw our reporting off. We didn't charge the company for the time."

"I respect your work ethic, but it's illegal for us to compel employees to work without compensation," he said.

"I know, sir. I made it strictly voluntary."

"They logged that kind of time for free drinks and football tickets?" he asked.

He knew about that?

He studied my face as I groped for an answer.

"They didn't stay because Mike picked up their bar tabs," Dennis said. "They stayed because they respect you. They respect you because you protect your employees and give more than you demand from them." He settled back in his chair and studied me over steepled fingers. "You could have explained Mike's requisition error and gotten an extension."

He knew about that too? He was scary.

"I promoted you because you have an admirable amount of common sense and an extraordinary work ethic. Don't allow the second to outweigh the first. You have maintained a demanding pace here over the last twelve months. I'd like to see you dial back your hours, although I can't stop you from working off the clock. I would feel better knowing you're no longer hurtling toward burnout."

That confused me. Didn't everybody want self-starters on their team? Was I supposed to be average now?

Reading the distress in my face, he said, "Your value to me is your ability to see the bigger picture when you examine a problem, to understand that you have to look at more than numbers to find solutions. I'm selfish enough to worry that if you lose that perspective, I'll be reading a lot more of these." He nodded his head to indicate Craig's huge report.

When I smiled, he laughed. "That might be the first crack I've seen in your work armor. Look, we don't have quarterly taxes due for several weeks. I'd like you to consider taking some time off. Start today. Consider the rest of the day a comp day for all the overtime this week. Give everyone who worked with you a comp day next week."

"Thank you. That's generous."

"Don't give one to Mike," he said, smiling.

When I started to defend Mike, Dennis held up a hand. "Don't worry. I respect someone who will put the time in to fix his mistake, but I'm not giving him a day off for screwing up in the first place."

I swallowed my objection.

"Take your day off and do *nothing*," he continued. "I need you fresh for a hairy project coming up in two weeks. You'll curse my name before you're even two hours into it."

"Sounds fun."

"You have no idea. I'm putting your team on support for Apoor's project right now. Get out of town for a few days. Apoor won't require much more than autopilot. It's so routine, it's Mike-proof."

"I won't be going anywhere. I don't have plans or anything," I said. "But I promise to cut back to forty hours."

A reluctant smile tugged at the corner of his mouth. "Since the only other way I have to keep you out of here is to fire you, I accept your compromise."

Compromise. I was in the position to make a real one with Ben now, ready or not.

They say to be careful what you wish for because it might come true. That goes double for prayer. A big, fat answer had just dropped in my lap.

* * *

Katie had already gone on her well-deserved lunch break when I left Dennis's office. Mike sat in her desk instead, lulled into a Zenlike state by the drone of the paper shredder.

I stopped and waved my hand in front of his face to snap him out of it.

"Jessie! How did it go? Did we save more than Craig with our proposal?"

"When you really look at the numbers, yes. Dennis loved it," I said.

He looked relieved. "Craig came through here a while ago talking like he ran circles around you."

"Mmm, he almost had it right. He did run around in circles, which is different."

"Dude, that guy is such an idiot," he said.

"At least that *dude* caught the test data, so maybe we should keep the gloating to a minimum. *Comprende*?"

"Got it," he answered, looking humbled. "So did Dennis find out about the data switch, or do I still have a job?"

"He does know about it, yes, but you have a job." His expression mirrored his relief.

"However," I added, "you're the only one who pulled overtime this week who won't be getting a comp day next week."

He nodded, clearly resigned to this slap on the wrist. "I deserve that. Does Craig's team get comp time?"

I shook my head, and he grinned. "They didn't have to work over a hundred extra hours to fix their reports," I reminded him.

"Ouch."

"Take your forty hours and be glad you get to work them at all," I advised him. "I don't know how he found out about it, but I think it's pretty generous of Dennis to keep signing your paycheck."

"It's actually a computer generated signa—"

"Mike!"

"I'll shut up and shred now."

"Good idea."

I continued to my office, growing lighter with every step. I didn't have to eat lunch at my desk today. I didn't have to eat dinner there either. I could have my breakfast at home tomorrow instead of grabbing a plastic-wrapped muffin from a street vendor on the way in. When I flipped on my computer, I would not wade through yet another audit report on a long-forgotten timesheet. I could catch up on interoffice e-mail or work on some of my own miscellaneous filing.

Yeah, awesome. I was so not into that. I picked up the phone and punched Sandy's number in.

"How did it go?" she demanded as soon as she answered.

"We smoked him," I said.

"Yes! I knew it."

"Care to have a celebration lunch with me?"

"Sure. Let me tell Susan I'm leaving. I'll meet you at your office."

"Sounds like a plan," I said and hung up. Instead of finding some busy work for the next five minutes while I waited, I spun around to stare out the window—and did nothing at all.

"I'm not interrupting anything, am I?" Only one person could inject his tone with such complete condescension. I took a deep breath and prayed for patience before I turned to face him.

"What can I do for you, Craig?" I asked.

"I wanted to make sure you're okay," he said.

This should be fun.

"I'm great. Thanks for asking."

He wandered in without an invitation and perched on the edge of my desk. I hate when people do that. I've never been in the habit of parking my behind in anyone else's personal space, so I didn't understand the comfort level there. But with Craig, it was probably some kind of alpha-dog territory marker thing.

"Have a seat, Craig. It's a comfortable chair," I offered. He took it and then, crossing his legs, prepared to make himself at home.

"That's nice of you," he said. "I thought you might be mad."

"About . . . ?"

"You know, how the meeting with Dennis went this morning."

"And how was that, Craig?"

"I definitely compliment you for being able to generate a report after your oversight on the test data, but come on," he said.

"Yes?"

"I hope you weren't embarrassed by the inequity between what I produced and your little slideshow."

"Right, that." I leaned back in my chair, amused. I studied him for a moment, noting the way he propped his wrist on his knee to display his watch to full advantage. His posturing should have annoyed me.

But I didn't care.

I didn't care that he sat there thinking he had bested me. I didn't care that his silence cost me hours of overtime. I didn't care that he probably had a plot hatching at that very moment, designed to thwart me again. I didn't even care enough about beating him to muster the energy to set him straight on his "win." With perfect clarity, I could see that we would replay variations of this scene, sometimes with me ahead and sometimes with him, ad nauseam.

With the genius of hindsight, I could see that Dennis would have granted me an extension without any penalty, tangible or otherwise, if I had gone to him and explained our screw up. He had enough faith in my judgment to allow me the time to reach my own interpretation of the data. He would have disciplined Mike, but Mike deserved it and was already serving his sentence anyway. The pressure I felt to complete the audit by the original deadline wasn't Dennis's fault. I couldn't even blame Craig that I took his bait every time.

I prided myself on not making the same mistake twice, never mind the half dozen times I'd already butted heads with him in the two months since my promotion. That gave me a choice: I could level Craig with a rundown of his report's analytical reasoning flaws and then refuse to ever engage in a round of schoolyard one-upmanship again. Or I could smile and let him win, this time and every time, and simply not care. I could focus on the job I did and that my team did and direct all my energy to that outcome instead of dividing it between my results and Craig's.

What an easy choice.

I chose to let Craig sweat.

Delivering a courteous smile, I reached across the desk and offered him a handshake. Confused, he accepted it.

"Your team did a great job," I said. "You deserve all the recognition Dennis gave you."

His perma-grin showed signs of suspicion. "Thank you. I find Dennis responds better to cold, hard facts."

"You're so right about that," I agreed.

His suspicion grew. Before he could probe further, Sandy interrupted from the doorway.

"You ready to celebrate?"

He turned to her, confused. "Celebrate?"

Noting my frantic headshake behind Craig's back she said, "Yeah . . . because it's Friday."

"Yep. Love those Fridays," I said cheerfully. "If you'll excuse us, Craig, we're going to go grab some lunch."

He looked unsettled. "You don't mind if I discuss the audit findings with Mike, do you?"

I could tell he wanted to rocket out to Mike's cubby and interrogate him.

"You better wait, Craig. He has a lot of shredding to do right now, and I don't want you to distract him." I escorted him to the door. "You should get out for lunch today. It's not good to spend all your time at your desk."

He gaped at me, dumbfounded by this bit of wisdom from Jessie, goddess of overtime.

Sandy moved out of the doorway to speed his exit. "Bye, Craig," she prompted him.

"Bye," he said grudgingly as I gathered up my purse and black peacoat.

As the elevator doors closed, I could see him loitering near my office, staring after us, probably wondering what had put such a bounce in my step. When we started down the eight floors to the building lobby, Sandy burst out laughing. "He doesn't know you beat him?"

"Nope."

"You're a strong woman to resist rubbing his face in it," she said.

"It's not strength. It's exhaustion. It's too hard to keep up with his garbage," I responded.

She studied me thoughtfully. "So you're done with him?"

I shrugged. "Dealing with him is not part of my job description. He can be Dennis Court's headache. So, yeah. I'm done."

"Hallelujah!" she said. "Lunch is on me!"

I smothered a smile. "Control yourself, woman. They have a security camera in here somewhere."

"Oh yeah? Look me in the eye and tell me it doesn't feel amazing to deliver a better presentation *and* break out of that vicious cycle you two have had going on, all in the same morning."

"It does feel amazing."

"Show it, girl!" she urged me.

"Yay?" I said.

She snorted. "You've risen above the Craigness. Give me something worthy of that!"

Grinning, I dropped my coat and purse, threw my hands in the air and did an endzone dance, which is how the head of purchasing found me when the elevator doors dinged open on the third floor. I dropped my arms and tugged on my blazer to adjust it then folded my hands neatly in front of me. Shooting me a bewildered look, Mr. Li scooted inside the elevator, but as far from me as possible. I hedged closer to Sandy to give him more room, elbowing her in the ribs to stop her from shaking with laughter. We rode the remaining three floors down in silence, broken only by suspicious squeaks from Sandy, who was still trying not to laugh.

When the doors opened into the lobby, Mr. Li scurried out, not returning my sweet, "Have a good afternoon!"

I glared at Sandy. "Are you done?"

"Are you kidding me?" she asked. She grabbed my stuff, piled it into my arms, and dragged me toward the exit. "We're barely getting started!"

Chapter 32

"YOU'RE EVIL," I COMPLAINED, PUSHING my plate back with a groan.

"And completely unrepentant," Sandy agreed.

The crumbs of four slices of cheesecake littered our table. When we polished off our pasta and couldn't settle on a dessert, Sandy had declared that part of our celebration entailed getting any kind of cheesecake we wanted. Insisting we taste all four flavors I had dithered over, she'd ordered the classic New York cheesecake, the Oreo madness slice, and a piece each of the sensuous strawberry and key lime versions. The waiter's eyebrows had shot up. He was obviously torn between earning a tip on a larger bill and saving us from ourselves, but he warned us, "Ladies, these are large slices. Perhaps you would like to share one?"

Glancing at his name tag, Sandy had purred, "Tony, don't I look like a woman who should get exactly what I want?"

He had snapped his order pad closed with a smile. "Of course. Four pieces of cheesecake coming right up for the lovely women at table six."

Sandy had smiled back sweetly and shooed him toward the kitchen and the cheesecake.

And now I slumped in my chair, devoid of the desire or will to move.

"Too much," I moaned.

"No such thing," Sandy mumbled, dazed.

"Not even four slices of cheesecake?"

A big sigh. Then, "Yes. Maybe four is two too many."

"Too many twos."

"Too many cheesecakes," she muttered back.

"You ordered them," I said in accusation.

"Because you couldn't decide. How come you can't be as narrow-minded about cheesecake flavors as you are about other things?"

I struggled to sit up straighter. "What am I narrow-minded about?"

"Working versus socializing, for one," she said.

"What else?" I demanded.

"Tofu."

"You can't win an argument where tofu is your defense," I said.

"Fine. Then I default back to working and socializing."

"What are you talking about?" I asked. "I've socialized more since New Year's than I have in months."

"I'll give you credit for the first three weeks. But the last two? Not so much. No Ben. No sharing Ben's e-mails or texts or phone calls. I'm mad at you."

"Me! Why?"

"Who am I supposed to live vicariously through if you're blowing off Ben for work again?"

"I see. This is about you," I said.

"Yes," she said lazily. "Me, me, me. But I'm buying lunch today, so be nice."

"I'm only going to be nice because I'm too full to do anything else," I said.

We both subsided, reserving our energy for digestion.

After a while, I roused myself to speak. "I'm seeing Ben tomorrow, you know."

She cracked an eye open and stared at me. "No, I didn't know. I wondered if you had dumped him for Craig."

"Ha."

"Well, you've spent a lot more time focused on him than Ben lately," she said, no apology in her tone.

"That's true."

Her other eye opened, and she narrowed them both at me, confused. "You're not going to argue about that either?"

"No. You're right. But in my defense, it's Ben's fault."

"Wait. It's Ben's fault you've been spending so much time at work?"

"It's his fault we haven't been talking. He didn't want me to call him until I finished this project. And the only thing I've heard from him is a text message wishing me good luck today."

"That was thoughtful," Sandy said. "So are you going to call him now?"

"I can't."

"Because you hate happiness? Sure you can. I'll show you how to work your phone."

"Very funny." I filled her in on the Ben ultimatum. I'd intentionally neglected to tell her any of it before because I knew she'd nag me to no end, wanting to know what I would do. Sure enough, she laid into me as soon as I explained the arrangement to show up for dinner on Saturday night.

"Ben's leaving in a month?" she asked.

"Yeah. He told me last week. His contract's almost up, and he's going back to Arizona."

"He said that?"

"Pretty much. It's not like he's going to stay here for me." I knew I sounded defeated.

"For a take-charge girl, Jessie, you sure are letting him call all the shots. You should shake it up," she said.

"Like how? Not show up tomorrow?"

"No. I mean, why not go over there tonight instead? Put this back on your timetable while still meeting his terms. You're done with your project, and you're ready to talk. Why wait for tomorrow?"

"Because I'm *not* ready yet, for one," I objected.

She rolled her eyes. "It's been two weeks since you saw him. How long is it going to take you to be ready?"

"Calm down. I meant, I'm not ready to talk to him tonight. I need to think about what I want to say. I'll be ready by dinner tomorrow."

"But what's to think about, Jess?" she pressed. "Are you going over there to profess your undying love or something?"

"No!"

"Then how hard do you have to think? You show up and say 'I figured out Craig was a total time-suck, and I'm ready to date you now. I'm cutting back to forty hours. Kiss me, Ben!'" She pressed her wrist to her forehead, Scarlett O'Hara style.

"Stop it!" I begged when I caught Tony staring at her antics. "It's not that easy."

"Yes, it is that easy," she insisted. "You're making it hard."

"This whole leaving in a month thing is tripping me out now. It changes everything."

"How? Does it suddenly make your feelings speed up or slow down? That's not possible. You feel what you feel. Emotions aren't subject to time constraints."

"That was almost profound."

She shrugged. "I'm channeling Oprah again. Seriously, Jess. What do you feel right *now*? Because that's what you should focus on."

"I feel overwhelmed and insecure and confused. What's the point of hanging out for a month if he's going to leave?" I blew out an exasperated breath.

"Why do you need to have this planned out?" Sandy asked. "Just go over there and see where it takes you."

"Good idea. I'll show up at his house, knock on the door, and stand there and say nothing. I'll stare at him, all mysterious, until he's creeped out and slams the door."

"Or you could let him do the talking. Hear what he has to say and trust your gut to know how to respond."

"My gut hasn't been so helpful in the past."

"What past? You never depend on instinct. It's always think, think, think with you."

"I trusted my gut with Jason, and that was a disaster."

"No, you didn't trust your gut with him. Remember telling me how things seemed off when he got home from his mission, but you ignored it, thinking it would go away?"

I nodded reluctantly.

"That was your gut, and you didn't listen. That was the mistake. Maybe you should hear Ben out and trust yourself more."

"That's crazy talk," I protested, but Sandy grinned, knowing she had scored a point.

Tony wandered over, check in hand. He laid it facedown on the table and backed away. Sandy flipped it over, and I reached for my purse, but she waved me away.

"I told you, my treat."

"Yeah, but you didn't know I'd order four slices of cheesecake."

"You didn't order them. I did," she said, fishing her own wallet out of a bright orange Coach purse.

"Only because I wanted them," I argued. "Let me pay. I can afford it."

This elicited another grin. "I hate to burst your bubble, Jess, but I get a bigger paycheck. I'm paying."

"What? You do not. How do you know that?" I demanded.

"I know everyone's salary because I have to make offers to new employees, and we want to stay competitive."

"I'm raising your rent," I said.

"Okay, but I won't share my closet with you."

"Fine, I won't raise your rent."

"Good. *Mi armario es su armario.*"

"I thought you took French in high school. When did you learn Spanish?" I asked.

"Spanish language CDs in the car on the way to work. Life makeover and all. Oh, hey, since you're not working crazy late hours anymore, we can carpool, and you can learn Spanish too."

"Uh, I know Spanish."

"Huh." She thought for a minute. "I'd be willing to switch to Japanese."

I squinched my nose.

"German?" she tried.

"Thanks, but no thanks. I think I'll stick to my iPod and news radio."

"*Que lastima.*" She slapped some cash into the payment jacket and declared, "Let's roll."

"More like roll ourselves out of here."

"Right. That's what I said."

We headed back to work and parted ways. The rest of the afternoon at work stayed blissfully uneventful. I assigned my staff to complete our project documentation and finish any leftover filing or shredding. I spent a couple of hours hammering out a support strategy with Apoor Gami, figuring out what my team needed to do to help. It would be a light rotation; Apoor was easy to work with and already had things well in hand.

By three o'clock, I had a clean desk and no crises to occupy my time, so naturally, my thoughts turned to Ben.

Sandy was right. Ben wasn't at the root of my confusion and insecurity. I was. How many times did I have to figure this out? I had hunkered down in a bunker constructed out of work excuses and then bludgeoned him over the head with overtime to keep him away. Could I complain because I was a tactical genius at self-sabotage? And as for him leaving in a month . . .

Well. I liked him.

I mean really, *really* liked him.

I liked him more than chocolate and at least as much as ice cream. And I wanted to spend all my free time soaking up the month with him.

I was in serious trouble.

Chapter 33

WALKING THROUGH THE DOOR BEFORE four o'clock on a Friday afternoon was a novel experience. On the one hand, traffic was worse when I left work early. On the other hand, I made it home hours earlier than usual, and I had nothing but time on my hands. No overstuffed work bag, no jellied Chinese takeout.

I plopped down on the sofa in satisfaction, surveying my domain, thinking for a moment. My current plan was to reveal my new worldview to Ben at dinner tomorrow, but I didn't want to wait a whole day to finally see him again. I had the overwhelming urge to live my own movie and show up on his doorstep tonight with dinner in hand and an announcement: I was ready to redirect my extra work energy toward our relationship, to give us the time to find out if we truly had something together. I hopped up, grabbed my keys, and headed for the grocery store, determined to act spontaneously for once. By the time Sandy walked through the door at six, the rich smell of a roasting chicken wafted out to meet her.

"Whoever you are, come out from the kitchen slowly with your hands up. I've got pepper spray," she called.

I poked my head around the wall. "Why would an intruder break in and make dinner?" I asked.

"Oh, it's you," she said with exaggerated surprise. "You actually left work on time."

"I left two hours early. I told you I wouldn't work late."

"And I've heard that before. This is the first time you've backed it up."

"So you're saying it's going to take you awhile to accept my conversion to the forty-hour workweek?"

"Yeah, that's pretty much it," she agreed. "Do I remember this correctly? You've recognized that you did wrong. You're going to confess and make amends to Ben. So that leaves the forsaking your long hours part. Is that what you're doing?"

I retreated back to the kitchen. "Fine, don't believe me," I called. "But I'm not sharing my big dinner secret with you until you accept that I've changed."

"In a day? Ha," she scoffed. She wandered in and sniffed the air. "Besides, I gave up red meat last week, so you can have dinner all to yourself."

"It's roast chicken. And you're not getting any of it anyway. It's for Ben."

She turned to stare at me. "You're kidding."

"Nope. As soon as this is done, I'm packing it up and heading to Ben's to have that talk."

"That's amazing!" she squealed. "I demand details as soon as you get back!"

I smiled and waved her off then headed to my room to change. What do you wear to say, "Sorry for being an idiot, but I've seen the light"?

It was hard to believe I hadn't had any contact with Ben for a week. It hadn't taken long from our first e-mail for him to stake a claim on part of each day, whether in a phone call or face to face, and I missed that. I couldn't wait to see him. I definitely had questions and maybe even some answers for him, but mostly I looked forward to him scooping me up in one of his hugs.

After that, we could talk. He would say, "I'm totally into you and want to be with you," and I wouldn't fidget or blush this time.

I would say, "I want to be with you too," and turn only a little bit red.

He would say, "I changed my mind about your work commitment. I like you so much that I don't care when you can see me; we'll find a way to work around your crazy hours."

And I would say, "Thanks for being willing to support me. But I figured out that Craig was a waste of energy, and I'm ready to date you now. I'm cutting back to forty hours. Kiss me, Ben," and Sandy would be stoked that I'd used her line, and I would ignore her gloating in favor of smooching Ben.

We might talk about what him leaving in a month meant and what might happen during and after that month, and we'd work it out. Because this was Ben, not Jason. Ben, who had been up-front with me from the beginning, who carried himself with a confidence Jason didn't have, who knew what he wanted and asked for it. This was not a newly minted returned missionary trying to figure out what he wanted to be when he grew up, too inexperienced to know how to communicate in sticky emotional situations. And despite the number of third dates I'd turned down in the last several years, this was probably not the first guy who could handle himself like an adult in relationships; however, this was the first guy I had given that chance.

I took a leap right there in front of my closet with that decision. A leap of faith. Faith that Ben was the guy he said he was, that asking me to balance my work hours more implied a commitment to growing what had budded between us. I was about to dump a box of Miracle-Gro on that bud and watch it shoot up, blossoming in direct correlation to the excitement burbling inside me.

I discarded four outfits before throwing on a black cashmere turtleneck, some old Lucky jeans I had snagged from DownEast Outfitters in my Provo days, and my trusty Converse. I wanted to look sophisticated and trendy without looking like I had tried too hard. Even though I totally had. Ten minutes in front of the mirror took care of makeup. I could hear Sandy stirring in her room. She'd be in to inspect me and send me off on my mission but not until I glossed to her satisfaction. Swiping some fruity peach gunk over my lips did the trick. Examining my handiwork with a critical eye, I smiled and hoped Ben would like what he saw.

No one could resist peach lip gloss and my mom's rosemary roast chicken recipe. Ben Bratton was as good as mine . . . I hoped.

The oven buzzer chimed, and I rushed to turn it off, my nerves skittering. Sandy popped back in as I tried to figure out how to transport the minifeast. Besides the chicken, I had whipped up some garlic mashed potatoes and some carrots in a honey sauce. I wanted to be at Ben's house by six, early enough that I figured he wouldn't have eaten dinner yet. She watched me without comment while I waffled between plastic wrap and aluminum. In a calmer state of mind, I would have remembered that you should always use foil when dealing with heat. It helped keep it in and all.

Ultimately, Sandy's impatient, "Foil!" interjection reminded me. Like I hadn't heard the same thing from my mom before every potluck we ever went to. But my jangling nerves interfered with normal brain function, so I just reached for the foil, thankful someone in the house was keeping her cool.

When I had dinner neatly packed and stacked, I turned to Sandy. "Am I presentable?" I asked.

"I can only speak for the top half of you. The bottom half you're hiding behind the counter could be a polyester trouser disaster, but from what I can see—you've got it at least half right."

I stepped all the way into the living room for her approval. She gestured for me to do a spin. "I probably can't talk you into boots, can I?" she asked.

I shook my head.

"Well, Converse are their own kind of classic. And with your turtleneck, the whole effect is kind of funky."

My eyebrows snapped together.

"The good kind of funky," she clarified.

"Oh. So I look okay?"

She nodded. "You look kinda hot. You're like a hipster chick, but the kind that washes her hair and smells good."

"Thanks?"

"Yeah, no problem. Nice gloss. Too bad it'll only stay on for about two seconds once he sees you."

I dug out the tube from my back pocket. "I'm totally prepared."

She smiled. "I wish I were going to be there to see his face. I want a dramatic reenactment later, okay?"

"Okay, but it'll be the G-rated version."

"That's the one where they cut out all the kissing," she objected.

"If you do a load of towels, I'll give you the PG details," I bribed.

"If you don't spill the PG details, I'll revoke your lip gloss privileges," she retorted.

"How do you always win these arguments?"

"Because I have all the cool girl stuff," she said.

"You're right. That's why. I'm going to have to hit the Nordstrom cosmetics counter soon to stock up, or I'll never have leverage over you."

"Good luck with that. Unless you can get the mythical Smashbox George and Wheezy eye shadow duo, it'll never happen."

I shook my head but knew I didn't have time to spar. This meal and talk with Ben, my favorite computer nerd, would mark a reboot for our fledgling relationship, complete with programming updates and debugging solutions to help speed things up.

Sandy helped me load my meal on wheels into my Accord and then scurried back inside to escape the chilly evening air. Wishing I had brought a jacket, I resisted the impulse to go searching for one, knowing I'd better point the car toward Ben's house before I could change my mind.

Chapter 34

For the entire twenty-minute drive to Ben's house, my stomach flipped. This was it; I was going to be a grown-up, one who made big-girl decisions and talked things through like an adult. One who took calculated risks to improve her happiness and welcomed open communication.

Exhilarated, I cranked up the local classic rock station when Journey's "Don't Stop Believin'" blared out of the radio, and I sang along. I didn't care that the song had been overplayed since its resurrection on *Glee* or that it was one of the greatest slices of cheese in the classic rock canon. The unapologetic optimism in the lyrics fit my mood perfectly.

As I neared the turnoff for Ben's neighborhood, I entertained myself by imagining his expression when he opened the door and found me standing there. It felt good to be turning the tables on him for once, to be the one showing up at his house with food in hand and a challenge to take another step forward.

I peered at the street signs and looked for landmarks. At last, I recognized a small bungalow on the corner marking his street. Its remarkable shade of pink made it memorable. I suspected the owners had intended to create some kind of mellow Mediterranean terra cotta effect. Instead, they got a shade of salmon, its freshness questionable.

I hung a left and peered at the left side of Ben's street closely, looking for his house. I spotted his car in the driveway. My nerves would have exploded if I'd had to sit and wait for him, wondering if every pair of headlights turning onto the street belonged to him. I parked in an empty spot two houses down, got out, and retrieved the dinner sitting on the floor mat. I had learned the hard way never to transport food on a seat after a childhood incident involving a sudden stop on the way to a Church dinner and a massive pot of chicken and dumplings sloshing to the floor of our minivan.

Hefting the awkward bundle of baking dishes, I managed to navigate onto the sidewalk and up to Ben's walkway. I stood at the foot of it for a moment, taking in the sight of the house and enjoying the warmth that came with knowing I had made the right decision about my love life, for once. I stepped to the door and awkwardly shifted my cargo to one arm so I could knock.

When the door opened half a minute later, I smiled, eager to see which expression would win out on his face.

I got shock.

Ben's lips parted but instead of puckering up to kiss me hello, they formed a wordless "oh," and consternation creased his forehead. My confidence faltered as he stared at me. "Jessie. Hi. What are you doing here?"

He didn't sound delighted like I thought he would in my daydream, but I pressed ahead. I had resolved to be a grown-up, and I would see this through. "Hi. I didn't want to wait until tomorrow night to talk stuff out. What are you doing right now?" I tried to make the question sound flirtatious.

When he flinched, I knew I had failed miserably. "Uh, now?" he asked, casting an uncomfortable glance over his shoulder.

"Sure, now," I answered, feeling stupid with my arms full of a chicken.

"I totally want to talk, but tomorrow would be a lot better. I'm kind of in the middle of—"

"Ben?" a soft female voice interrupted. A hand appeared on his bicep, resting there comfortably, tipped in manicured pink fingernails. Whoever the voice belonged to stood out of sight, hidden by the door frame. "Who is it?" she asked.

A flush suffused my face, and I backed up, ready to retreat. Ben took a step toward me, a hand outstretched. His shift created enough room for a pretty blonde to take his place in the door, her hand fixed firmly to his arm. When she saw me, she tightened her grip possessively. "Who's this?" she asked coolly.

I could see Ben's reluctance to make introductions written all over his face, so before he could walk us through that particular exercise in humiliation, I jumped in. "I'm Jessie," I said. "Ben's friend from church. I was assigned to fellowship him so I stopped by with some food. You should have some. It's from one of my mom's recipes," I babbled, amazed I could lie so easily. And I only lied to save Ben from a tough spot so he wouldn't be on the hook with this girl. Who I didn't even know. Which meant I had lost my mind, so I switched into escape mode, desperate to get away.

"Anyway," I continued with my word vomit, "I've got a busy night, so I'd best be going." Not knowing what else to do, I turned and set the food at the edge of the porch and whipped around, heading for my car.

"Jessie!" Ben called, shaking off the hand on his arm and taking a few steps after me.

I turned and said, "No, Ben. I don't want to intrude. Enjoy the meal, and maybe I'll see you around."

"Ben, what's going on?" his guest asked.

Good question. I knew I didn't have the presence of mind to stick around for the answer, so I picked up my pace and focused on getting to the car before I did something even more embarrassing. Like cry.

I cranked the ignition, cursing the loss of my favorite casserole dish to Ben, and fought the instinct to burn rubber in my mad rush to get away. When I safely navigated out of the neighborhood, I found a business park already closed for weekday business and pulled in. I put the car in park and idled the motor, radio turned off, my hands gripping the wheel like it was the blonde's neck.

I forced myself to relax my death grip after a few minutes and dropped my head back against the headrest. Then I did it again, and three more times for good measure, but the cushion prevented a satisfactory thump. What was I thinking, going over there unannounced? I dropped my head to the steering wheel and replayed the awkward scene in my mind: Me, standing all fresh-scrubbed and eager with a homemade dinner for Ben on a Friday night. Ben, standing there, looking slightly disturbed to see me. Blonde Girl, her pink-tipped claw wrapped around Ben's shirt sleeve and the disdain in her question, "Who's this?" And me again, practically throwing the food at Ben and hightailing it out of there.

How humiliating. I started the deep breathing exercises I reserved for getting myself through dental visits, trying to exert control over my emotions. On my third deep breath, the phone rang. A sidelong glance showed Ben's number on the caller ID screen. I grabbed the phone and sent the call straight to voicemail. It's not like I could form words at the moment. A beep twenty seconds later told me he'd left a message. I turned the phone off completely. I didn't want to hear anything he had to say at the moment.

What *was* going on? I had to give it to the blonde. She asked good questions. I'd love to know the answer to that too. Who was she? She clearly felt comfortable enough with her place in his life to be at his house at dinner time on a Friday evening and to demand explanations about his visitors. *Maybe it was his sister,* I rationalized. But I knew she was away at BYU–Idaho.

Carie.

It had to be her. No one else would have felt justified in acting so possessive. Not even me, not even after he'd confessed his feelings and the things he'd said had haunted me all week, forcing me to realize how much I liked him. I had no claim on him because I'd been too chicken to stake one.

I drew several more deep breaths before I calmed down enough to drive again. I spent the return trip home in a weird, numb shock. I blessed it because without the numbness, I think a suffocating sense of idiocy would have overwhelmed me. When I pulled into my parking space, autopilot took over, and I found myself pushing through my front door, unaware of even leaving my car.

Sandy glanced up from a bizarre yoga pose in surprise but took one look at me and unwound herself. I walked straight to the table, pulled out a chair, and sat down, staring at my hands on the placemat in front of me. She sat down directly across from me and said nothing for a while. Then she asked quietly, "What happened?"

"He—"

My throat closed up. I cleared it and tried again. "He had company," I said.

"Company?"

"Yeah. Some girl."

Her face tightened. "He had a girl over?"

"Yeah. His ex, I think."

Her face darkened further, but she said nothing before jumping up and heading for her bedroom. A minute later, she returned, a sweatshirt over her yoga tank and a purse in hand.

"Where are you going?" I asked as she charged past me to the door.

"For ice cream. I'll be back in ten minutes with a big carton of something bad for you."

"Oh." I hesitated. "Sandy?"

She turned, pushing the front door back open and poking her head in. "Yeah?"

"Could you find me a really big spoon while you're at it?"

Chapter 35

An hour later, with my stomach full of Jerry's (Sandy had inked out the "Ben and . . ." part of the carton label before handing it to me), I stewed. It felt better than being a useless lump, which is what I'd been until the ice cream had kicked in. Then I began processing my humiliation.

I had a litany of things I was mad at: me, for going over there; Sandy, for giving me the idea to do it; the blonde, for being at the house; and Ben. He had a whole list of things that made me mad at him. Like, that he was breathing. And those were the rational things I could think of.

The adult and responsible thing, which I had set out to do tonight (before Blondie's intrusion had blown it all sky-high), would be to stay calm and find out exactly what was going on. But as a smart girl with math skills, I could add up the facts and find no good outcomes. An irritatingly pretty girl, probably his ex-fiancée, had clearly marked Ben as her territory and acted very at home in his house. Plus, Ben hadn't felt the need to inform me of said girl coming around. Plus, Ben looked uncomfortable to see me. Not delighted, not excited.

Uncomfortable.

And worst of all, I had left work early to make him a stupid roast chicken for no reason, and I had dropped it on his porch and run away. All that equaled me being an idiot. *Again.* Well, time to fix that. I hopped up, startling Sandy, and raced over to the fireplace mantle to snatch up the rock sitting there. The words "This is just a rock" were still scrawled across its face, written in my burst of empowerment a month ago. With one Sharpied motto, I had turned it from a souvenir of my failure at love into a statement about my readiness to move on. It was supposed to symbolize that if I let go of that failed relationship, maybe it would lose its grip on me.

I felt the sudden urge to do with the rock what I should have done when I plucked it out of Jason's hands years ago: toss it in the ocean and not look back. Maybe if I had done that then, I wouldn't be living in that old shadow, practically repeating the same mistake. I was into a guy who was juggling feelings for me with feelings for someone else. Again.

"I want to go to home," I announced.

"Um, hi. You're here already?" Sandy said.

"No, I mean, *home* home, to California. I want to eat at my mom's table and have my dad refer me to fifty different scriptures related to this mess, and I want to throw this stupid rock in the ocean and figure out what to do next."

A knock on the door cut off Sandy's answer. Since I was closest, I peered through the eye hole, and my stomach dropped.

"It's Ben!" I hissed at Sandy. "What do I do?"

"I don't know," she said. "I mean, do you want to talk to him?"

"Should I?"

"I have no idea what you need right now. If it were me, I'd open the door—but that's me."

"Jessie, I can hear you through the door. I know you're home. Can I talk to you, please?" he called.

I hesitated for a moment and then yanked it open and turned around, walking to the sofa. Sandy got up and, after casting Ben an ambiguous smile, headed back to her bedroom. He stood in the middle of the living room, wavering for a moment before moving to take a seat on the opposite end of the sofa from me.

"You'd better sit there," I said, indicating the oversized matching chair instead.

He nodded and sat where I pointed. He shifted a few times, eyeballing the rock in my hand.

"Are you going to throw that at me?" he joked.

The joke fell flat when I set the rock on the floor but otherwise declined to answer.

"You're mad," he surmised.

"No."

"Okay." He didn't believe me; I could tell. Smart man. "So that was Carie at my house."

"I figured." I kept my expression blank.

"She surprised me by showing up about a half hour before you did. She wasn't supposed to be here today," he said.

His phrasing caught my attention. "You mean, she wasn't supposed to be here today, but she was supposed to be here at some point, like on a different day?"

"Well, yeah, but—"

"Oh, that's fantastic," I bit out.

"It sounds bad, but it's not, I promise. I wasn't expecting her until next week."

I snorted. "This gets better and better. Next week, meaning after you and I talked so you could let me down gently and be free and clear to pick things back up with her?"

"No! Of course not. I've been looking forward to seeing you for days and hammering out this thing between us."

"Oh, I can save you the trouble. The thing between us now is Carie," I retorted.

"Jessie, please. I need you to understand—"

"What? That Carie was conveniently on tap for next week if I didn't show up tomorrow? You had your plan B all worked out until she and I both came up with the embarrassingly unoriginal plan to surprise you tonight?" I realized I was contradicting myself and making no sense, but I hurt too much to care. "You're so good that you ended up surprising the two of us instead. I hope she bought the whole fellowshipping thing. I don't want to be the reason things don't work out for you again." I lifted my chin and stared him down.

He jammed his fingers through his hair, frustrated. "Jessie, listen. I agreed to see her because—"

"Stop!" Suddenly I didn't want to know. "I don't have time for this. I came over tonight instead of tomorrow because I'm going out of town, and I didn't want you to think I was standing you up." Well, the going out of town part was true as of that moment. "And I need to be getting on the road soon, so you should go."

I got up and walked to the door, a clear invitation for him to leave. He sat for another moment, looking like he wanted to argue. Then he sighed and stood up. "Will you call me when you get back?"

I didn't answer.

Looking defeated, he shoved his hands into his pockets and walked out.

When the door shut, Sandy walked back into the living room.

"Are you okay?" she asked.

"Yeah."

"So what did he want?"

"To explain."

"And?"

"I don't know. It was his ex-fiancée. He was expecting her but not today."

"Wow."

"I don't even know what to think about that," I blurted. "He admitted that she came so they could talk. How many girls does he have to define his relationship with anyway?"

"Uh, I can name at least two."

"Very funny. Not."

"Okay," she said. "How do you know it wasn't all her idea?"

"I don't, but it doesn't matter," I responded. "If he's willing to let her get on a plane and fly all the way up here to see him, that already tells me a lot."

"So . . . what next?" she asked.

"I'm taking a road trip, I guess."

"To your parents' house?" she clarified.

"Yep."

"I can't believe I'm going to ask you this, but what about work?"

I shrugged. "Dennis Court as good as told me to take a vacation. I'll shoot him an e-mail and let him know I'm taking advantage of that for a few days. He'll probably do a hooray cheer."

"Dennis Court? I don't think he cheers."

"Okay, he'll say, 'Excellent plan, Ms. Taylor,' and start in on another spreadsheet. But believe me, he won't care if I'm out of the office for a few days."

"All right! California, here we come!"

"We? Not we. You have to work."

"Jess, you don't think I'm going to let you have all the fun, do you? I'm not shivering in my long johns here while you're soaking up the sun at the beach."

"Not to burst your bubble, but it's not exactly beach weather in January, even in California."

"Fine, but at least it's not Seattle. Besides," she grinned, "it turns out I have a couple of sick days to burn. Susannah can't fire me because there wouldn't be anyone likeable left in HR."

"Can you be ready to leave in an hour?" I asked.

"An hour? Who taught you to pack for a spontaneous road trip? I'll see you out here in thirty minutes." And she flew back to her room.

I shook my head and went to dig my cell phone out of my purse. When it powered back up, I saw eight missed calls from Ben. Ignoring them, I hit speed dial number two.

"Mom?" I said when she answered. "I'm coming home."

Chapter 36

I STUMBLED INTO MY PARENTS' kitchen for breakfast Sunday morning. Sandy already sat at the table with a steaming plate of scrambled eggs in front of her.

"Good morning, sweetie," my mom said from the stove, where she stood monitoring the progress of another frying pan. "Would you like an omelet or squiggles?" she asked.

"Squiggles?" Sandy echoed.

"That's what Jessie used to call scrambled eggs," my dad explained from the doorway. He wandered over to the table and dropped an absentminded kiss on the top of my head before he sat down and disappeared behind the Sunday paper.

"That's so cute," Sandy cooed.

"Shut up," I grumbled.

"Be nice, Jessie," my mom admonished me.

"Yeah. Be nice," Sandy parroted.

I picked up a fork from the place setting in front of me and rotated it methodically in my fingers.

My dad watched me over the folded corner of the paper for a moment. "You'd better move," he told Sandy. "I think she's going to stab you." He disappeared behind the local section again.

He knew me well.

Sandy grinned but scooted her chair another foot out of reach. "So, Jessie was like this back in the day too?" she asked.

"Only if you ask her to function before she eats," my mom confirmed.

"Yeah, that's the same," Sandy said.

I couldn't find the words I needed to say, like, "Stop talking about me like I'm not here. I'm cranky because I'm hungry. I'll be fine once I get food," so I growled instead.

My mom brought the skillet to the table and slid some scrambled eggs straight onto my plate. "We'd better not wait for an omelet," she said.

I dug in and, after three mouthfuls, said, "Thank you."

"Of course." After letting me finish a few more bites, she took the empty seat beside me. "Are you going to church with us?" she asked.

"Yeah. What time do you guys meet?"

"Nine o'clock. Your dad has meetings after church, but I don't, so you girls can ride with me if you want, and we'll come straight home."

"Sandy won't—" I was about to say, "be coming with us," but Sandy cut me off.

"Sounds good, Sister Taylor," she said. "I'm not in a hurry to get back into Jess's car anytime soon. Eighteen hours between Friday and yesterday is enough."

Even leaving within the hour on Friday night and cruising comfortably above the speed limit all the way down, we hadn't stumbled through my parents' front door until midafternoon yesterday, bleary-eyed from sleep deprivation and road weariness. Office gossip and iPod disagreements had filled the first ten hours. The last few hours had passed in quiet as we took turns sleeping and driving.

"We'll be ready," I said.

"Good girl." My mom hopped back up and headed for the sink with my empty plate. "There's something you should probably know before you go to church. I meant to tell you this before you came down for your next trip, but you surprised us with this one."

I dropped my head to my hands. "I have a feeling I know what's coming."

"Jason is back," she said. "He's living in his parents' house while they're gone."

Brother Stewart had been called to serve as a mission president in Chile almost a year before.

"I wouldn't worry," she said. "They're in the other ward now. But I thought you should know."

"It's okay, Mom." I got up and hugged her. "More okay than I thought it would be. Thanks for the heads up."

"Good." She patted my cheek. "You go on up and shower, honey. You smell like road trip." We'd spent most of Saturday afternoon catching up on sleep and watching old movies in my parents' den while they attended a high priest group social at the church. With all my movie-watching and wallowing, showering hadn't made it on my list of things to do yet.

Sandy grinned. "Yeah, you stink, Jessie. Go wash while I help your mom."

When she joined my mom at the sink, Mom took the dirty plate Sandy held in her hand and said with a smile, "I think you're wearing the same road trip perfume. Why don't you go on ahead too. We have a big hot water heater."

It was my turn to grin when Sandy looked amused and trailed me out of the kitchen.

"Your mom's pretty cool," she said. "I can see why you would want to come home."

"Yeah, she kind of rocks," I agreed. "Do you have anything to wear to church?"

"I think I shoved a skirt in my bag somewhere."

"Okay. I'll meet you downstairs in half an hour?"

"Sure. But you need to learn to do your makeup faster." My jaw dropped as she said this, moving past me to the guest bedroom down the hall. Sandy was the mirror jockey in our condo. Scowling at this latest jab from her, I hit the shower to finish waking up. Since I skipped a hair washing (I'd scrubbed it thoroughly before heading off to see Ben), I made it down to the living room ten minutes early in a simple gray merino wool wrap dress and black tights with black high-heeled Mary Janes. As I finished off my dad's discarded business section from the paper, Sandy made an appearance in a tweed pencil skirt and a chocolate brown turtleneck. On me, it would have looked frumpy. On her, it looked sharp.

"How long have you been sitting here?" she demanded.

"Half an hour," I said.

"Then you got ready in negative five minutes because we weren't even upstairs that long." She squinted at me. "You even did your makeup," she said. "I went as fast as I could, and you still beat me."

"I had to fight four sisters for bathroom time growing up here," I said. "Must be my genetic memory powering me through."

She sniffed, took a seat beside me, and sorted through the rest of the paper. My dad wandered in after a moment, looking vaguely distracted, a distinguishing trait of professors everywhere. When he saw me, he smiled and gestured me over for a hug.

"Sorry we didn't have time to talk yesterday. Maybe we can visit after dinner?"

Because of the social the night before and the fact that I'd been too travel-weary and emotionally strung out, we hadn't dug into the reasons behind my sudden appearance anyway. I felt slightly more human and coherent now.

"Sure, Dad," I said. "It's no big deal."

He arched an eyebrow at that. "Well, you showed up with almost no notice, so it must be kind of a big deal," he replied.

"It's not. Sorry I worried you."

He sighed but said only, "I'll see you at church." No sooner had the garage door closed behind him than my mom appeared, dressed in a neat black skirt and red silk blouse.

"Ready to go?" she asked.

"Ready," I said. But then Sandy's cell phone shrilled from upstairs.

"Sorry," she said, looking embarrassed. "Let me go get that. I'll be right back." She bounced up the stairs and down the hall. Instead of bouncing right back down, I heard the low hum of conversation. It went on for at least five minutes. My mom shifted anxiously, but good manners kept her from commenting on Sandy's detour.

I didn't mind though. For the first time in a long time, I didn't feel like being at church. Parading through the hallways of my childhood chapel smacked of regression, and I dreaded the questions from well-meaning members who'd known me as a kid. I'd bet on at least ten "Are you dating anyone?" inquiries, and that didn't even count Relief Society. For a couple of years, the breakup with Jason had given me immunity as people held their questions out of pity. After that, though, they clearly expected to hear any day that I had moved on and was engaged to be married, like Jason was six months after our ugly beach scene. I didn't begrudge their expectations; they only wanted me to be happy. But some of the older ladies grew more comfortable every year with ignoring the social niceties and had no problem wading into everyone's business, especially mine when I showed up in my home ward only twice a year.

I followed my mom out to the car when Sandy reappeared, apologizing for the delay. I didn't want to give Sandy a reason to bolt by describing the hordes of nosy old biddies that would descend on me as soon as I set foot in the meetinghouse, so I said nothing and eyed the clock in the dashboard. I had a shot at making it in time for the welcome from the bishopric but no chit chat if I dragged my feet from the car to the chapel.

I sat back and sighed. This would be one long Sunday.

* * *

I waited for the Gospel Doctrine teacher to wind down. Brother Stevens was a nice man and had an encyclopedic knowledge of the scriptures. Those two things together didn't necessarily add up to a riveting lesson. In fact, his encyclopedia tendencies had taken over and had turned our New Testament lesson into a bit of a Middle Eastern travelogue. Finally deciding I couldn't sit still any longer, I abandoned Sandy to my mother and headed out for a sip of water. It's not like I was getting much out of the lesson anyway.

Since there were a few minutes left before the bell officially rang for the third block, the halls stood relatively empty. I took my sweet time wandering back to the cultural hall, reading the bulletin boards lining the corridor. Pictures of youth activities and Scout outings papered one; another bristled with announcements and fliers from the activities committee. I paused in front of the one belonging to the singles ward. The institute class schedule hung on a fancy piece of CES cardstock and was illustrated with a group of clean-cut young men and women all raising their hands enthusiastically to participate in whatever the teacher asked.

I stared for a while. At the university here, while I worked on my undergraduate degree, I had attended institute diligently, volunteering to help with activities and making lots of friends to fill the time until Jason came back. I wondered if the students in the brochure's idyllic picture had any idea that the future wasn't always as bright and shiny as their faces. I hadn't when I'd sat in their places after high school. Back then, I'd thought things went how you planned them.

In the middle of my mental tirade, I heard a soft voice call, "Jessie?"

I froze. I hadn't heard that voice in four years, but I knew it immediately. I turned to face Jason. He held a blonde girl about three years old on his waist, his arm crooked to secure her, his other hand anchoring a baby carrier under a blue blanket.

"Hi, Jason." Of course. Like I needed this. The universe seemed bent on forcing me into a nervous breakdown. Nausea churned in my stomach, and the sensation of stepping outside of myself for a split second disoriented me. I swallowed down the sick feeling and struggled to focus.

"Hi. Wow. How amazing to see you," he said. "Are you visiting your parents?"

"Yes. For the weekend," I answered, trying not to let my discomfort show. Which meant I probably looked as awkward as I felt.

I gestured to the children. "Are these yours?" I asked. Duh.

"Yeah, yeah. This is Maddie, and my boy is Hunter," he said, nodding down toward the sleeping infant.

"Congratulations," I said. I hadn't heard about his kids, but then, I had made it clear that I didn't want to keep up with him after my mom had delivered one of her Jason updates a few years ago.

"Jason?" A pretty blonde drew even with him in the hallway and reached over to take the little girl from his arms. He turned to her and smiled, and I could see his affection in that simple expression.

"Sweetie, this is Jessie," he said, gesturing toward me. "Jessie, this is my wife, Stacie." She looked delighted to hear my name.

The strange detachment returned as I stepped forward to accept her handshake. Was this the sister missionary from his mission? The one he'd dumped me for? How was I supposed to act? I fell back on manners. My mom would be proud.

"Nice to meet you, Stacie," I said. It was like I was observing myself on film in a scene titled, "Girl meets ex-boyfriend and his wife."

"No, I'm thrilled to meet *you*!" she cried. "Ever since we moved here last fall, I've gotten a chance to meet the characters from all of Jason's childhood stories, but I thought you were long gone. I can't believe I'm meeting Jessie, star of ninety percent of those stories."

Okay. I wanted to hate her. But I couldn't. She meant it. I relaxed a fraction, and my nausea subsided.

"Take those with a grain of salt," I cautioned her.

Whoa. Adult conversation with someone I had once held responsible for bringing my life arc to a grinding halt. Not bad.

She laughed. "Oh, no. He gives you full credit for being the voice of reason. I think you're the only reason he didn't break his neck at least a half dozen different times."

"Hey!" he protested. "I wasn't that wild."

At his wife's skeptical glance, he grinned. "All right. Maybe five times she saved me."

She smiled back at him. Their easy rapport sent a pang through my bubble of detachment. I shifted uncomfortably, searching for something to say so I wasn't standing there with a big social smile papering over my confusion. "So you're back here."

"It was time," he said. "I finished up my business degree back east, and now I can take over for my dad."

"Maddie, this is Jessie," Stacie said. "Can you say hi?"

Maddie ducked her head but gave me a tiny wave. A real smile tugged at the corner of my mouth. She was pretty cute. "Jessie story?" she whispered loudly in her mother's ear.

Jason laughed. "Yes, honey. This is Jessie from my stories."

"Where Twoy?" she asked. Troy was Jason's other childhood friend.

"Troy's in Utah, I think," Stacie answered.

"Meet Twoy?" Maddie asked.

As simple as that, I had been reduced to nothing more than a story, like a hundred others her dad had told. Interchangeable with Troy, his affable sidekick through our school days.

The bell startled me, and people surged into the hall. Jason looked over his shoulder to the chapel, wincing. "We were almost on time today," he said. "We better go before they close the doors for prayer. It's good to see you, Jessie."

"Yeah, you too," I answered automatically. I watched as he carefully transferred the weight of the carrier to his other hand and headed toward sacrament meeting. Stacie smiled and turned to follow him, but after a couple of steps, she spun around and hurried back.

"I'm glad I met you," she said. "I've always wanted a chance to apologize for how everything happened with Jason. I was madly in love with him for months on my mission before I admitted it to myself. I had no idea you were waiting for him until he told me when I got back. I'm so sorry it went down like that."

I studied her for a minute, taking in the apology and the sincerity in her voice.

"Thank you," I said.

She hesitated then nodded and followed her husband down the hall.

"Stacie?" I called when she reached the closing doors.

She turned.

"It's okay," I said.

She smiled and slipped inside before they clicked shut.

And I thought that maybe I meant it.

Chapter 37

"SORRY!" I SAID AS SOON as Sandy stepped out of the cultural hall.

"For what?" she asked.

"For bailing and leaving you in Gospel Doctrine. I am a bad friend."

She looked at me strangely but said only, "Don't worry about it. It's Relief Society now, right?"

"Yes. Although I can run you back to my parents' house if you're churched out," I offered.

"It's fine. I'll stay. Where'd you disappear to?"

I didn't answer for a moment, instead leading her down the hall to the right room.

"Um, I was chatting with Jason and his wife," I said.

She stopped, and I had to backtrack a few steps. "What?" she asked.

"You heard me."

"*Jason* Jason? And his *wife*? Should I be getting you water or a fainting couch or something? How do you feel?"

"Fine-ish."

She continued to study me.

"Seriously," I said. "I don't think I'm going to lose it. They were both pretty cool about it."

"Realllly." She drew the word out. "Cool, huh?"

I nodded.

"Good. Can I see them? Let's peek through the doors."

"No, crazy. We're going to Relief Society."

"Party pooper!" she accused.

"If the ruins of my life are your party, that's a sad commentary on you."

"You said you were fine," she reminded me.

"I said fine-ish. In the neighborhood, but not quite the same thing. Let's hurry, or we're going to be stuck on the front row."

"Don't act like you're not a front-row sitter," Sandy said. "You're a nerd from way back."

"Yeah, in calculus or chemistry or something. I like the back row in Relief Society."

We slipped in for the opening hymn, "Where Can I Turn for Peace?," and that tickle swept up the back of my neck, the tickle that tells you to pay special attention to the lesson. The tickle that says, "Today, this lesson is about you."

After the announcements, my mom stood to give the opening prayer, and then a young woman began the lesson. She looked my age, and a simple gold band circled her ring finger.

She'd been assigned a general conference talk about forgiveness for her lesson, and she solicited stories and experiences from class members who were eager to share. At the end, she bore a simple testimony about forgiveness. "Forgiveness brings us peace," she said.

Oh man. I didn't know whether I loved or hated Sundays when the message burrowed right into my heart.

* * *

"How did you like church today?" my mom asked us over a lunch of roast beef sandwiches.

I waited for Sandy's response.

"I thought it was pretty great. It's a lot different than I remember," she said.

Well, that was a surprise.

"How so?" my mom asked. Good. I could eavesdrop on the answers.

"It seems like all the activities are different. I remember it being more old ladies teaching lessons and the activities being about canning stuff or sewing aprons. Not that there's anything wrong with that."

I could tell this amused my mom. "Believe me, we do plenty of that too, but we try to branch out and attempt new things."

"Yeah. The whole organic cooking sounded interesting. And the volunteer thing where you go read. That's kind of cool," Sandy said.

"Maybe you could find something similar to do in Seattle," my mom suggested.

"Good idea," I added. "It could be part of the life makeover. I bet you can't throw a rock in Seattle without finding someone to teach you organic cooking."

"Throwing rocks at people got phased out in the makeover," Sandy said. "But replacing that with the volunteer reading thing sounds like a possibility."

"You would be marvelous at something like that," my mom declared. "You're so personable. The kids would really respond to you."

"I don't know. I haven't been around them much." Sandy mulled the idea over briefly. "I can't believe I'd be the only one into doing it. I wonder if I could set up some kind of corporate outreach program through our department to coordinate volunteer stuff in the downtown area."

"That's fantastic!" my mother exclaimed. She and Sandy were off and running in a brainstorming session before I could blink.

I checked out of the conversation within seconds and jumped onto the train of thought I'd been riding all day since my out-of-body experience with Jason and his family. I still didn't know what to think.

I guess in the hundreds of times I'd imagined it, running into Jason had gone much differently. I'd pictured him with a growing paunch and thinning hair, his bedraggled and lumpy wife trailing him and eying me in jealousy. I would be dressed to kill, and I would greet him all calm, cool, and collected. His eyes would fill with regret, and I would give him a smile that said, "Too late."

Instead, I'd barely avoided stammering when he'd caught me off guard in the hallway, and I had stood there, dim-witted from lack of sleep, incapable of soaking up the moment. I wished I could claim that my mental filter kept me from saying anything truly stupid, but the reality was that my brain had worked too slowly to open my mouth and incriminate me. I'd walked away feeling confused, not triumphant. Or I had until the lesson in Relief Society.

I dug into my purse and pulled out the rumpled quote the teacher had handed out at the end of the lesson, a reminder about how focusing on old wounds couldn't offer any peace.

But until Ben showed up, I'd had peace, hadn't I? I had a nice home, good job, pleasant ward, and no drama. Peace oozed out of my ears. So why did I feel like the quote spoke to me?

I must have looked like a space cadet when my dad walked through the door almost twenty minutes later. I shook myself to alert status and tuned back in to my mom's conversation with Sandy. Somehow, it had veered from volunteer opportunities to a conversation about needlepoint. I didn't even try to retrace those steps.

"Hi, sweetheart," my dad said, giving my mom a squeeze.

"Hi, sweetheart," he said, turning and giving me the same treatment.

Sandy watched with a small smile.

"Hi, Daddy."

"Uh oh," he said.

"What uh oh?" I asked.

"I know that tone of voice. You only call me 'Daddy' when you need something. Will this cost me money?" he asked, his eyes twinkling.

"No. I need advice, I guess."

Sandy listened to the exchange with interest until her cell phone rang faintly upstairs. "I'd better go get that."

My mom got up too and murmured something about finding an embroidery book for Sandy.

Dad watched in amusement as they left and then eyed my half-eaten sandwich. "What are the chances of you finishing that?" he asked.

"Slim to none. How about you finish it off, and I'll make you another one all for yourself?"

"Deal," he said.

I waved him into my seat and rummaged through the fridge for more sandwich fixings. We chatted about my sisters while I crafted a meat-and-cheese masterpiece for him, and a few minutes later, I plunked the double-decker beauty down and pulled out the chair opposite him. Settling into the worn wooden seat, I glanced around and smiled, recalling the countless times my dad had counseled one of us girls at the table. Usually, it was because we asked his opinion, but I had been invited to take a seat a time or two when he had something on his mind. In my case, he wanted me to dial back on the stress in my life and take it easier.

"What's on your mind, stinkpot?"

The goofy term of endearment dated from early childhood, but it comforted me. "I ran into Jason today," I blurted.

He finished his bite before answering. "Your mother warned you that might happen. How did it go?"

I shrugged. "I met his family. Cute kids. His wife seems nice."

He waited. When I made no other comment, he picked at his sandwich and asked, "How are you feeling?" He took two more bites while I struggled with an answer.

Finally, I came up with one. "Confused?"

"What confuses you?" he asked.

"I don't know. Because I'm confused. Get it?"

He laughed. "Yes, I get it. Are you confused about your feelings for him?"

I thought for a minute. "Yes." Hmm. "No."

He laughed again. "That's about as clear as mud."

I slumped in defeat.

"It's not that bad, Jessie," he consoled me. "Why don't you tell me what you felt when you saw him?"

"Shock. And a little nausea."

"Of course," he said, his tone understanding. "You didn't expect to see him right then. What did you feel when the shock wore off?"

"I'm not sure it has yet," I said.

"Do you feel happy that you saw him?"

"No . . ."

"Do you feel sad?"

"That's not it, exactly," I said, frustrated with myself.

"Do you maybe feel confused because when you saw him, you felt neither happy nor sad? That you felt nothing at all?"

I let that sink in. "Yes, that's more what it is. After I got over the surprise, it was kind of . . . I mean, I was embarrassed but not . . ." I trailed off, clueless about how to explain my state of mind.

"Hurt? You weren't hurt?"

"No," I said, shaking my head. "That wasn't it. It's like you said. I felt nothing. Not mad or anything. Maybe conspicuous, but that's it."

"Ah." He fell silent, eating his sandwich and letting me think. After a while, he asked, "Was this the kind of nothing that feels like being numb?"

I poked around inside and tugged at my unraveling confusion. "No, not numbness," I pronounced. "It's just . . . nothing."

The realization stunned me. It was so simple and so obvious. My inevitable confrontation with Jason in my imagination had always been fraught with emotion; in my other favorite version, I would stand there triumphant while he groveled and confessed his idiocy. I would say something cutting like, "Too bad I outgrew you years ago," and walk away, leaving him crushed in my wake.

In reality, I hadn't felt triumph or humiliation or anger. Or anything. It wasn't numbness. It was indifference. I remember reading once that indifference, not hate, was the true opposite of love. Somewhere along the way, any real emotion for Jason had sort of . . . faded. And with that realization, a couple of things snapped into perfect focus.

I poked around inside my brain again, testing my new theory.

Yeah, that's what I thought.

Dang.

Chapter 38

SEVEN HOURS LATER I SAT squished between my mom and Sandy on the couch, fighting to keep the blanket we shared from slipping over my head again. My dad reclined in his favorite armchair with a tattered copy of *Don Quixote* in his hands. We pursued the less refined entertainment of watching a Lifetime disease-of-the-week movie. Tonight's special starred Denise Richards as a terminally ill mother whose house burns down, car blows up, and kids get kidnapped, and when it can't get any worse, she attracts a psycho stalker. But a handsome doctor, played by Lorenzo Llamas, discovers a cure for her illness, rescues her kids, fights the stalker, and proposes, and everyone goes to live in his McMansion with a convenient extra Mercedes in the driveway to replace her exploded car.

At least, I assumed it ended that way. I only got as far as the doctor showing up before I caught myself in a yawn. Guessing the ending, I slid off the sofa.

"Are you going to bed already?" Sandy asked. "It's not even nine o'clock."

"I got almost no sleep last night, and I want to wake up super early tomorrow."

Her face was suddenly guarded. "You do? Why?"

"I want to be at the beach."

"Oh." She thought that over. "Is it pretty close?"

"Kinda, I guess. It's about five miles."

"Are you going to drive?" she asked.

"What's with the twenty questions? Yes, I'm going to drive."

"I wanted to borrow your car."

Even my dad put *Don Quixote* down to stare at her this time.

"At six in the morning?" I asked.

"Um, yes. There's a yoga place I looked up online. They do daybreak yoga, and I thought I'd try it, that's all." She flushed.

"Oh. Well, I'm not sure how long I'm going to be at the beach, so why don't you drop me off, and I'll call you when I'm done," I offered.

"Sure." She sank back into the couch and turned her attention to Denise Richards and her poorly done pancake makeup intended to mimic grave illness. Lorenzo Llamas in a doctor's coat soon snagged my mom's attention.

I headed upstairs and changed into sweats with my high school's logo across the chest and down the leg. I'd found them sitting in the bottom drawer of my old dresser, overlooked in my move to BYU and grad school. My mom had stuck a sachet in there, and the sweatshirt smelled vaguely of lilacs. Taking a few minutes to give credit where credit was due for today's realizations, I said a prayer of thanks and set the alarm on my cell phone before tumbling into bed, exhausted.

It went off about five minutes later, or it seemed that way when I cracked my eye open to check the display. But it said 5:50 a.m., which meant I had gotten a full night's sleep. Stifling a groan, I rolled out of bed and dragged my feet down the hall to knock on Sandy's door. I had barely lifted my hand when she opened it, already dressed in turquoise yoga pants and a crisp white hoodie.

"I hate you," I said. "Let's go."

"I can wait while you get dressed."

I looked down at my San Luis Obispo High sweats. "I'm dressed."

"Right. You look . . . warm," she said. "But I have a cute sweater you can borrow instead if you want."

I glared at her.

She sighed. "Okay, no sweater. Let's go."

When we slid into my car, I took the passenger's seat. I figured she'd remember the route better if she drove it herself, so I gave her the directions to the beach. "Are you sure you don't want me to wait in the car until you're done with . . . whatever?" she asked, eyeing the gray dawn as we pulled into the parking lot.

"Yep. Only beachcombers come out this time of year in the morning, and they're harmless," I said. "Go do your yoga."

She looked relieved and didn't argue when I shut the door and headed for the trail winding down to the tide line. I didn't look back when I heard her pull away.

At the water's edge, I found a spot out of the reach of the receding tide and sat down. I wished I had remembered to bring a blanket for the chilly sand, but again, early morning? Not my thing. Reaching into the pouch on the front of my sweatshirt, I pulled out the rock I had lugged all the way from my fireplace mantel in Seattle. I rubbed my finger over the marker on the front, feeling the heft of its solid weight in the cup of my hand. I had intended to give it back to the Pacific ever since we'd embarked on this crazy road trip, but my motive for why had changed since my epiphany in the kitchen yesterday afternoon.

At first, tossing the rock back into the water was supposed to be a defiant thing, a big "In your face!" to Jason and Ben and every other guy who had strung a girl along. But seeing Jason had changed his part in it. I couldn't stay angry at a guy who was so clearly with the right person for him. It even reassured me that two people could find their perfect fit so well, the way he and Stacie had.

By the time my dad had eaten his Sunday sandwich, Ben's role had changed too. When I'd sat there with my dad yesterday, thinking about how love and indifference are opposites, I also had to acknowledge my anger at Ben. And my hurt. And someone you're indifferent toward can't hurt and anger you like that. But someone you . . . love . . .

Well, someone you love can.

And in that moment, I had to accept that Ben had breached my defenses in record time; he had wiggled under and through all my most creative relationship repellents and insinuated himself somewhere in my heart, inside the walls. So I had run a thousand miles and found myself face to face with the guy I used to love and now felt nothing for before I finally figured out that the guy I loved now was probably not going to speak to me again since I'd kicked him out of my house and ignored almost two dozen phone calls.

I had intended to chuck my rock as far as I could, feeling vindicated about the emotional lockdown I'd maintained for four years. But if Jason felt for Stacie even half of what I did for Ben, I couldn't begrudge him one molecule of his happiness or the choice that day on the beach that had led him to it.

I examined the rock and thought about what Jason had said so long ago, about feeling like he was being worn down and letting life happen around him. I understood now. I knew as I fingered its smooth curves that if I stayed in the emotional hidey-hole I'd created for myself, eventually I would wear away too. Into a lifeless lump without any interesting planes or angles or texture.

Lurching to my feet, I stood and flung the rock as far as I could, watching it sail through the air and land with a plop in the trough of a wave. I sat back down and considered what to do next. Call Ben? Jump in the car and race a thousand miles back to his house? Sandy might kill me if I tried to drag her back so soon. But I didn't want to wait. I didn't want to think through a careful plan. I wanted to make things right, to make Ben see that Carie was crazy for letting him go, and that I'd staked my claim in her absence. And that I would tolerate absolutely *no* claim jumping.

I jerked my phone out of the hoodie pocket to see if it was too early to call Ben. I wasn't sure what I would say, but I wanted to hear his voice, to find some way to apologize. The sky had lightened enough for me to see, even without the screen light, that it was at least an hour too early to wake him up. In fifteen more minutes, the sun would be above the horizon, and normal people would begin to stir. But I should wait.

I dialed my voicemail, picking up Ben's messages for the first time. The first few dated from Friday night. Ben sounded stressed as he offered several variations of, "Hey, Jessie. I need to talk to you. That was Carie, but it's not what it looks like. Call me back, please." The time signatures on the voicemail switched to Saturday morning.

"Jessie, call me," Ben's voice pleaded. "I hate that you're upset. I hate that you're mad at me. I can make this better. Call me." Five of those came in a three-hour period.

There were several from Saturday afternoon, tapering off toward the evening. The messages picked up again yesterday, cajoling, pleading. "Jessie, call me. Carie's gone, and she's not coming back. I'm not getting back together with her, and I never was. She wanted to talk, and I owed her that much, but I needed her to see my face when I told her we were completely through. She's already gone, Jessie. Call me."

Several more like that followed, laced throughout the day.

Dumb, dumb, dumb, dumb me. But the anxiety in his voice gave me hope that maybe all was not lost; maybe he wouldn't kick me to the curb when he saw me again. I dropped my head onto my folded arms, holding onto my bent knees. I checked the time again. I would wait until 7:30 to call him but not a second longer.

I listened to the last few voicemails, each getting shorter and sounding more terse. "Jess, call me. I am not going away. We need to talk," and "Jessie, I will sic Sandy on you and disrupt your ice cream supply if you don't call me back soon." I smiled at that one, but the smile faded when I got to the last voicemail. He said only, "I'm done calling, Jess."

A tear slipped down my nose and formed a perfect circle when it plopped to the sand below. I sat with the phone pressed against my ear, hitting replay again and again on that last message when the chirp of a text message startled me. I lifted my head to look at the screen.

Jess, I love you, I read. It was Ben's number.

My heart stopped for a moment. *Okay, breathe,* I ordered my lungs. I sat frozen, trying to decide what to do. The lap of the waves thrummed in rhythm with my heartbeats echoing loudly in my ears as blood rushed through my veins, trying to keep up with my pulse.

Breathe, I ordered again then jumped to my feet. I would call Sandy, get my car back, and pack it for an immediate return trip to Seattle. I whirled around toward the parking lot, ready to pace its length while I waited for her, when I saw my Accord already sitting there.

Ben leaned against the hood.

Chapter 39

I STOOD THERE MOTIONLESS. EVEN when Ben pushed off from the car and walked toward me, my only thought was, "My sweats are so ugly." With him now strolling my way, hands in pockets, I could see Sandy sitting in the driver's seat with a huge grin on her face. Her gentle wardrobe coaxing this morning made more sense.

I watched, mesmerized, until he stopped about four feet away.

Cocking his head to the side, he said, "Hi."

Dazed, I answered, "I love you too."

A crooked grin teased his lips.

I shook my head, trying to clear the cobwebs. "I meant, hi. And also, I love you." Then I stared, having no idea what was going on.

He pulled an apple from his pocket and held it out to me. "Sandy said I might need to feed you before we could talk this morning. This was the only breakfast type thing in the airport vending machine."

I took the apple from his hand and pulled it toward me in slow motion. I stared at it, perplexed, then tossed it over my shoulder and threw myself into his arms.

Laughing, he caught me and swung me around, but I couldn't get any dizzier than his presence had already made me.

Setting me down, he leaned back far enough to ask, "You're not mad?"

I stared at him, mute, and shook my head.

"Good. Then you probably won't smack me for doing this." And he lowered his lips to mine for a long kiss. A loud series of honks from my car broke it up.

I shifted to glare over his shoulder at my roommate banging on the horn. She stuck her head out the car window and grinned again. "Yuck!" she yelled.

"I'm going to kill her," I said.

"Go easy on her," he said. "She's the one who helped me engineer this whole thing."

"Come to think of it, how did you get here?"

He turned to wave at Sandy, who leaned the driver's seat back as far as it would go and made herself comfortable. He slid his hand down to mine and took it in his own, tugging me back down toward the sand.

"I panicked when I couldn't get you to return my phone calls," he said. "I went by your place yesterday morning to see if I could catch you before church and see if you'd talk to me in person. When I got there, I found a note on the door from Sandy, telling me to call her."

That explained her detour upstairs while my mom and I had waited for her so we could leave for church yesterday.

"So I called," he continued, "and she told me where you guys were. I think she took pity on me because when I asked her what I had to do to get you to listen, she said to get on a plane because you couldn't ignore me if I flew down to find you."

"So you did. Just like that?"

"I called Sandy with the details yesterday afternoon and took the first flight out this morning. She said she'd pick me up and then beat you into submission if you didn't listen. I guess I don't need to call her over though?" There was a question in his voice.

"No, I guess not." I smiled.

His face grew serious again. "Jessie, Carie came to—"

"It's okay," I said. "I listened to the messages. All of them."

He winced. "Yeah, there were a lot."

"That's good. I should have given you the benefit of the doubt."

"I know it looked bad," he said. "I wasn't expecting her until this week, and I meant to tell you on Saturday night that she was coming and why."

"And what else were you going to tell me?" I asked, fishing shamelessly.

"That I love you." He grinned. He leaned over for another kiss, which was interrupted after a few seconds by another honk.

I rolled my eyes. "She's taking her chaperone duties too seriously," I said.

"Do you forgive me for being an idiot?" he asked.

"It's not your fault Carie surprised you," I said.

"No, I mean about more than that. For being a jerk about your hours and not calling you or just accepting the time you could give."

"I didn't like it," I admitted. "But it's probably the only way you could have made your point. I can be hardheaded."

"You?" he gasped.

I butted him playfully with my shoulder. "I cut my hours back, you know."

"You did? For me?"

I shook my head. "No. For me. It was the only way to get what I wanted."

"Which is?"

"You," I smiled. "I wish I would have known you were leaving Seattle so soon. How do you feel about packing the next four weeks with craziness?" I asked.

He took a deep breath. "What would you think about me picking up a permanent contract in Seattle?"

I turned to look him in the eye. "I think that sounds exactly right."

"Good," he smiled, "because I don't think I could fit enough 'I love yous' into a month."

And this time the horn went off for a long time.

About the Author

Melanie Jacobson is from Baton Rouge, Louisiana, where she grew up in a rich tradition of storytellers. After graduating from Brigham Young University, she enjoyed a career in fashion retail before pursuing her true passion: teaching literature and writing. Realizing she was still missing something, Melanie tried Internet dating for a few years. She now considers herself a retired Internet dating expert after searching the World Wide Web to find her husband, who only lived forty-five minutes away. They live with their three children in Orange County, California.